Advance Praise

"*Miss Lucy* is essential reading for anyone interested in Bram Stoker or his best-known work, *Dracula*. Orem, who is obviously knowledgeable about Stoker's life, and especially his work with the Lyceum Theatre, has created a haunting novel that explores possible origins. Anyone interested in Bram Stoker or *Dracula* must read *Miss Lucy*."
    —Carol Senf, author of *Dracula: Between Tradition and Modernism*

"Orem has gifted us with a vivid glimpse into the life of *Dracula* author Bram Stoker. A combo of exquisite details and hallucinatory prose (think Louis Bayard or Iain Pears) illuminate how the vampire plot and characters may have come about. Oscar Wilde and Walt Whitman have cameos. Yet it's the empathy Orem holds for Stoker's tragic life that will haunt you."
    —Richard Peabody, editor, *Gargoyle Magazine*

"A compelling and creative work that subtly illuminates how elements of Stoker's life, both real and imagined, may have inspired his most famous novel."
    —Majorie Howes, Associate Professor of English and Irish Studies,
      Boston College, Editor, *Bram Stoker's Dracula*

A master-chef's layer-cake, *Miss Lucy* serves up delights for every taste. It's got Gothic nightmares to make the skin crawl, illuminating portraits of 19th-Century Dublin and London, X-ray insights into the workings of money and class, deft appropriations from a sumptuous library (Oscar Wilde, anyone?), and above all the tormented humanity of its central figure, Bram Stoker, author of *Dracula*. Orem dreams Stoker to life with terrific vividness and subtlety, fluent in all the languages of late Victorian society. The story may, over a single long night riddled with shadows, travel from bejeweled aristocrats at the theatre to the reeking slums that allowed Jack the Ripper to flourish. It offers a vision at once perverse and transcendent, a miracle that eludes the crush of history— a *tour de force*.
    — John Domini, author of *A Tomb on the Periphery* and *MOVIEOLA!*

Other works by William Orem:

Fiction
Zombi, You My Love
Across the River
Killer of Crying Deer

Poetry
Our Purpose in Speaking

Miss Lucy

William Orem

Arlington, Virginia

Copyright © 2019 by William Orem.

This is a work of fiction. Names, characters, businesses, places, events and incidents are either the products of the author's imagination or used in a fictitious manner. Any resemblance to actual persons, living or dead, or actual events is purely coincidental.

All rights reserved under International and Pan-American Copyright Conventions. Printed in the United States of America.

With the exception of brief quotations in the body of critical articles or reviews, no part of this book may be reproduced or transmitted in any form or by any means, graphic, electronic, or mechanical, including photocopying, recording, taping, or by any information storage or retrieval system, without the permission in writing from the publisher.

Published by Gival Press, an imprint of Gival Press, LLC.
For information please write:
Gival Press, LLC
P. O. Box 3812
Arlington, VA 22203
www.givalpress.com

First edition
ISBN: 978-1-940724-20-1
eISBN: 978-1-940724-21-8
Library of Congress Control Number: 2019948111

Cover art: © *Kriscole | Dreamstime.com*
Author photo by Lauren Proll.
Design by Ken Schellenberg.

For Lauren: *There are darknesses in life, and there are lights; you are one of the lights.*

Author's Note

This book is a work of fiction, written out of admiration for Bram Stoker and what he was able to create, as well as a lifetime love of Gothic literature. As fiction, it reconstructs both interactions that are known to have taken place as well as those that must have occurred, in some form—though of course no one was there taking notes on what was said, or (what is of far greater interest) what it meant. It also invents other events purely for the sake of art.

For those interested in a detailed historical account of Bram Stoker's life, I recommend *Something in the Blood* by David J. Skal, as well as Barbara Belford's excellent *Bram Stoker and the Man Who Was Dracula*. There are many other books and articles to which I am indebted, as well as the societies, organizations, fans, candlelight tours; Stoker has become a world.

As Muse is the daughter of Memory, so
every book is a sepulcher. It contains,
just underneath its surface, the outline of
each corpse that inspired it to be written.
> Alix Boulloche, *The Critic as Ghost* (trans. Duprés)

What is history but haunting?
> Charles Ting

Prologue

"The Pang of Famine": Dublin, 1852

1.

Arrive the Castle— Loneliness. The Kiss.
Author's Draft Notes
for *Dracula*, Chapter One

THE BOY'S NAME IS ABRAHAM BUT WE KNOW HIM AS BRAM. ABRAHAM suggests biblical strength, but this boy is not strong: disease lies in him, unannounced. It has entered his body in cryptic fashion, showing as yet no sign. True, the delivery was troubled, and for a time he seemed dangerously weak. True, baptism had been delayed. But now his limbs are lean and sturdy, see, in a manner that promises a handsome adolescence; his features healthy, if severe; the round, pouty mouth and especially the prominent forehead oddly assertive for one so young. It is the heyday of phrenology, and when adults pass him in Clontarf and surrounds they take a second look, impressed by the capacities in that brow, though unsure of their direction.

His father favors young Bram, who can answer already the responsorial prayer, showing a facility beyond that of his siblings. This child, the proud light in his father's eye says. *This* child! Abraham Stoker is a narrow, responsible gentleman who keeps large masses of hair on either side of his jaw, the peppery beard shaved underneath to his little knot of chin. With a parent's intuitive favoritism, he has named his second son after himself, Abraham and Abraham, pleased father of a fast-growing man. *And how are we, my boy, this day in the morning?*

Bram basks in parental favor. How good it is to stand at the fire, the black grate warming your finger ends; to step only on the dyed parts of the parlor rug, as if it were a bridge over a swiftly running stream; to run from behind the hallway door and throw oneself at Father's calves, and to feel the warm rough wool as his face laughs down. *Now then, my little man.*

It has been a damp Irish autumn, full of contrary gusts that smell like the sea. Tonight they will do the prayer and response, a performance he and Father have planned since Sunday last. Diligent, proud, Bram takes his chair by the smoldering peat. The odors of a dinner just enjoyed, cabbage and crubeens, a hot black pudding with spices, festoon the waiting air. Abraham Senior begins reading from *The Young Worthy's Book of Prayer* but, after a few turns, Bram finds himself choking. Mortified, he labors to pronounce *spirits kind to watch my sleep* but the syllables turn ugly; on the third try his voice squeaks horribly in his throat. Tonight's audience, a moustache-laden barrister at Dublin Castle and his wife, are uncomfortable. It feels like blasphemy, this spasm in the child.

Charlotte Stoker rises and makes excuses; it seems as if she will sweep her younger son physically up in her skirts. After all that she has experienced in the West Country her empathy for suffering can be intense, even overwhelming. Following an embarrassing interlude she rustles the boy upstairs to bed. Hot and cold rages the fever in his brow, his skin is crawled across by invisible hands. When Charlotte snuffs the oil lamp Bram presses his cheek, livid with shame, into the brocade covers. They smell of lye soap, of his mother's hair.

Within the covers' darkness, he dreams a deeper black. Images, as if from hell, flood through his convulsing brain. A terrible carriage, whose name is DISEASE, is rattling madly across Ireland, hands and feet dangling from its sides. Its hunched driver cannot be seen, save for a leering, toothy grin. Bram fears the crook-backed driver, that black carriage hurrying closer on its insane race of destruction.

All night Bram struggles in the wild grip of meningeal fever. In the morning, he is paralyzed.

2.

By week's end the Stokers know their youngest child is going to die. Both the family physician and a Dublin surgeon have examined him and the latter suggested, behind the parlor door, that Bram be given the holy sacrament now "as precaution." In such mysterious cases, life may expire without warning. But Abraham Senior balks at summoning the minister. The Stokers are men of Science; and then, this boy is his apple. To lose him with such unaccountable swiftness would be an offense. Behind this sentiment, unrecognized, lies Abraham Stoker's own fear of the damp grave: having given the second son his name—the first so often withers—he has laid a cautious wager with the universe. Little Abraham was meant to carry the *pater familias* forward into time. To lose him would be to lose his own bearing on tomorrow.

Bram's mind perceives this disaster in the limited palette of a child. Its complexities outstrip him, but a primal awareness of threat lances sharply into his heart. He has disappointed Father; the shameful performance in front of the barrister was unforgivable, the inability to stand, or to feel his own body at all past the navel, his fault. This much he takes in, a bitter cup of dread.

Quietly, the man on whose brow had rested pride begins to withdraw. More and more his daily expressions of love have a resigned, obligatory feel. Almost imperceptibly he turns toward Bram's older brother, Thornley—touching casually *his* shoulder, asking after *his* day. For the first time, an evening passes in which he forgets to kiss Bram goodnight.

3.

By evil coincidence, Bram's condition resembles the effects of the famine Charlotte Stoker herself endured in her native Sligo. Such mysterious fevers have been known to move through the countryside after each wave of starvation, like echoes of a macabre song. How the cholera hit when she was a girl she has often told her children by moonlight: tales of men flung naked into mass graves, lime-sprinkled, some awakening days later to find themselves weighted down on all sides by cold, rubbery flesh. Of the madness that came over cholera victims, and how they would wander the dirt lanes, lock-jawed, moaning. Of a Catholic priest who stayed jolly and plump while his parishioners starved and who, when they broke into his sacristy, was discovered there eating the dead.

But the boy does not have the cholera. Gradually his pallor abates, leaving him with an expression faintly slack, as if struggling to respond to a schoolmaster's query. What has happened to me? the expression asks. What has happened to my life? It is a visage, at once sorrowful and alert, he will carry all his days.

4.

AFTER A MONTH, THE STRANGE LASSITUDE IN BRAM'S LOWER HALF HAS become a shadow in the Stoker home, a presence that is everywhere felt and yet must pass unmentioned. In the smoking room, Uncle William sucks his habitual cigar while assuring Abraham Senior that the famine is now wholly spent, and was, in essentials, only a matter of "transitional economics." This phrase he repeats frequently, dawdling over it as if savoring the term with the acrid flow of smoke. They did well, William says, to move out to Clontarf, where the sea breezes blow pestilence off. Soothed in blue haze the men discuss Tory doings, emancipation, the societal effects of the Tithe War. Awkwardly balancing himself on his old hearthside stool, Bram tries to chat amiably once more, to rekindle that former high spirit. But something has been broken, and his almond eyes, mournful above the heavy silk collar, fear desperately it may never be mended.

In an embarrassing arrangement Thornley helps him to his toilet each morning. *Come on then, bab. Let's have this part done.* Other times Charlotte carries Bram about like an oversize doll, arranging him by his sister on throw pillows or couches in an awkward imitation of health. A rickety, mothcolored wheelchair is secured, and the family takes him to the sea. The water is black and ungiving, its cold horizon suggesting eternity.

The child must not be treated like a shame.

... weak... little thing...

Abraham, for pity. He can hear you.

By this time the Stoker family has, with the vague guilt aroused by protracted illness, quietly resumed its routines. Abraham Senior spends long days laboring at parliament, often rising before dawn and not returning until twilight has painted the skies over town. It is one of many images that impresses itself deeply on Bram's forming mind: the dominating father, both longed-for and feared, who disappears, each day, with the rising of the sun.

5.

NOVEMBER ARRIVES WITH ITS DAZZLING CHANGES IN WEATHER. BRAM, still in the upstairs bedroom, watches from the window seat. Though his flesh remains half crippled, his brain is frightfully awake. At times he worms his sweaty torso entirely onto the ledge where he stays, watching the rains coming over the docking slip, watching the clipper ships inch out of Dublin Bay. He tries to imagine himself as seen from above, or from behind his own head; himself as a cloud; himself in the body of a dog. More and more his imagination serves as the only release for the world of emotion that is bundled within him. He wills himself into a gull rising over the water, feels the chill air trembling its wings. He lets his breath fall out of him, out of him, as far as he can blow. He imagines the sound of his own final suspiration: *e —h —h —h.* He pictures the funeral they will hold for him, the black wreaths on all the windows, like the ones they saw that day in Malahide Road. Charlotte weeping, Father holding the blue coat and flowers. He imagines Thornley dead, Matilda dead, everyone in Ireland dead, their bodies dropping into the bay like the rain.

The surgeon has been wounded in a riot and Uncle William bleeds him instead, pressing the leeches silently to Bram's temples. Uncle William no longer speaks of transitional economics; something in his manner has changed, though in shirtsleeves and cabled vest he still seeks to project a fine optimism. In his heart, William Stoker is convinced his young nephew will die. Trained in what will one day be called viral diseases, he has been seeing among the blackened, stinking fields and overfull corpse pits of his country the mounting signs of plague. The creatures he holds out to young Abraham Junior are cold and repulsive, little globules of black mucous. When full, each is dropped in a porcelain bowl, where the water sits faintly pink.

But Bram does not die. Instead, leaned up against the mullioned window on the second floor, he watches.

A coal-laden vessel is lying at anchor, with rigging that flashes in its copper braces. By the viaduct in the distance, the Dublin-Drogheda train is starting up, drawing smudges of steam against an apricot sky. The servants are dancing lightly in the yard, a small tuneless song to keep away evil. It is autumn, it is winter, another year; Uncle William has fled to the continent now and Abraham Senior must perform the necessary task. Tired, pale, the scowling man picks up the leech bowl without comment, signaling his once-beloved to open his shirt.

Papa, Bram thinks, not understanding how much has been lost in these years, not understanding his own unmet need or the haunting complexities of love. *Will you not kiss me?* The leeches are fixed to his bare skin, his torso, his throat.

Part One

The Woman in White

Chapter 1 (October, 1878)

> But who hath seen her wave her hand?
> Or at the casement seen her stand?
> Tennyson

1.

THE FIRST TIME HE SAW THE GHOST, BRAM STOKER WAS HIDING BEHIND the safety curtain that hung neatly out of sight by the wooden proscenium, and which he himself had insisted be installed, at some expense, only a fortnight earlier—conscious, as any Acting Manager had to be, of the ever-present possibility of fire. Such catastrophic events swept across the London theatre world with distressing frequency, owing in most cases to the presence of filmy costume material left hanging near candles, the use of cheap, highly combustible greasepaint, and the current popularity for ever greater and more elaborate pyrotechnics than had been witnessed the season before. He himself had seen—only last month, at the Theatre Royal on Drury Lane—an entire parade of African slaves smeared head to foot in blacking, every mother's son of them sporting lit torches as they cavorted beneath a slew of drapery meant to suggest palm trees. He had been nearly unable to remain in his box that night, eyes flicking over and again to the Drury's exit while his brain pictured the sudden brightness that would no doubt appear as the paperboard sets began to catch. Next would come the shock of the players, some of them still delivering their lines; the well-dressed audience, uncertain at first whether this blazing spectacle, too, was only the latest in stage craft... then the stampede would begin...

In the end, he had managed to maintain his seat for the Drury show, but had accompanied his wife Florence into the damp evening afterward with a decided sense of having escaped a calamity whose outline they had already witnessed in full—with the exception, merely, of *when* it would unfold. And he had turned his steps, the next morning, toward the Lyceum with a renewed determination to leave nothing to chance.

Bram Stoker at thirty-one was a physical, redheaded presence on the London scene, broad in the chest, with a slow, sonorous voice, the precise opposite of what early life would have predicted. The childhood paralysis, never explained, lasted for years. So too did the great hunger that ravaged the island of his birth; before it was finished, over one million corpses littered the muddy fields, with an equal number emigrated to anywhere that would have them: to Boston, to Brisbane, to far-off Argentina. In New York, the Irish formed the bulk of the new poor, trading one species of suffering for another. Bram still remembered the brittle autumn when families first started appearing outside his sickroom window, shadow people that had fled the worst parts of the country on foot. In streams they gathered around the docking wall, foul rags begging food, begging passage on the ships.

Where are they going? he had asked Mrs. Kirwan, the Catholic domestic who cared for him during that time. She herself lived through the worst part of the blight in Eaksey, where along with two of her sisters she had survived by creeping onto a landlord's estate after dark, using a gentleman's razor to cut the haunches of cattle and sucking the hot runoff. *All those people?*

Whitechapel, most like.

Why?

An who can stay here, with the devil himself up and walking about?

Bram felt deep distress over the starving crowd and their suffering faces. The walkways of Clontarf were cobbled with stones that had been pulled from the fields to allow desperation planting, and in the evenings the emigrants wandered them up and down. Some begged food, or blankets; some merely drifted, like leaves. The twilight road was haunted by their numbers.

Aren't they afraid?

Hunger, child, Mrs. Kirwan had grimaced, closing up the blind. *Hunger will make you do anything.*

Most painful to Bram from that time of horrors, though, had been the total loss of his father's affection; the goodnight kiss had never returned. But infirmity, once lifted from his shoulder, had been banished forever. One afternoon—had he been seven? eight?—he could abruptly feel three toes, and a patch on the top of his left foot. By season's end, the paralysis had leached back out of his flesh as inexplicably as it appeared, and a young man took his first, wobbling steps. In his teenage years he developed an athletic streak, as if in repudiation of all weakness. His limbs grew thick, his body massy. He began sporting a copious, crimson beard. At Trinity, he took medals in hurdles, vaulting, long-distance walking, swim-meets, returning from the rugby field with blanched shins and heroically bleeding nostrils. Yet it was as if Bram had been rendered permanently invisible by the disease. Try as he might, the old man never stopped regarding him as something already dead.

It was only a year ago now (was it so little? yes, barely more than a year) that the *second* great miracle had occurred in Bram's life, a miracle that, like the recovery of his ability to stand, had altered his prospects with the swiftness of a summer storm. Twelve months ago, he had been living in Ireland still, working as a civil servant at Dublin Castle, both his personal and professional life for at least the next three decades as predictable as the setting on a table. Tonight, instead, he found himself *here*, at the noble Lyceum Theatre—found himself at the opening performance of *Hamlet*—found himself (was it even possible?) Acting Manager to the most powerful Shakespearean in a generation.

From his position behind the baize curtain, Bram could see the actor waiting, as the saying went, in the wings, head tilted low as if at prayer, so that his swept-back hair shone in silvery tints above the absolute blackness of his cloak. The man had his long librarian's arms draped behind himself, fingers interlaced, listening to each line that preceded his own appearance onstage with the intensity of a chemist trying a metal for imperfections. It had been made quite clear in rehearsals that nothing would be permitted, this evening, short of excellence.

What, hath this thing appear'd again tonight?
I have seen... nothing!

Cautiously Bram eased himself another half-foot into the narrow gap between fire curtain and house, struck by the notion that he *had* seen something odd. It was an uncomfortable feeling. The demand that no element be amiss during *Hamlet's* opening applied just as sharply to him as to any of the crew, and likely even more so, as he was an outsider to both island and profession, and it was in every sense incumbent upon him to prove himself.

Only a few yards away, their hush audible in the manner of full theatres, sat a capacity crowd of well-dressed Londoners. Bram's searching eye could just make out the ground floor orchestra, the first dozen rows illuminated by stage lamps, with here and there a playgoer's visage thrown into garish relief. Above the ground, a wedge of the dress circle, likewise filled, and a small section of the mural that ran from the back wall to the head of the western stair. The Lyceum was old and of grand construction, yet hardly what purists might call a "concise" structure. There were little peculiarities in the way this theatre had been built, quirks that a casual eye would overlook, but that lent it a feeling of never quite being at right angles. Stairways came to abrupt conclusions, before the foot expected them; sounds could be heard emanating from unusual directions, or no direction at all. One of three major windows—Bram had discovered on examining the immense structure that had, almost overnight, become his responsibility—was a good eleven inches lower than its companions, a defect he had covered with an advertisement banner.

Owing to one of these awkwardnesses, at the top of the western staircase, between two rows of audience members but concealed from both, was formed a little containment called the "Nook of the Stair": simple wasted space, like an abortive hallway, too stunted to serve any purpose. He remembered having fretted over it in the first weeks after arrival, finally deciding that it would not be possible (due to an unexpected curve in one side of the plastered wall, but not the other) to hang even a candelabra there. And it was in that confoundingly disordered space, not visible from any position but his own, that his eye stopped. For a moment, he was quite certain someone was standing in the Nook.

The figure was just past the point where deep shadows fell. It appeared to be female, pretty enough, slight of build, and vaguely outlined in something white. Even from a distance, this person gave off a peculiar feeling of *stillness*, as if she had kept watch in this unwitnessed spot for a century already, and could do so for another; but at the same time there was an equally strong sense of *activity*—the motionless species one sometimes perceived in persons intently engaged in addressing some vexing, inward problem. The arms, shrouded to the wrists in that same white material, hung loosely at her sides. Bram could see an oval face, with its gleam of forehead surrounded by unruly hair, and underneath it, catching lamplight, two eyes that were—he realized with a start—pointed in his direction. Then there was nothing.

It was only later, after the relief and celebrations of opening night were concluded, after red beefsteak and wine at the *Plough and Harrow*, after his employer had gone on for almost an hour over precise alterations to be made before *tomorrow* night's performance (everything from costume details to a change in Fortinbras' blocking), only after all that, in the quiet of his bedroom with Florence once more, the last minutes of October silent save for the cross-town carriages rattling through the fog, that Bram remembered the definite impression of someone—a young woman, he had thought, in the grip of strong emotion?—standing, quite impossibly, in the shadow of the Nook; and, remembering his mother's frightful stories on Hallowe'en night, wondered whether there were, in this world God had created, such actual things as ghosts.

And if there were, what any such creature should want of *him*.

Chapter 2

1.

ONCE UPON A TIME, AN IMMORTAL TURNED HIS RED EYES TOWARD LONdon.

Invasion, and domination, and an endless host of fresh victims on which to feed: but to achieve his goal, he needed assistance. An amanuensis was required, someone both perfectly malleable and competent enough to handle the myriad details of the daylight world.

For a time, it hunted.

2.

ONE YEAR AGO, WHEN THE ENGLISH ACTOR HAD FIRST BECOME INTERested in Bram Stoker, he had not yet known his name. The thespian was in Ireland only briefly, performing a trial run of his *Hamlet* before its English debut, and had a letter sent, on crisp expensive paper, to the editorial offices of *The Dublin Evening Mail:*

> Sirs,
> Mister Henry Irving wishes to meet the author of flattering *Hamlet* review in recent edition. Should that person wish to accept Mr. Henry Irving's invitation to dine, we are obliged if you would instruct him

to arrive Thursday evening, 6:30 sharp,
bearing with self the following items…

There now, young man, the editor said, flapping the blue-edged envelope on which was stamped the golden crest of the Shelbourne Hotel. The editor and joint proprietor at *Evening Mail* was Sheridan Le Fanu, tall birch of a fellow, already lauded as the author of *Haunted Lives, The Wyvern Mystery,* and *Passage in the Secret History of an Irish Countess.* Lean, with tight hair and waistcoat, Le Fanu had also just published *Carmilla,* a hair-raising gothic about two women, rumored to have questionable undertones.

Le Fanu's rough clothing, like the office itself, was tobacco scented, sleeve ends tinted with newsprint from his habit of absently rubbing the hems. *It seems your labors, Mister, ah… Stoker… your labors as theatre wag have not gone unnoticed.*

Yes sir, Bram responded. *Or, rather, no.*

Bram received the envelope like a fragility spun out of glass. For several months he had been penning theatrical reviews for the *Evening Mail* (no by-line, no pay, a fool's task) simply as a way to vent his confined soul. Clerking at Dublin Castle had long since become suffocating, the ancient building itself, set like an echo at the center of the noisy city, a man-maze of dust and futility. He had entered the ranks of Junior Clerk immediately after Trinity, but almost at once the place had begun to feel like the prison for which it had been designed. He was still young; a strong desire burned in him for adventure, for a thrilling exploit. He wanted to travel, to act, to sing in public. Like many young men, he secretly wanted to *write*—not rent files and tickets, but stories, novels, something with *life* in it.

Well? What say you, my boy? Le Fanu asked, his glad eyes dancing. *Will you meet this Irving fellow?*

Oh, I don't know… I really hadn't intended…

No?

Henry Irving! The thing was unprecedented. Bram had snuck out of a file-and-sort only the week before to see the actor play at The Royal, standing enthusiastically at the fifth act and cheering with the rest of the overflow house. Only after several minutes had Irving returned to endure three lengthy rounds of bows, fairly scowling at the ebullient Dubliners, as if he were superior to their salvos. Bram's blood-gush of a review the next morning (so Le Fanu had dubbed it) had been passionately in favor of the Englishman's craft. But it had never occurred to him, somehow, that the actor himself might read it.

He doesn't say what he wants. Bram turned the paper around.

Ah, then you won't know, unless you ask him.

Well—well.

Bram was caught in a feeling not unlike embarrassment. Though his sentiments ran deep, he was only a secretary; as regards the higher echelon of fine arts, he had more enthusiasm than experience.

Add a line to your next piece, why not? Le Fanu's monocle dropped and hung flashing from his vest. He was marking edits with another stringer in time for the morning run, the other man waiting, one finger pressed on a page. *Quote him if you can.*

… it is a rather busy moment just now at sessions…

Oh, take the chance, lad, Le Fanu returned. In the novel *Dracula*, the role of this person—the employer who sends our protagonist into the villain's company—will be found in Peter Hawkins, Esquire. In the first, and finest, film adaptation, F. W. Murnau's *Nosferatu, Eine Symphonie des Grauens*, this same character will become *Mr. Knock.* As in, death comes knocking.

Go ahead and meet the man, Le Fanu's thin skull grinned. *Who knows where it might lead?*

3.

WHEN WORD OF FATHER'S DEATH HAD REACHED BRAM FROM NAPLES— both his parents had spent their golden years traveling the continent, where more healthy airs could be taken than in Dublin—he stood on the front hall of his modest rooms on Harcourt Street, staring at the tip of one boot he had already removed. The boot lay there, its brown upper neck limp, bespeaking nothing on the rough-hewn entryway. He had a long passage, he knew, between that moment and the funeral service itself. He would need to prepare himself for travel… train schedules, Baedeker guides… but instead he had remained, only staring at the boot. Out front could be heard the ubiquitous gulls, that cry that had always seemed to him both laughter and weeping; the hiss of street sweepers; the old vendor singing prices as he nudged almonds 'round the black roasting pan. These commonplaces, these comforting things, were themselves about to be swept off. Like a character in a penny dreadful, he would be traveling now to an uncharted country, summoned by a dead man.

At the Funeral Home for English outside *Cava di Terreni* Charlotte and his sister Margaret attended him, somber in their mourning dresses. The coffin lid had been screwed down when an exhausted Bram finally arrived, and he stood silently before its panel, thinking how like the closed doors of his childhood home was this final sight: Father concealed from Son, the great mystery kept to the last. Had there not been, in Abraham Senior's rejection, a kind of anger—even a hatred? He remembered the old man, required one morning to carry him to toilet, stumbling and dropping him on the stair. *Stand, damn you, boy. Will you not stand.*

Oh, what was the point? From the first days of life Bram had built up his body in apology. He had driven his brain until he took top prizes in mathematics, in oratory, until he had been awarded a position on both the Philosophical and the Historical Society, all to no avail. Nothing had ever persuaded Father his weakling boy had within him anything of worth, no learning, no excess of physical or intellectual skill. To Abraham Senior, he had always been the dying thing in the bed upstairs.

Without warning Bram thought he might sob, but what had come was worse: a tearless, silent racking of the chest, so that he raised and struck mutely his breastbone in slow, even strikes, like a muffled bell. Charlotte and Margaret decided to walk the dripping gardens of remembrance and Bram found himself alone with the corpse, surrounded by bland ovals of dewy, cheerless light. Shakily lowering himself to the knee-pillow he had experienced the overwhelming sensation not that the old man was locked inside this wooden box, but that he, himself, had been locked out.

4.

On Thursday Bram arrived at the Shelbourne Hotel early, nodding overconfidently to the indifferent doormen. Nervous—so obviously nervous! It was the first time he had ever entered the famous structure on St. Stephen's Green, and, having achieved the polished and radiant lobby, he found himself immediately at a loss. Was Mister Irving already here? The Shelbourne was the most expensive hotel in Dublin, conscious of its place in history, having sheltered *literati* from Thackeray to George Moore. In one direction was a smoking room, in the other a glass lounge for the sifting of this week's papers. Dark streams of carpet poured themselves across the central floor, closely piled and soft underfoot; at the foyer's far end, like the ascension of privilege, rose a grandly rising stair around which cherubim and seraphim played. The very ceiling was animate, twin pillars arcing toward a series of plaster vaults like the surface of a cake. Silk dresses rustled past him left and right, Britons of note arranging themselves by the overlarge paintings without comment, in the manner of those who do not address art, but are addressed by it.

It is... you know... they were quite sen-sible.

Oh... the lady would...

Oh... from family.

Bram ran an awkward finger along the nameplate of the nearest painting. *Autumn Spires* by S. B. Lemonwood. *Lemonwood, Women's Blood,* his anxious mind played; the mental rearrangement of letters was a trick he had learned at the *Mail*, watching the typesetters move lead blocks around the printer's rack. Initially disconcerting, the experience of seeing words broken into moveable units had proved fascinating, so much so that he eventually found himself unable to write *Othello, Iago, Desdemona* without seeing *To Hell I Go, A Sad Demon, O!*

Helplessly he began to study the fronds of a potted palm tree, as if he were merely a horticulturalist on an off-hour. Around his hot ears rippled the muted tones of affluence, that stream in which Empire waded without ever disturbing its subtly lapping surface. In the dining area he showed his hopeful face: no response. Behind a brass rail at one end stood a painted globe, outposts of progress helpfully identified with the Union Jack. He stepped aside to allow an elderly couple past; the gentleman, on his absurdly wide collar some ornament from military service, did not acknowledge him.

How should he introduce himself? Mister Irving, of course, did not know his name. Suddenly he did not wish to be *Abraham Stoker*. No, Abraham Stoker was that dead thing across the ocean, hidden in its box, concealed behind an eternity of glossy, black refusal. He was free of the old man, free... good evening... excuse me... and with that freedom must come liberty, too, from the name that had heretofore chained their destinies. *Abraham* no more. If he was to find the new life that he sought, he needed a *nom de plume*. Something with verve, even a bit of Byronic dash. Perhaps...

Good evening, a low voice intoned from a leather booth. Bram started. It was Irving, his sharp features appallingly close. The actor had been at his ease, watching Bram pace, two fingers playing insouciantly with a large silver ring. Bram caught a whiff of red wine. There was something cruel, almost, in the way he had chosen to bide his moment, as if entertained by a younger man's suffering.

Bram brought his stumbling body to order—damn this jacket, the cut was all wrong—nodded, entered the chandeliered inner space. Nodded a second time, bowed—was it ridiculous?—offered his own hand.

The author of the Hamlet *review in the* Evening Mail?
Yes, sir.
I read your work. Something about the sentence, delivered with a dropping intonation, seemed to carry with it a host of implications.
Yes... thank you indeed, sir.
Do you have a name?
But what was his name? What was it?

5.

They dined; they sipped *rosato*; Irving talked, without break, about himself. He was thin to the point of gauntness, his bone structure throwing across his forehead and cheekbones an architectural quality, so that listening to the actor at proximity was like being addressed by a Roman bust.

Even in his prime (he could hardly have crested forty) there was an antiquity to the man's bearing. The hair, parted in the middle and falling in both directions over large ears until it touched the collar, was an indifferent mixture of silver and black. The nose was aquiline, with arched nostrils and a sharp, judgmental cartilage, set like an exclamation between thrusting brows. Most expressive of all, though, were those wildly lustrous eyes, which glimmered in contrast to the motionless irises themselves. There was about the man's unbroken gaze—yes, Bram spotted it again, with a sensation not entirely devoid of discomfort—a *calculating* quality. Irving seemed to be not just looking at him, but *watching*, like a hawk at a barn door, as if to determined to catch something live and wriggling, should it appear.

The actor drained his glass and signaled another, the line of his speech uninterrupted. Immediately they were seated, he had begun speaking forcefully about art—art in the ideal sense, *universal* art—seen as a phenomenon of both *immediacy* and *eternity*—do you see? Bram tried to follow the convoluted diatribe with almost desperate attentiveness while the food, a hot vegetable medley, escargot in a sauce, warmed and filled his gut. Once, he set his palm almost giddily on the silk tablecloth before again lowering it to his lap. He had to restrain himself from doing something daft.

Indeed. Mister Irv… I think… yes, certainly. I quite agree.

Do you, young sir? Have I found in you a compatriot?

I … do.

Jewel-toned carafes of port were ferried through, trailed by bread baskets, hotly laden gravy boats wrought in silver. From around their table sounded the low grunts of aristocratic mouths closed over red beef and fowl. Nothing in Bram's life had prepared him for this dazzling interior, for the intensity of this man: he felt his brain reeling. In two of the dining hall's corners, burnished copper statues in the Punjab style held up flickering lamps, the light-bearers gracing eaters with the compliantly bowed heads of creatures who know themselves colonized.

I… as you say.

Are you with me, sir? Do I have you?

I do, Mister Irving… to be sure.

Irving's cravat was precisely set, collar high, the steely hair pushed off by three fingers. He was brilliant, of course he was brilliant; Bram's own ideas about drama, one or two of which he had dared venture into his reviews, were rendered dust. He hardly registered any more *what* was being said, not longer than the moment it took to bow his own neck in concession. A distant facet of his mind recalled the Ancient Mariner, how he traps the Wedding Guest, hapless naïf, in a flung net of words. Indeed, if any living person had the Mariner's capacity, it was Irving. The effect of those unblinking pupils was almost overpowering.

Yes, sir. Yes, Mister Irving.

I... yes, sir, Mister... Irving...

That is... quite.

There was a pause, in which Bram could hear his own heart. The hawklike features seemed to reach a decision. Abruptly, the actor stood.

Come.

Bram coughed into the palm he had been in the process of extending. Was their meal over? Together they ascended the stair, Irving maintaining his theme, as if monologue itself were a strong hand on Bram's elbow. What did Bram—you did say *Bram*, did you not? Well—what did he think, then, of Hamlet? Not the play, dash it all... he had read the review, he had known right away that here was a young critic to know better... but Hamlet, Hamlet! Was he not odious, a mere Danish theologian? Why, your red beard asks? Because the fool believed himself *damned by an absence*—by the absence of his beloved father. And yet the feeling of damnation was in itself *a theological one*, so that Hamlet pursued his own destruction as a way of maintaining balance in his cosmos. Did he not agree?

Bram nodded until his shoulders tired. The only plank he grasped was the possibility that his stunned incapacity had come across as thoughtful silence. They had completed the first long flight of steps, past brass lamps shaded by pearly glass covers; past a series of ivory miniatures, set on velvet of Kendall; past a long, polished rail, ending unexpectedly in a cobra head, the jeweled hood open and the barbed mouth agape. Still they were rising, the foyer visible now from above. Irving had not paid for his dinner, only summoning it as he summoned Bram himself, stepping away when he deemed it uninteresting. Surreptitiously, waiters below them were removing his plates.

And yet one saw the contradiction buried at the very soul of the Danish delirium... did one not?... the undiscovered country from whose bourn no traveler returns... He could *say* this, having just spoken to one who did...?

I have lost my own father recently, Bram blurted.

The thespian, for the first, fell silent. They had entered his suite, a series of ivory hued rooms fronting the hotel, with a view of St. Stephen's Green. The walls were papered in a silver scheme that was picked up by the carpet, overlarge paintings of Greek and Roman ruins framing the sitting area. Furniture that appeared more ornamental than functional had been spaced about the floor, like pieces in chess. Irving's white hands lowered themselves into his pockets. Bram could hear the tapping of a mechanical clock on the mantle.

Softly, the other man approached. Drawing four fingers from their place, he pressed them startlingly onto Bram's heart. His eyes closed with fellow feeling.

So I understand. My sympathies.

The pain welled up in Bram like a rain-swollen bank, overspilling. This man, this great good man, would understand his suffering, would lend him, as none had done, a sympathetic ear. A distant note sounded concern—for how *could* the actor have known of his loss, when they had only just met? Had he researched Bram for some purpose?—but his mind was a blind rush, and the hot desire to be fathomed, to be known to exist, was overwhelming.

I am afraid he and I never...

Sit.

Bram closed his teeth, on the edge of confession. Irving's three fingers lowered him to a chair that had been positioned against one wall.

I shall now deliver a poem.

Abruptly the actor turned his back and strode to the long bank of windows. Bram was staggered. A poem? Had they not been on the verge of great, even profound depth? And then it all seemed irrelevant, whatever he had been about to say. What kind of fool had he been to interject a note from his own life into the actor's muse? His was not to speak, but to take his place obediently. He was a fool, a blubbering, emotional fool; he prayed, he prayed the moment had passed unnoticed. From Sackville Street came the metallic hiss of the trolley, a fishmonger shouting prices, some children repeating a naughty word, over and again. Irving positioned himself so that the lowering sun threw his expression into flame.

This poem tells a tale, he informed the waiting air. *Of unbearable regret.*

On the penultimate word the actor spun fiercely, and, as if seeing Bram for the first, took three dominating strides forward. Bram's fingers clutched the velvet armrests. At the third step Irving had come stupefyingly close, towering over him like a monolith. Those vulpine eyes flashed cold fire.

> *'Twas in the prime of summer-time...*
> *An evening calm and cool...*
> *And four-and-twenty happy boys*
> *Came bounding out of school...*

Captured in his chair, Bram was washed over by a rioting mix of emotion. He knew the poem, of course he did. It was Thomas Hood's *The Dream of Eugene Aram*; all schoolboys memorized its singsongy verse. What could the actor be trying to do, descending from their high talk of Hamlet (Irving's talk, Irving's! His place only to listen) to this childish entertainment? But the boyhood doggerel was transformed by the very intensity of its presentation now, refashioned into something novel and sinister. Bram felt his bowels shift.

> *And, long since then... of bloody men...*
> *Whose deeds tradition saves...*
> *Of lonely folks cut off unseen,*
> *And hid in sudden graves...*

Minutes passed, discarded by the mantle clock. There was no escaping the towering doom, mounting in its awful power. Basked in chaotic light, Irving told the tale of ghost-chased Aram, told how carefree youths grow to guilt-hounded men, helpless before the spectres that haunt, that *hound*, that *harass!* until

> *no peace for the restless clay,*
> *Will wave or mould allow...*
> *The horrid thing pursues my soul—*
> *It stands... before me... NOW!!!*

At the final syllable Irving thrust his hands brutally forward. His brow was sweat-dotted, his trembling lips open. The delivery, like Aram's life, had come to its hideous stop.

Bram was in a state of terror. Mortal, undistilled terror. His very veins closed off inside him, his life energies completely halted. His jaw hung slack, eyeballs brimming. He feared he might urinate in his trousers.

Wiping at sweat, his cravat pulled askew, Irving limped back toward the window casing. He remained a long time, fingers clutching the curtain pull, observing the ruined sun drop through the chimneypots of Dublin. Eventually, he turned.

Get on your knees, he said.

But this part was a dream: it came to Bram later, though it stayed with him for weeks, a primal image written into the very stage dressing of his brain. In it, he fell compliantly to the rug, throwing himself down before the awesome sublimity of this man. Meek, grateful, he clasped the actor around one calf, feeling the scratchy wool press against his cheek.

From this day forward, you shall be blood of my blood. Flesh of my flesh.

Master.

You shall enable all my designs.

Yes. O yes, master.

And in return... I shall give you life.

Peering obediently up, Bram saw his father's face. When he woke in his own bedroom, hours later, he realized he had been crying.

Chapter 3

1.

Hamlet was in its third week when the ghost reappeared. Bram was trying to press himself unnoticed along the western wall in order to be present in the foyer during intermission, where he would be required to make conversation with the evening's most eminent patrons. The extra task, on top of his usual load, was odious; yet Mister Irving's command was law; and so, having only just assisted a stagehand in swapping out a candle that had begun to sputter (when he spotted the line of thick blue smoke rising from behind Elsinore, his heart had come to full gallop), he found himself obliged to violate decorum and walk quickly through the ground floor seating area during the performance itself. His dark formal clothing obtained its purpose, and he stole out from behind the stage and made his way almost to the foyer doors without being spotted. At that moment, however, his eye crossed the Nook of the Stair.

Someone was standing there. Though hidden in shadow, this was no trick of the foot lamps, whose fluttering reflections had the tendency to illuminate strange corners of the theatre, revealing for an instant a brass candle stand or the distended eye of a carved eagle in full, angular detail. No, this thing that had appeared once more was solid, as solid as the carved imps and satyrs that surmounted the balcony (a tribute to *Midsummer*, rather inaccurate, and commissioned before his arrival). It was the woman—Bram could make her out clearly this time—thin, almost willowy, and dressed all in white. Her hands hung lightly again at her sides, palms turned outward by only a degree, as if pleading, or in preparation to receive something. She seemed to be watching the performance taking place onstage, on her features an expression too complex to call sorrow.

For a moment his own body was frozen in place, and he stood, staring blankly. Then her eyes snapped toward him, and Bram felt all his skin jump. He hurried through the double doors, heart alive in his neck.

Midway through the third act he made his way, carefully, down the carpeted hall, arriving at the Nook from the opposite direction, but finding it (had he truly expected something else?) quite empty. A cold sensation crawled up his backbone. There was no mistake this time, he had seen what he had seen. Yet to pursue the matter further would have been unprofessional, however one might do that, and he returned to his duties, not clear in his own mind as to what these experiences meant. He did not believe in what were called "wild" occurrences, mesmerism, table-tipping, voices that whispered through the mouths of oriental women in trances. In potboilers, to be sure, such things made for entertaining device, but his concept of "the breathing world," as he sometimes phrased it in discussion, was not one in which outright violations of nature could occur.

Yet neither was his mind wholly closed on the subject. He had never experienced that other realm so many believed went whispering and drifting alongside our own, making itself felt on special nights, when the trees were bent by a gale and the gas lamps sputtered. But his mother certainly had. Of all the frightful tales she had spun for him of the cholera years—stories of entire households dying off in a single night, of the graveyard bell that rang itself, of a mongrel dog they had seen worrying something on the side of the road that turned out to be a woman's head—most fascinating, and most terrible, were the stories of disease victims who returned from the grave pits, not understanding they had died. Their numb fingers sliding down the windowpanes after dark, their gravelly voices asking to be let back in.

The back of his neck tingling, Bram returned to his position at the Lyceum's front entrance. He opened the doors and looked out for a time on the fog-locked street before returning to the lobby. From where he was standing, he could just make out the long hallway that curved toward the Nook. Was he destined to discover that there was some mystery attached to that corridor, a tragic suicide perhaps, death by violence, a hushed-up chapter in Lyceum's past? What if he were to see it again, now—a female shadow where no shadow should be, unnaturally long, gliding in his direction? Looking at the twisted glove in his hand, he realized he had pulled out a stitch.

Do you see nothing there? Irving's stentorian voice boomed from center stage. Act three, scene four: Prince Hamlet is visited by his father's spectre. Queen Gertrude would just now be tilting a slender arm toward the audience, as if seeking confirmation against her mad son's words.

Nothing at all. Yet all that is, I see...

2.

It was nine o'clock by the church tower before Bram found himself home once more in the rooms he and Florence now shared. Cold at the windowpanes tonight: winter coming.

And how thrives the world of English theatre?

Ovations once again, Bram sighed, relieving himself of his jacket and formal restraints. His whole body was fatigued, the muscles in his face weary. *Mister Irving had to return seven times for bows. Seven bows!*

Is that very many?

It's... darling, it's extraordinary. Florence did not understand theatre. She had been pleased enough to appear for the opening week celebrations, in a seagreen pagoda dress whose price Bram shuddered to consider, but had not sat through the production. The occasional light comedy by Goldsmith was to her liking, but nothing as difficult as Shakespeare. *Of course, Mister Irving is something of a taskmaster, I am finding. He will have perfection in his theatre, and no mistake! One feels a bit put upon.* She was not listening.

Well, Florence offered eventually, frowning at some china plates. *I am sure you are doing an admirable job.*

Thank you, my dear.

In truth, Bram's situation was proving significantly more difficult than he had admitted. Henry Irving was a kind of magician, and the wild enthusiasm of the show's first weeks had made his powers clear. It was to the sorcerer's apprentice, however, that fell the heavy load of bringing off the illusion every night. There had been little enough time to commission the complicated backdrops, or period costuming, or to arrange for the presence of certain noteworthy persons whose presence in the boxes would be material to Irving's success. Irving's name made the tea-talk, but it was Bram's own labors that were legion—from the small business of arranging vendors to the moderate challenge of constructing programs to the tremendous challenge of handling the Lyceum's finances (all its finances!) in the very teeth of performance.

Vaguely he began fingering his moustache in the hallway mirror. *I do feel the amount of absolute work... the great many things I am called upon to oversee... it is rather much. But, of course,* he amended quickly, *I am more than pleased to assist such a man, more than pleased!*

Come. I had Cook make us a late something.

Bram passed through the front room and into the kitchen, drawn by Florence's hand. His wife of less than one year was a notable beauty, frequently commented on; her hair, flat as still water when combed, as the pure black of certain Irish women, the stuff of ballads. Her waist was slim and tight under the dress material, the bosom pleasantly defined. Barely out of her teens, she had already perfected that feminine ability—secretly Bram wondered whether they did not practice it, behind curtains—to glide across rooms, only touching ground when her destination was achieved. And she had certainly taken right away to her role as the Lyceum wife, entrancing roomfuls of admirers with her moments of pretend helplessness. *Oh dear, oh... ! Will no gentleman assist me?* In her own way, Florence was as much a performance as any stage.

He seated his tiredness in the little alcove space. In the morning he had to rise early, once more, and assist with the backdrop changes. He must not forget...

Do you believe in ghosts, Florrie? He was not sure why he had raised the issue.

Florence resettled her chair.

Why? Have you seen one flapping about Covent Garden?

Oh, I don't know. Bram was suddenly unsure about discussing his experiences. Though she was social by nature, Florence was not sensitive to things. She had no strong feelings about music or painting, and there was something of an aesthetic receptivity needed to discuss the otherworldly. Was that not true?

When I was a girl in Artane, my Aana heard the banshee creeling, Florence said, reclining into herself. The hour was late, and showed in her eyes. It had been kind of her to stay up. *This was just before the Conway brothers died. Falling in the stream and catching their deaths of cold, all three.*

Oh? And how did it sound?

Like music it was, Aana said... *like someone singing to you, over the hills. Only the tune always going wrong.*

Bram pushed away his spoon, oddly moved. *It's a strange world.*

Theatre men keep strange hours, of that I am certain. She rose, touching his shoulder. *Remember that tomorrow I will be having luncheon with the Captain Andersons.*

Good night, my dear. I want to sit up for a bit.

... night...

Bram eased himself into the cushioned purple chair, stabbing the coals. How quickly he had fallen into the rhythms of married life! He had only begun "stepping out" with young Florence Balcombe the year before. Their acquaintance had been rapid. Several friends had persuaded him to a social event in the spring; he would have declined, but the afternoon had already been arranged. Then, when he arrived at the home of his companion, this lovely nineteen year-old had fairly charged off the porch, taking his arm with such surety it was as if they had known each other always.

Now, sir, you will be that Abraham Stoker of whom we have been hearing such naughty things!

The whole afternoon, in which the four of them had ridden together to St. Stephen's, taken in certain gardens that belonged to the Bishop's Men, had come off marvelously well. He had called at the Balcombe residence again, with a partner, and a second time, on his own.

Don't you love the sound of a breeze in the lindens? I might say I do.

Well, Miss Balcombe. If ... if it pleases you, I am certainly in favor.

Oh, do call me Florrie in the end. We are hardly such strangers as all that.

She was a bit rough-hewn. He had heard her say *bloody* once, under her breath. She enjoyed being fawned over, too; in the brief time of their acquaintance he had seen her draw men into competition, who shall twirl her about, or bring her ices. He was likely not the only gentleman whom she had rather aggressively taken in hand. There was a rumor, in fact, that she had already been close with a Trinity boy called Wilde, brother of Bram's friend Willie. Young Oscar had given her a silver cross with his name inscribed, a somewhat questionable intimacy. Still, Bram had been pleased to report to his family that he found the company of Colonel Balcombe's daughter distinctly agreeable.

Then had come the overwhelming afternoon at the Shelbourne, the great sea-change. Afterward, the telegram that had arrived in Bram's postal box had seemed both incredible and, somehow, inevitable:

```
WESTERN UNION
REC'D AT CFP/CRT 1201PM 1878 DUBLIN A8 DUBLIN
MISTER ABRAHAM STOKER

LYCEUM MINE    YOU WILL BE MY ACTING MANAGER
ALL RESPONSIBILITIES YOUR SHOULDER
LEAVE IMMEDIATELY CURRENT EMPLOYMENT
MAKE YOURSELF PRESENTABLE ALL RESPECTS
YOU MOVING TO MAYFAIR MONTHS END

IRVING
```

The possibility of *refusing* the actor—of thanking him for an extraordinarily generous offer, but begging off on any number of grounds, least of all his unfitness—had not seriously entered his mind. He had told himself that here, at last, was that higher possibility of which he had dreamt: a chance at a life not of dusty consignments at Dublin castle, but of *artistry*, in association with genius. Irving's telegram (Bram argued to himself, in the mad days that followed) was a crossroads in blowing darkness where separate carriages beckoned him down contrary paths. On one, he would remain in lackluster Dublin, a civil servant, only half-alive. Down the other lay adventure.

Yet how much had been contained in that PRESENTABLE ALL RESPECTS! He understood well what was being said. Irving had sounded him, and found his mettle good; but he demanded more than good, he demanded perfection. The actor would excuse his Irish blood. But if he, Bram Stoker, were to serve as the public face of the Lyceum, a gentleman he must become in all outward respects. A presentable wife, and preferably son, would be a necessity.

The next day Bram had ridden south to Clontarf. As bad fortune would have it, he had visited the Balcombe residence just recently, passing most of a wet afternoon under the family portraits with the Colonel and his wife. Finding some small excuse for his return he struggled through a tedious second conversation with the elderly fellow, who examined Bram's reappearance on his parlor rug quizzically out of his good eye. From the other one a thin, pinkish scar ran vertically to the man's upper lip, reminder of his accidental collision, while on horseback, with an unsuspected Wych Elm.

As if in pantomime, they repeated several lines of discussion only recently covered in full, Bram hoping the senior man's memory was infirm. His family was well, yes; his brothers, Thornley, Richard, both physicians now... indeed it was a shame to lose their father that way, no one should be called to his maker while off native soil... this pabulum, barely supportable, had continued until he spied Florence gliding through an outer chamber. She was wearing an eggblue crinoline dress that held her form marvelously. On her right cheek, the beauty mark accented her secret smile.

Why, Abraham Stoker! What a pleasure to see you once more, and so soon.

Bram stood brightly. The Colonel, invoking the privilege of age, had appended to this show of manners only a gesture with his cane.

He and Florence had spoken again, he hardly remembered what, something about the sparrows in the shed; yet Bram *must* forgive her dishevelment. He had come upon them this afternoon, and her most of all, unprepared for visitors of any description... no, no... surely he could not mean those too flattering words. This foolish dress was all she had at hand... and so on. When he suggested they might take a turn, Florence had given him the twinkle that was hers alone, the one that said you are the sole interest of mine, see how completely I am in your power.

Unchaperoned, the two of them walked the grassy park as if it were the gardens at Versailles. She had slipped her fingers more gently into the crook of his elbow and, laughing at a foolish magpie, recited the rhyme: *One for sorrow, two for joy, three for girl, four for boy.*

But I see only the one, Bram returned, *and surely an afternoon so fine as this could not have been made for sorrow.*

Only the one, poor fellow! Florence searched playfully the light-dappled grass. *Do you think he is lonesome?*

Inside the house once more, Bram had steeled his resolve. Now. The moment was now. They were more or less alone: the Colonel, and a fading grandmother, were within earshot, but not in the very chamber; it might be his only opportunity. But as he went on one knee, Florence had retreated in shock.

Madam, I recognize this declaration to be rather sudden—

His voice freezing inside him, Bram felt the full weight of his absurdity. *Indeed, I had cherished notions that you and I might take advantage of another full season together. For to witness the springtime blossom in your company a second...*

He had planned out his oration, run it over several times like a Trinity debate, but in the execution it fell terribly. Kneeling in the Balcombes' cramped dining room, before the undisguised shock of this girl's expression, the whole task felt hurried, disrespectful in his mouth. He had failed, utterly failed.

Florence took a moment to recover from her surprise. *My dear friend*, she began.

That had been it, then: the smiling, downcast eyes, full of gentle pity, a species of vinegar to the suitor's wound. She was arranging her obvious rejection—and Bram, seeing all lost, had dropped the entirety of his text and simply told her what had come about in his life. How he had been plucked up by an English artist, one unlike any he, or the world, had ever seen. How he was upending all connections, sailing to London at month's end in this same man's service. How there was already dawning for him an entirely different social sphere.

With this information, a sudden stoppage had come across Florence's demeanor. One carefully trimmed eyebrow rose until it stood a full half-inch higher than its twin.

—London, you say.

Indeed so; his passage was already ticketed. It was madness to be throwing over his present career, but if he was ever to find the life of which he had dreamed...

And... London.

Yes, London. At the end of the month.

Florence gathered her wit. While he spoke, a hasty revolution had been completing itself behind her blinking lashes. The idea of *marriage*, she now reflected—though, to be sure, rather sudden!—was one to which she found herself not *entirely* unamenable…

3.

AND SO IT HAD BEEN DONE. IN THE END THEY HAD MARRIED, SAILED, ALL within a string of weeks. Like all Victorians, Bram dreaded any inkling of scandal as he would the pestilence. Social censure, and its avoidance, was the solder of the time. Yet for this chance, alone, he had been willing to enter into risk. The marshy clay of his origins was washed clean by so great an elevation. Henry Irving had made him a man. In a stroke, his English hand had created *Bram Stoker*—husband, Londoner, a respectable servant.

All Bram's connections to his former career at Dublin Castle were severed, rendering him incapable of drawing a pension, a decision that had prompted the cashier to drop his lower lip sharply in a frown. *You understand, Mister Stoker, that such a decision is quite binding in terms of any—I repeat myself, any—future benefit.*

I do.

Forgive me for the presumption, the cashier had continued, returning his pen nib to the stained box, *but what offer have you in hand… I assume, as I must, that it is well in hand… that so predisposes a man of your relative youth… to part with a sound means of financial well-being?*

Life, Bram answered.

The hurried marriage ceremony had been worked through, in the end. Colonel Balcombe, his frail chest trimmed out in rose and golden medals, was visibly displeased with the proceeding, but unwilling to cross his self-willed daughter.

Abraham, a word.

As many as you like, sir. I answer now to Bram.

Abraham, the unhappy moustaches repeated, *I have given you, this day, my daughter's hand, which holds in it my family's name. Do you trust this fellow—Irving?*

With my reputation, Bram said stiffly. He would have said: With my soul.

An... actor. Colonel Balcombe's wincing intonation, perching on the steps of St. Anne's Church, had carried in it all the bundled outrage of his disempowerment.

A Shakespearean, I would call him. A great—
Do not expose our family to disrepute, sir. You risk a great deal.

The fool, the shriveled old mushroom! He *had* risked a great deal, had indeed put himself into a position that was precarious. His side of the family was dispersed, and could not be counted on. The severing of ties with the Castle meant that he had cast himself professionally adrift—to say nothing of the personal risk in plighting his troth to a woman, a girl really, of whose deepest, fundamental character he knew almost nothing.

Failure, here, could be disastrous. But success held within its folds the tantalizing whispers of immortality.

4.

BRAM RAISED HIS STARTLED CHIN, REALIZING HE HAD DOZED IN THE FIRE-side chair. The air in the parlor was chill now, reaching under his collar. Had he been sleeping for some time? All the servants were abed, Florence long since retired. They had spoken about his exhaustion, at the Lyceum... he remembered... some bits about her plans for the morrow; he had told her he would only sit up briefly. How late had it gotten to be?

The walls around him were littered with blue shadow. What fire was left in the twisted grate had fallen down to embers, giving the Stoker family portraits that slight, disturbing sense of motion offered by trembling light. The atmosphere seemed full of portents.

He had been dreaming—something about a female figure, pretty in a vague, troubled way, standing in a hidden space. In the dream, the figure had been reaching out to him, as if to beckon, or to warn of some danger. Bram had seen the expression on its visage, almost haunted.

Can ghosts themselves be haunted? he wondered, thoughts glowing and dimming once more like the cinders. The hallway was full of night, and his sleeping face passed the mirror. *Who haunts the haunters?* His foolish mind began rocking the words, a little childlike prattle.

Who watches the watchers? Who haunts the haunters? Carefully he made his way into the bedroom, where that mystery, his wife, was a shape, lying in the darkness.

Chapter 4

1.

*H*AMLET PASSED ITS FIFTIETH PERFORMANCE IN THE NEW YEAR, TO STILL-mounting ovations. The house continued to rise, the dress circle, the stalls, the boxes, like a moving tide of adulation. In an uncharacteristic moment the stage manager, a snowy-headed man with enormous, drooping moustaches and the unlikely name of H. J. Loveday, slapped Bram between the shoulder blades. There was talk, already, of a record setting run.

Bravo, Bram shouted over the applause, conscious of re-ordering his face into what he hoped was a less fatigued expression. He stood once more by the edge of the stage, one arm easing out the safety curtain to block himself from view of the hollering house, as Irving came away from his bow. Just before he would have become visible—so quickly he might have denied this was what he was doing—Bram glanced toward the Nook of the Stair. No one.

An outstanding fifth act tonight, Henry, outstanding. Braviss—
You will invite me to your home.

Bram's mouth went dry, but he straightened himself quickly in this evening's brushed velvet jacket. The shock of the comment mixed inside him with a confused sense of flattery. *Why, Mister Irving, you may certainly honor my wife, and myself, with your presence any time you desire.*

Tonight, then, let us say. After finish.
Tonight?

The floor was demanding Irving's return once more, a dull, suppressed thunder. Ellen Terry, already onstage where rose wreaths were being flung about her ankles, beckoned him back with one silver-gloved hand. Other actors were backstage, removing costume pieces, there was more work to be done… but Irving had taken the stage again like a soldier returning to the field, leaving before Bram an expression, briefly witnessed, that lingered in the air. It struck him uncomfortably that the man would make a fine Mephisto.

2.

SOUTHAMPTON STREET WAS FRUSTRATINGLY CROWDED EVEN AT THIS hour, with strolling couples around whom Bram was obliged to dodge: violin players, jugglers, a lightning sketch artist under the lamp, doing faces for a shilling. The evening had lingered on fine and clear, a surprise after wet weeks that had plastered the cobbles with watery leaves. *He is coming*, he called in near panic, flying into the front room and shaking down his scarf. *Mister Irving is coming, this evening. Drinks, some food perhaps, I don't know what all.*

This evening? Florence cried. She had been trying on different earrings and was wearing a mismatched pair. *Tonight? I had no warning.*

Tonight. Now. Now.

Bram laughed despite himself, his fingers arranging pointlessly a china bowl of fresh lilacs. 'My dearest love,' he tried to quote the Scottish play, 'the king comes here tonight!'

Thinking things out rapidly, Bram believed he had divined the purpose behind this late, sudden, unlooked-for visit. Irving was "checking up" on his new Manager—seeing for himself whether his personal life would project the image that was key to Irving's larger plan. That plan he had already enunciated in the papers: to bring a new dawn of *morality* to the English stage, to elevate theatrical arts, long regarded as low entertainment, to a position of utmost respectability.

Florence was agog. Her natural vanity had burned somewhat brighter since their arrival in England; used to being the focus of male attention back home, here she had been exposed to a greater field of admirers, and from wealthier stock. Already she had fashioned herself into a hostess *arriviste*, arranging at-homes in which she herself could perch like a flower among gentility. But the jewel, to be shown at advantage, must be turned to the light. Unscheduled appearances distressed her utterly.

And must this unexpected wonder be tonight? The servants have already left.

Yes...

Nothing in the front room is prepared. And my dress—! Abraham, my dress! Clothing had become an issue, as well. She must have the latest style, coming from the continent, or disaster.

The Chinese Ambassador was in the audience this evening, in yellow satin. Bram grinned pointlessly. *The Marquis!*

Well and good, but the Marquis is not coming under my roof. How long have I to prepare?

The actor arrived at ten o'clock, his expensive suit smelling of cigar smoke and previous engagements. A light supper of *coq au vin* had been dashed out—last minute, but admirably—by the returned cook, with insistent input from Florence. Cook was hardly younger than Florrie herself, and their proximity in age required his wife treat her with especial severity; behind each woman's cast Bram had seen something of the animus that drove females, most especially those who ought, by nature, to be sisters, but whom the vicissitudes of class had flung into differing fortune.

Irving's demand to be hosted, followed by his delay, was unkind, but, Bram reminded himself, one must make exceptions for the exceptional. Artistic temperaments were not to be judged in the plebian court. Down a fogged alleyway in his consciousness there emerged, for a moment, a recollection of how Irving sat and watched him pacing unhappily in the Shelbourne, taking evident pleasure in his discomfort.

Do come in, Mister Irving.

Florence corrected with flourishes Bram's hesitation, which had left the actor posed on the stoop. In less than an hour she had transformed herself into a well-composed vision in saffron and pink, appearing now as if she had been casually waiting all day for the opportunity of hostessing. She had seen Henry Irving at opening week festivities, but only long enough to curtsey before he had been borne away, and was determined, now, to make her impression.

Yes, yes. Bram hurried forward. *Do come in, Henry.*

You must call me Henry as well, Irving declared in his baritone, capturing Florence's hand and leaning over until his thin lips had made touch. She mirrored the gesture with a pleased, prepared smile—a gift, Bram knew, that she offered her male friends. *Lovely creature. I can see you are my Abraham's muse.*

I am his wife. I rather believe you to be his muse.

Charming! Stoker, take my gloves.

The late supper was announced in the dining room, which had been gussied with winter violets, trinkets, some unread but respectable books Florence had liked, on one of her many expensive jaunts. The gas flame was hooded in a green crystal globe, giving a restorative effect to the less successful items of furniture. Irving took his food abstractedly, launching, without preamble, into a discussion of plans: *this* was how he was going to transform drama, now, in their day. He was Napoleonic in his vision, seeing himself as a hinge-point in cultural history. No longer would players be regarded as lowly creatures, drawn from the dark edges of life. No longer would the stage be taken as a mere diversion, touching upon immorality. No more! There was a time, do you know, Mrs. Stoker, when actresses were seen merely as a particular type of mistress?

Bram balked at the dreadful word, uncertain whether he feared for his wife's sensitivity or her response. So much was riding on their hospitality. Irving must be kept amused, must be charmed, he must think himself the font of all seven wits. But Florence was untroubled by the vulgarity, watching her guest, rather, with a look of interest while Irving, cutlery in hand, hammered toward his conclusion. The upper echelons of society, Chelsea, Kensington! The drawing rooms of Parliamentarians, the plump, tithing-fed homes of Bishops—*none* should refuse the new priesthood of the stage. No longer would tilted noses exclude *him* and *his* kind from the profit and celebration of life. No longer!

Pudding was brought in, Bram realizing only then how tightly he had been holding his napkin ring. Was the house to Mister Irving's liking? Despite the actor's emphatic self-regard, Bram wanted desperately to be pleasing. The place they had rented was a bit narrow, but papered instead of painted, with a curlicue pattern of scrolling vine leaves. The effect was Grecian, and the rooms kept the heat. On one wall they had massed the Balcombe silhouettes, mounted in polished blue frames. On another, an arrangement of gilded pinecones. Would the artist find fault? No; Irving had begun again…

For a second time the great man circled through his theme, unaware of, or indifferent to, the repetition. Lyceum was his vessel, and he was sailing it now into Victoria's waters. With its arrival in harbor, he should liberate drama, he would elevate acting to the purest of the arts. Under his tutelage, English theatre would become *noble*. Do I have you?

Irving refused coffee but took port. Bram laid out a brass cigar case, purchased exactly for such occasions, which Irving ignored. He had not thanked anyone. After a pause his employer, abruptly swallowing, checked his half-hunter and stood. At the door Bram knocked away the flustered serving girl and assisted Irving into his furry greatcoat, his walking stick, his silk-banded top hat. Fifty nights of *Hamlet*! It will run for a hundred, or I miss my guess. And a thousand bows already, five thousand, Henry, I should think! It has been both an honor... but the actor was not listening. He had turned those glittering eyes on Florence—bowing to her, this time deeply, as if onstage once more. She offered for a second time her hand, her face tilted in a particular gesture that made Bram wince. Irving took, and kissed, the skin of her wrist.

To the muse, he smiled.

Chapter 5

1.

IN THE DREAM, BRAM WAS STANDING ONCE MORE AT THE FUNERAL HOME outside *Cava di Terreni* where they buried Father. Charlotte and Margaret attended him, both wearing the floor-length dresses of mourning, their faces obscured by veils. Unlike most dreams, though, a feverish clarity infused this scene: he could make out in perfect detail the eight-sided chamber, the turned-around mirror, he could smell the smoky Italian candles. On a dais at the front of the room rested the coffin, black, polished wood. This time, however, the lid was raised.

Bram approached his father's body, overwhelmed by a feeling of horror. Abraham Senior's brows had been clipped and straightened by the mortician's brush, his in-fallen cheeks rouged, almost strumpet-like, in the disquieting manner of corpses. The dead limbs had been dressed in a formal coat, with the high collared shirt and linked vest it had been his habit to wear in life. Kneeling on the awkward pillow, Bram whispered the *Pater Noster Qui Es in Caelis*, and then—with the strange logic of dreams—began reciting from *The Young Worthy's Book of Prayer*. But the breath seized up inside him. The old man had opened his eyes.

Bram jumped awake in the overstuffed seat where he had dozed once again, exhausted by his workday to the point that he had not even made it to the bedroom. His skin was tight all over, even his upper lip dotted in sweat. He tried to walk down the loathsome image, circling the room like an animal in a snare.

Madness, senseless and tangled! What, after all, were visions? Mere nothings, random disturbances in the deep lake of the mind. Yet in his bedchamber, undressed and lying next to Florence, the dream came again. The frightful Italian room, the knee pillow, the open coffin. This time, however, it was Henry Irving's face that jumped toward him, staring out of the coffin with a wolfish intensity.

In a panic Bram tried to pull away, but an icy hand had grabbed hold of his wrist. The thing in the box was pulling him down, closer, its dead lips tearing apart the mortician's stitches that held them with a popping sound.

Will you not kiss me, Papa? it hissed. The mouth was breaking into a terrible smile, the ratlike teeth grown hideous and sharp.

Part Two

The Muse of Night

Chapter 6

> She walks in beauty, like the night
> Of cloudless climes and starry skies;
> And all that's best of dark and bright
> Meet in her aspect and her eyes.
> > Byron

> Well I know that, did I move and speak in your London, none there are who would not know me for a stranger…
> > *Dracula*, Chapter II

1.

A SHADOW FELL ACROSS THE UNEVEN FLOORBOARDS. CONFUSED, BRAM looked up.

Sir! Excuse me, sir.

She stood just shy of the paper-strewn rug, as if she had emerged alchemically from the discarded scripts. His first impression was of a great profusion of chestnut hair, held down by an unfortunate boater hat; without its careful constraint, the unruly mass would have been thick and extravagantly wavy. Even with the bulk of it tied as it was, escaped ringlets framed the young woman's features here and again in a charming spirit of rebellion. She was of medium height, a bit olive complexioned, and pretty—no, that was not right; she was *not* pretty—but striking, perhaps, in an unusual way: *laid jolie*, as they said, with full, wide lips, high cheekbones, a rather assured nose, and above all, an unexpected, almost luminous expression that brightened the whole from within. Much of the startle Bram experienced when first seeing her had been due to that look of *alertness*—its presence, especially in female lineaments, adding a surcharge that commanded one's attention.

His initial shock (he had thought himself alone at this hour, tediously making his way through a pile of scripts whose suggestions—*would Mr. Irving consider the enclosed; I feel this character quite right for Mr. Irving; Mr. Irving will not refuse this drama I have penned with him especially in mind*—it was his duty to sift) gave way to an involuntary smile. Covering the gesture with a cough, Bram rose.

Good afternoon, miss! You rather took me off guard. I am afraid I am quite by myself in here.

He was in the office once more, the one he, Irving, and Loveday shared, with its low, tight ceiling, darkly paneled walls, and hanging portraits of famous players past. He had not intended to work past closing hours yet again, but had turned to the play scripts in a frustrated attempt simply to clear his own, small desk.

I should not come in?

You see, I am only finishing up, Bram stumbled, uncertain in which direction lay decorum. *The others have all gone home.*

He should be home, as well. It was a difficult thing that he was not home already. The property manager had been the last to leave, almost—Bram checked the hanging clock—an hour past. But the demands made on him showed no sign of lessening. Too frequently, of late, he found himself returning to his residence only after Florence had retired for the evening. Sometimes a small supper was left hanging in the downstairs fire, herring and mushy peas, with a covered plate of salt. The gesture was dutiful; yet the food, waiting in the silent house, felt awkwardly like an offering to a spirit, soul cakes left for the departed. Worst of all were the nights he returned home too exhausted to stand, but unable to rest, and lay for an hour in his sleeping robe, staring helplessly at the yellow ceiling. On those occasions Bram had been painfully aware of his wife's distance, lost in the depths of some dream unknowable to him, some life in which he had no role. One night Florence had laughed in her sleep, so sharp and heartless a sound that his blood ran to ice. There had been in her dream-laughter the quality of cruelty, something he had never heard.

Bram smoothed his disturbed tie with one hand. *So, then... miss... of course you understand.*

But the curly hair seemed not to understand, neither the implication of Bram's not being home, nor the indelicacy that could result from his entertaining a female guest, unobserved, at this hour. Who was she? Twenty something, still in her freshness, but with that strange percipience in the bearing. No urchin from the street, but neither a member (the imperfect manner of dress revealed it) of the safely middle classes. Of her clothing, all the major elements were worn: second-hand garments from one of the markets, perhaps Bermondsey New Road, where inexpensive extras could be obtained. Around her shoulders, a cheerful enough muslin wrap, though tattered. The tips of her boots showed marks that an owner of more substantial means would have buffed. Even the boater hat, with its carefully pinned ribbons, was only an imitation of refinement, something toward which the wearer was aspiring more than the quality itself. Bram had the distinct sense, in itself not unendearing, of a poor woman who had dressed in the finest she had in order to "make her impression on the wax."

Yet his visitor held herself with no sense of inadequacy, without any of the common gestures of self-effacement one was used to from the lower rank. She faced him directly, two open, deeply brown eyes to go with the hair, and that vibrant expression that was so damnably difficult to characterize. Part wonder, part incredulity, with a touch of something that was neither. Bram, his own gaze flicking once to assure himself the hallway was empty, decided to risk impropriety.

All right, then, yes. Come in, please. May I help you?

I trust so, sir.

She had called him "sir" and not "Uncle Bram," a pet name given him by some of the actresses. So she knew *of* him, evidently, but did not know him, and again he struggled to place her. Was she an employee?

You have found me out, sir.

Have I? Well, then. Indeed.

... yes.

The woman shifted uncomfortably. Bram, realizing after a moment that he was holding it, quickly set down the lorgnette he had picked up somewhere.

Won't you sit?

Thank you, sir. I thank you.

She turned with doubtfulness about the room and Bram had to summon his momentarily fled wit.

Mister Loveday's throne has, for the evening, suffered abdication. He gestured elaborately with one palm. *The King's, of course, should not be risked at any hour.*

Though all three of them made use of this cramped office, it was Irving all over: shelves and bookracks groaning with reviews, musical scores, Tyler's *Sonnets*, a stuffed, glowering rook under glass. The scent of Irving's tobacco hung permanently in the air. *His* chair was the portentous Louis XIV in oak, set before a grand lacquered desk with ornamented sides. Suspended on the wall behind it were the actor's most prized trophies: the sword Edmund Kean had used as Brutus, Kemble's scarf, a Circassian dagger from Lord Byron's own hand.

But Bram's attempt at whimsy had misfired. Perhaps his language had been obscure. A foreigner, then?

This chair, here, is available. And now, what may I do for you, my dear? I mean to say... have you not found me out?

Yes, a foreigner. She had a definite accent, somewhat angular in its effect. The *f* was extended—*you haff fount me out*—in the German style.

Found you out, my dear? Well, now... as to that...

But his unexpected visitor gave him no assistance, only resettling herself pertly on Loveday's beaded cushion, spine straight, fingers laced over one thigh.

And... whom do I have the pleasure of addressing? He was suddenly afraid he had been staring. *Now, before you answer, my dear, I must say I feel I have seen you before.*

You have, sir. I am thinking, more than once.

I suspected as much. Then do I...

And abruptly the singular face—which from the start, some part of his brain had been laboring to place—flew into focus. He *did* know this young woman; he *had* seen her. The experience of recognition was like that of finding oneself staring at a carpet pattern for several minutes before even realizing it was there. *Why, you are the one watching the performances... the one in the Nook of the Stair!*

Swallowing faintly, she turned her gaze down.

For this I come to apologize. I be-leef that I am not seen.

I say!

I know, sir, that the girls must not come up. The recitation was rehearsed. *This has been made clear to us, and I trust...*

No harm, none intended, I'm sure, Bram interposed in a fluster. He found himself wanting to pat those cotton gloves to assure himself of her corporeality. *Only, you gave me quite a turn, standing all alone, in the dark. I... well, I half believed we had a theatre ghost.* Those feminine lips risked only a small movement, but the actual magnitude of their relief was mirrored in the rest of her features. Emboldened, he added,

And are you in our employ here, at the Lyceum?

Yes, sir. I haff work in the costumes.

Her English quite failed her there. "I have work in the costumes." *I see, then, I see. You are one of our... of...*

I am a needle-woman.

You are a seamstress, Bram amended delicately. Seamstresses, "needle-women," were very cheap labor, brought in to sew the various dresses, gowns, suits in which the dramas would be set. It was a common enough kind of work. The same hands that decorated the cast sewed the sumptuous fabrics of the ladies in the boxes, and not a few of the trouser hems.

But the theatre ghost, his curious dream! And here she was, *in carne*! Strange indeed, and somehow, more.

And what is your name, dear?

Lu—zee.

Bram examined a vest button quickly. *Your surname, of course, was all I intended.*

She hesitated, for just an instant.

West-Ender.

Lucy West-Ender? My dear.

Bram tutted, happy despite himself. Was this all some silly tease? But no, the creature was all earnestness, turning hesitantly about the room now, expression wide, as if she were seated in a castle of wonders. Every object on which her gaze alighted—the gilt molding; the humorous *Guardian* illustration of Irving as a Roman Emperor; the black marble mantle, with its curlicue edges—made its mark, which she was evidently not well schooled enough to conceal.

Now you are being playful, are you not? Bram drew her attention back. *Is that your real name, or a bit of an affectation?*

Aff... ec...? Miss Lucy West-Ender pulled again at her gloves. *I haff only work, here, in the costumes. Yourself, sir, and Mister Loveday, with the other girls, give me this work. You remember?*

Of course. To be sure.

A lie. All he had known was that the Royal Court of Denmark would need shirts with frogged cuffs that showed well in the foot lamps.

Mister H. J. Loveday, he gives us work in the costumes. We are from the shop on Goulston Street. But now... but now...

Yes?

Now—everything changes.

Here his unexpected visitor's expression closed down, as if they were entering on more difficult territory. Bram stiffened a little in his chair. To his knowledge they were alone, but the building was large, and he could well be mistaken (had he known she herself was present?). Discussion of a personal nature, after hours, would be entirely inadvisable. Still, he did not wish her to leave.

Cautiously he checked, for a second time, the long hall. No one there.

Do continue, my dear. How has everything changed?

I have seen, here... sir, I have seen!

Gradually the seamstress inclined her head until Bram could see the top of her hat. It was clear that emotion—real emotion, not the staged kind—paused her tongue. When she spoke again, it was with an honesty that shone through the fractured English.

What you do here, sir. What you do... it is wonderful.

—Ah!

Bram felt the warm tide of flattery lapping over him, an almost physical sensation. But how gratifying, after weeks of exhausting effort, to be offered recognition: after standing in the background while another man took the praise, to be noticed for himself! Of course, the glory was not his to share; he was only the serving man. It was Henry Irving whom all of London celebrated. But a bit of pride was not at all unwelcome. Bram could feel his cheeks turning up in another smile, one that he did not, this time, suppress.

Very kind of you, very kind. I take it you mean our plays?

Plays?

What happens. On the stage.

Oh, yes sir! She gestured, those ingenuous brown eyes widened by amazement. *Everything you do. I have never seen! Never!*

Too pleased to sit, Bram paced the little room. Now he had it; now he understood. New to London, possibly to any large metropolis, this curious ingénue had been plucked up for assignment at random, and, creeping along the stair after curtain-up, had begun witnessing sights that must seem, to her, to have emerged from some golden dream. The escalloped shells softening the footlights; the towering, fresh-painted pictures on the ceiling; the pit benches and the gallery. How must it all appear to a poor needle-woman, hidden there in the Nook?

Bram's obligation in the matter was clear. Discipline her, and return to work. Yet instead, he rose and paced in a semicircle, hands resting on and releasing small items.

The making of a play is indeed an excellent pursuit, he began, allowing himself to leave off responsibility for the nonce. *You have perhaps heard that, under Mister Henry Irving's direction, English theatre itself is being transformed from mere entertainment into a fine art. Something to rank, he and I trust, among the finest. It is a great*—here Bram risked a direct look, only to start a bit, as he found himself closely attended—*a great moral enterprise.*

... must I... ?

There it was. Was it *bad* that she should watch the plays in secret, a dusky head tucked in the dark? As she asked it, surely the actual question she had come here to pose, and for which she had dressed herself in the closest she had to respectability, that natural brightness began to waver. The trepidation that took its place, though, was of an interesting sort. She was not fearful of him, exactly, but of his power to deny her more of the visions.

Bram knew it was within his compass (indeed, as Acting Manager, it was his duty) to insist that all workers refrain from sneaking upstairs, most especially during performance. In was inappropriate at any number of levels. But, watching the little seamstress steal another look at the office furniture, he felt a softening in his heart.

My dear, I believe I shall wink at your, how shall we say, unticketed attendance at the play. A budding appreciation for the arts should not be casually stifled.

It took her a moment to understand, at which point her whole person showed the thrill of relief. Realizing, then, the actual risk he was taking, Bram sought to establish a more formal tone.

Of course, now, you must never interfere with the patrons in any way. No one must ever be allowed to see you, or become aware of our little arrangement.

No, sir. Thank you, sir.

Can you offer me assurance? She did not follow. *Can you promise me you will be... good?*

The needle-woman nodded, rising quickly to retreat with her prize. Bram leapt up as well.

Seamstressing is an admirable necessity, he said, hoping somehow to prolong their interaction. He should not have been speaking to a lower class female alone, certainly not risking professional censure on her behalf. He should not be detaining her now. *If... how may I phrase it... if you are favorably impressed by what you have learned, why, you too may take some measure of satisfaction in its creation. My part is small enough, to be sure. Yet all of us, great or small, who give to The Lyceum, share some aspect of its life.* Bram was growing warm with these elaborations, not even sure what he was saying. He had followed her to the paneled door.

Well, Miss Lucy of the West End, he tried to add casually, *you may continue to watch from the Nook, so long as no one is the wiser.*

Thank you, sir. Goodbye.

You must call me Bram, he spoke on impulse. *And I shall call you Spirit of the Lyceum.*

This was meant to be charming, but she missed it, responding evidently to something else.

—*Your name is Abraham?*

It is. Well. Bram paused. *My father's name.*

She seemed pleased by this. He could not say why.

Good day to you, sir.

Good evening.

After she went, Bram remained standing, hands locked behind his spine, rising and falling lightly on his toes. Much later, when he had finished the final script of the pile, he turned to his side and, blowing out the candle, was surprised to see that man smiling there, in the mirror.

Chapter 7

1.

Courage, Stoker. Tonight, he would do it!

This latest round of tasks—fliers, copy pages, even securing a heavy loan from Coutts Bank, one for which he himself must stand surety—it was simply too much. The workload at Lyceum, after months of the same, had grown to a killing weight, causing his pulse to flutter distressingly. Bram had even taken to checking his temples, wondering if he were indeed becoming ill.

Courage!

He had planned out his request half a dozen ways, practicing a casual delivery so as not to suggest he was *unable* to perform so many duties—able he was—only that he was looking for a bit of extra daylight, to experience London... no, that tack luffed the sail... was looking for a bit of extra daylight to pursue his own writing. As an artist, Henry, of course you understand.

You understand, Henry. You, as an artist, understand, Henry.

Bram had decided on this evening's dinner, when Irving would be basking in triumph, relaxed with drink. Tonight they were at *Ridley's Star*, a dozen cast members all crowded into the back room, where a gleaming, oblong table had been dragged by the servers. These public dinners, too, came at a price; with the record-breaking run of *Hamlet*, the amount of time he had been required to spend away from Florence had only increased. Lately, even the cold treat suspended in the fireplace had stopped appearing. More than once he had found himself standing, alone and forgotten after midnight, a ghost in his own house.

But now, all that would change. Squeezed in by the actor's side, Bram waited his moment.

I say, Henry. Can we...

There was a commotion; the French doors were swept back, and the *maître d'hôtel* presented Ellen Terry to the loudly cheering room.

Gentlemen, we make history, Terry announced, taking the carved chair from which Bram had instinctively risen. *The steam train Lyceum speeds on, with conductor, engineer... and its Stoker!*

Bravo, madam! Very clever.

Bram stepped aside from what had been his own dinner, making his way awkwardly to a spot at the table's far end.

The Bard was more than a playwright, Irving sighed, returning to his theme. He was speaking to his third glass of claret. *Mark me, gentlemen, there's rough magic in every line.*

In every word, Henry, every word! Miss Terry thrust herself into the conversation with a gesture quintessentially hers: hands high, wrists loose, chin daringly tilted. An appreciative murmur rose from the nearby tables. Wherever they went now, onlookers played witness to the *contretemps* between the "Lord and Lady of the Lyceum." Irving and Terry's own relationship had become as much a creation as the play itself, and more frequently commented on in the papers.

But as he tried to find another way toward Irving, her gaze pinned him. *And do you have the alterations?*

I—I do, Miss Terry. Or, rather, I shall.

See that you do. I shan't attempt it again in that straightjacket.

Bram's heart winced; the directive, in front of his employer, had felt like a rebuff. One particular dress, her mad scene garment, had proven to be a complicated affair. The latest version was found acceptable only after a certain "downward sweep" on which Miss Terry insisted had been stitched, for a second time, into the difficult collar. Now she was demanding still further changes.

Rough magic, I say. Irving was still bent on his idea. *The artist is alchemist, and like the mages of old, he draws the chalk circle to summon the spirits. If our alchemy is weak—if we fail—!*

Then we fail, Henry! Terry cried, in a supremely masculine gesture. *But screw your courage to the sticking place, and we'll not fail!*

It was a daring rejoinder from Lady Macbeth, and the small circle of diners patted their tablecloths. Her cleverness was sure to appear in the morning columns.

Bram had missed his chance, and frustration burned in his spleen. Forcing it down, he stood from his seat, small glass raised in one hand.

Players, he began, *one and all. It's a marvelous time in which we live. The many sacrifices we have each made, in dedicating ourselves to Mister Irving's vision, have begun to bear excellent fruit. I think often of how—*

Oh, get out, Stoker.

Slowly, Bram closed his mouth. Irving continued his discussion with Miss Terry, their volley of *bon mots,* sprinkled liberally with quotable lines. Bram hesitated where he had stood until Loveday, looking up, flapped a hand at him, as if he were shooing an irritating fly.

Of course… of course.

He forced himself to set down the glass, carefully to fold his napkin.

Of course, you will wish for some privacy after your triumph. Madam, sirs, I bid you all…

Irving swung his fork at the waiter. *You, there! The next course! Must the lady wait all evening?*

2.

Slowly Bram walked the darkened avenue alone, in one ear the distant sad shuffling of the Thames. What was that sound like? It was the voice of time, endlessly gurgling time: of names misremembered and finally dropped from conversation, portraits fading in back rooms, of days and years filtered away into nothingness. Brick houses of three stories rose on both sides of him, the lamps that had been erected for public benefit dropping hazy ovals along the sawdust. Between uncurtained windows he could see gentlemen conversing in smoking jackets, housemaids carrying children off to bed. The night out here was cold again, with a mist.

He must not take umbrage, Bram told himself. Mister Irving meant no disrespect. It was only that his personality was choleric, as was so often the case with visionaries. Yet tonight's rudeness had been rather concerning. If Bram's spine was bending under the load, the prospect of actually *losing* his position was far worse. But it would not do to think such things. The last-minute supper at the Stoker home, Florence's flirty performance (he almost wanted to call it) for his employer; all had been a success. And then, Irving had come to *him* back in Dublin, had singled him out—*descended* on him, one might even say—no, that was far too jaded an expression. Mister Irving had seen, in Bram, an aspiring theatre critic whose talents deserved better than the lowly circumstance afforded by Ireland. He remembered the first time he had risked showing Irving some of his own creative output, of which he had been proud:

Let us see, let us see.

Nothing, really. I had thought perhaps to send it out. A bit of a lark.

A writer of fictions as well, Irving had smiled, drifting through the pages. *You are a creature of various talents.*

How Bram's heart had exulted in that brief praise! Secretly, he still felt the desire to be an author… though he had never known what one wrote *about*, exactly… he had assumed that, one day, inspiration would alight on him, like an unexpected shower. In truth, he did not know whether Irving ever read the little sketch. He had not dared ask, and the older man never brought up the subject again. But Bram had felt seen, in that moment. Not invisible, not a person with no reflection.

Oh, get out, Stoker.

Get out.

Was it that sudden feeling of *visibility* that had touched his soul when the little seamstress mistook him for one of the Lyceum artists? He had enjoyed her naïveté, her mistaken sense of his importance, enough so to bend the official rules, even if he had taken a definite gamble. Were either Irving or Terry to discover he had elided decorum so far as to allow a menial access to their theatre during performance time, the effect could indeed be calamitous. Why had he taken such a risk?

What you do, sir. It is wonderful.

Bram stopped, shoulders tingling. He had the undeniable sensation that, somewhere in the street, someone was following him.

Cautiously he turned in each direction, but could make out only foggy cobble.

Hello...?

It was nothing. The moon overhead was a rider in the mists.

Hesitantly he walked on, debating an early return to his lodgings. Westminster was quiet at this hour, with only the clatter of cab wheels in the distance and a bobbie whistling his rounds. In truth, it was not the first night Bram had spent meandering the streets. More and more, the once-champion walker was becoming a Melmoth, a wandering spirit in the city that had promised so much. And perhaps he had to admit that there was, in his overwhelming business, something convenient as well. The distance between himself and his wife had deepened now. He loved her, of course; the marriage was something into which he was contracted for life. It was only that it was difficult to *reach* Florence, difficult to make any contact with her, in a fundamental way. He did not entirely wish to be home.

Without direction, Bram headed toward the water. The foggy lanes swallowed him.

Recently he had begun reading, again, the poetry of Walt Whitman. At Trinity (how many lifetimes ago?) there had been a point of just such *contact* between himself and the laughing American's verses, Whitman's brash frontier talk, his fearless, almost physically present lines. The colonial spoke of love as heroic, and a younger Bram had felt certain that such love would come rushing into his own days, lighting on him like an inheritance. Many times he had started letters to the poet, but never found the courage to mail them. There was some scandal associated with Whitman; critics spied a Uranian element in his works, and, for fear of perversity, dismissed what Bram took to be the actual theme of the whole, a clarion call for a life fully lived.

Once, in a mood of self-disclosure, he had tried sharing *Leaves of Grass* with Florence, but she was unmoved. Her features contracted and then lengthened at the attempt to make sense of what seemed to her merely a series of fulsome observations.

> *'s not Punch, is it? Who is this fellow?*
> *The King James Bible is written this way.*
> *And what has this fellow... this...*
> *Whitman.*
> *Is he a new King James, then?*

Bram had nodded hazily as if he too were indifferent, but another disappointment had thrown frost over his soul. What response had he expected? He and Florence were different types. In verses that did not rhyme she was entirely uninterested, as benumbed by modern aesthetics as he was by her endless socializing. Perhaps *this* is why their nuptial pillow had stayed... one blushed inwardly to think on such matters... had stayed rather cool. Of course there had been the wedding night itself, after that business with the scones set them laughing, and Florence plucking crumbs from his beard. He had taken her gown in his fingers, lifting it slowly, while unbuttoning himself; yet the act that followed had involved a sudden, unexpected sensation of *piercing*. Florence cried out, her eyes screwed tight in pain. And only moments later had come the blood, hot and wet across their thighs, so much blood that the sheets underneath them resembled a scene of violence. For days afterward, the image had returned to haunt him, as if the act in which they engaged had been something criminal.

Descendants were expected of him as a gentleman. It was part, too, of the professional pact; if his wife were not with child within a year, two at most, the absence would be imputed to failing on his part. But Florence only gritted her face when they were together, and inside his mind the image of her spilled blood seemed to swell up instead: the oval stain on the mattress glittering with menace, becoming more distinct: threatening to metamorphose into something else entirely, something that made him shudder as if naked in a cold wind. Because he knew, he recognized what this other, horrible thing in their bed was. It was the *leech bowl*—the terrible bowl from childhood, but *moving now*, somehow alive, like a round and blood-filled mouth, a ring-shaped, spasming mouth, surrounded by little white teeth, with at its center a single, queen leech, grown so black and swollen that it formed an eagerly pulsating tongue.

A church bell lamented the hour and Bram halted, rubbing one palm across his features.

Take heart, he assured his own repeated sighs. He had been working much too hard, abusing his poor brain. His obligation as a husband had not been met, but he knew he was physically strong. After all, had he not once taken the laurels in rowing, vaulting, cricket? The leech bowl—and that other, worse thing he saw, sometimes—need not keep him from his desires.

That *other* thing; yes. For behind even the weird fantasy of the leeches lay a much more frightening image. Did it not? A hideous, unfaceable image, more appalling than the most lurid gothic horror. That of a sad wheelchair, left behind in an empty room.

***

A dog howled somewhere, containing the forlornness of night. Bram shook his frame. How long had he been lost in himself? This close to the water, the buildings had fallen off, becoming squat, huddled shapes, vaguely menacing in their ambiguity. Not a window was lighted, and, after the animal barked for a while in pointless, unrescuable rage, no further sound touched his ear. But turning to go, the hair on his neck crept suddenly into pins.

There it was again. Was someone not standing in the shadows, watching him?

Hello? he called, more definitely this time. He raised his voice in order to hide its alarm. *I say, there.*

No… no, the stony walkway was empty. It had only been fog.

A phantom caress, he tried to laugh uncertainly, remembering lines from Whitman:

> *As if a phantom caress'd me,*
> *I thought I was not alone walk-*
> *ing here by the shore.*

Orienting himself by a church tower that had been strung with red lamps he began hurrying back. Be a man, he hissed at his too-anxious feet. Nothing was closing in, this weird sense of premonition was only in his brain. Florence would soften to him, Irving recognize his merit. His true potency, all proud and flag-flying, would soon show.

Soon—if only he did not feel that a tide of darkness was rising, in some subtle and unperceived way, against his life.

If only, like Hamlet, he did not have dreams.

Chapter 8

1.

CURTAIN-DROP, ANOTHER SHOW. THE LAUGHING PATRONS FILED OUT IN A wave. They were headed to gentlemen's clubs, to hands of whist, hot lobster and spirits. Alone, alone, Bram closed up the Lyceum.

He checked the gas room and the property room, the paint supply and carpentry shop, brooding under their odor of shaved wood. He closed up the extensive area designated for the construction of sets, with its gallimaufry of stuffed horses, complete suits of medieval armor, rolled flags, Elizabethan kirtles, paste necklaces, all overseen by the suspended face of a jester who was caught forever in his shriek of silent hilarity. Conscientiously Bram arranged, when all was secure, his thin coat, his muffler, his brown bowler hat, damping down the final lights. In the darkness the incense of snuffed wicks eulogized the flame.

O, sir! I am still here.

Why, Miss Lucy!

Bram felt abruptly caught out, struggling to force open the massive street doors. Then both of them tumbled through, like people trapped in a fire.

I did not see you in the hallway. She was giggling almost, and quite suddenly he could not help himself, he was laughing as well. She had frightened him like the bogey he had once taken her to be. *Did any passersby hear us? Did they?* The night outside was dim above the haziness of the lamps. It was too foolish, to be caught in darkness together, and come bolting out like school children. *I believe we are in the clear. Oh, dear. How lunatic we must have looked.*

Tonight her clothing was basic, a simple grayish frock. Her appearance was more relaxed than the day she had come to his office—though he noted she was still wearing the cheap, cotton gloves—and Bram found the change appealing. Hatless, her chestnut hair was wavy and soft as he had imagined it would be, kept away from her brow, this time, in a simple knot. His sudden gladness at encountering the seamstress highlighted the lugubrious state into which he had fallen. It was not simply the turn she had given them both, but that her presence seemed an unexpected boon, the way one is pleased to come across daffodils on a windy hike.

So, so! You remained for the whole of this evening's performance? I believe the Spirit of the Lyceum was to be seen, once more, in the Nook of the Stair.

Yes, sir. I am here.

Indeed. They walked carefully alongside each other. *You are certainly our production's most ardent fan.*

Miss Terry... she...

Yes, of course, Bram agreed, surprised by the bitterness in his own voice. Quickly he added: *She and Mister Irving are both masters of their trade. London is immeasurably enriched by their efforts.*

Hesitant, he looked around the thinning street.

I say... how are you to get home?

I walk, sir.

But where are your fellow—the other seamstresses?

They go. She sought the phrase, the pulled gloves expressing her effort. *When all the work is made.*

Do you mean to say that every time, each time you watch the play, you have been walking home afterward, unattended? It had honestly not occurred to him that the mysterious girl might be remaining for all five acts, still less to wonder where her place of residence was, or how she travelled there and back. *How far have you to go across the city?*

I walk an hour, sir... more, a little.

You...?

It is all right.

It is certainly not! You are alone—darkness has fallen—it is hardly done.

They had reached Victoria Embankment, where the nightly cloud was sliding off the river, bringing its odor of burning. From downriver came the clang of the barge: more fog on the way. Bram was torn in two directions, between his uncertainty over the foreigner's safety and the real risk he was taking in speaking to a young, unchaperoned female in the street. Cautiously he checked the faces of several persons walking nearest them. It would be unwise to be noticed together... *Why, you are crying!*

It is nothing, sir. It is not...

She turned away, but his instinct to defend any woman stood hotly to the fore. *Miss Lucy, come aside.* He searched for some private place. A bench, there, underneath a cowl of spreading oak. What a chaos of sentiment were the frailer sex, to laugh in one moment and weep the next! *What is it, my dear? Has someone been unkind to you?*

The little seamstress was unable to respond. Then it all leapt from her in a rush.

Oh, why does she do this, sir? Why?

Tears burst out completely with her words, spilling down both cheeks in sparkling lines. She had no shame of her emotion, making no effort at all to conceal the drops. Instead she only stared through them, as through something in her way. *Why? Why does she—?*

Who? Heavens, who, my dear?

Why does she make herself... in the stream, in the water?

The stream?

It is not good, fair. She should never have. Never!

My dear—are you truly beside yourself over the fate of Ophelia...?

The angry, open-eyed teardrops overflowed again, their perturbation dismayingly real. In half-formed English the seamstress hurried forward, talking about the terrible event, the drowning of the pretty woman who had been on the stage, who was so happy until the young man treated her that way and she went mad. Good lord, good lord, Bram thought frantically, searching his cloak pockets for a kerchief. Was it even possible? He tried in his mind to gather this together, to understand what was happening. It must have taken her many, many evenings—hidden in the Nook, and contesting, along with everything else, with a version of English that would have been near incomprehensible. Perhaps only one line, at first—one scene, roughly conceived—then a full act; then two, three—until finally, complete performances of *Hamlet* were happening before her every night, the Bard throwing his spells over an untutored mind, one with neither preparation nor guile. This poor recipient, fascinated by the action, captured in the shadows by she knew not what, watching, watching, until finally (had it been this very night?) she had achieved the impossible. She had understood the story.

Understood: and it had outraged her heart.

My dear, it is only art, Bram began to say, then stoppered the hateful sounds. How could he resort to so disgraceful a dismissal? This non-person had *striven* with a masterpiece, and it had cleaved her to the root. He could have laughed. How many of the Oxford-pinned gentry in the boxes had performed anything like her labor? It was rich, painfully rich. Had any of the grand English crowd felt what this waif, this unsuspected cipher on the stair, had felt—had anyone in the Lyceum actually *seen* the play?

One person had. And she was no more visible than he.

But the dark-featured seamstress was still staring at him, in her angry, tearstained expression the unanswered question. Why does she do this terrible thing? The kerchief unfolded slowly in Bram's hand.

Miss Lucy, what... what you are asking...

He hardly knew how to speak, what words might not be impotent. Why must Ophelia drown? She had turned to him as the keeper of these mysteries, him, Acting Manager of the miraculous. Before, he had felt pride. How should he speak now, and not expect his falsities to be turned into black daggers against his own breast?

I must say, Miss Lucy. Bram struggled, as with bitter drink. *I really must say...*

A hansom swung by, twin lanterns lit, and he pulled back. For a moment shadows swept them. But no one had seen.

Discreetly, he reestablished their original positions; he had been leaning a bit too close.

I must say, it is gratifying to find among the working people... among the workers... one whom I believe... one who so thoroughly responds to the finer aspects of theatre. Now, don't turn aside! You do credit to your class.

She did not need to die.

The statement was so bald, so painfully direct, that it had the absolute weight of a cry against the universe. All his posturing was dashed.

No... no, he murmured.

A cool river fog had begun to build around them, nacreous in color, condensing on the shells of the lamps. In the nearest houses he could see servants' hands drawing blinds against the thickening night. A bat made a rapid swooping circle, vanishing in the direction of the piers.

No indeed. She should not have done.

The embarrassing female tears had stopped, in the same direct manner in which they emerged. What was it, what did he find so captivating in the lines of this foreign face, the disjointedness that formed an odd harmony? Slow-clopping, a horse and rider ambled past, candle raised in hand. Its glassed flame trailed briefly, like the will-o-the-wisp.

Nine O'Clock. Nine O'Clock. Nine O'Clock.

Bram was glad for the leafy adumbration that concealed them both. He needed to consider his position carefully. If someone were to pass more closely—a newspaper man who recognized Bram's own face; a regular at Florence's garden parties; any of his own scores of employees—the misunderstanding, and its impact, could be serious.

Yet he could not allow this young soul to walk, unprotected, through the perilous byways of night. And then, something else drew him as well. For a woman, not even an Englishwoman, to be riven by *Hamlet*, to sob over a picture on a stage! He had seen some hint of strong capacities, but *this*. What kind of intelligence dwelt inside so unlikely a vessel?

Come, allow me to accompany you. At least part of the way.

Sir?

A few streets, at least. As precaution.

She wiped dry her cheeks. *Oh, no, sir.*

I insist.

She resisted, but he would not be swayed. It was unacceptable to have her undertake such a risk. And since he, as her employer, was in part responsible for the lateness of her commute... still uncertain, she pulled her shawl more tightly around her ribs and they began, at proper distance, to walk the embankment.

But she stopped and faced him.

Sir, it is not... you do not do this... have to do this... for me.

To be frank, Bram replied, *it has become my habit, of late, to spend much of the evening strolling. I should rather enjoy the company.*

You do not go home?

I have a home, he offered confusedly. It was not what she had asked. *I am not expected there until quite late, often after midnight. Such is the life of the theatre man.*

He had not mentioned Florence, though it would have been natural, at that interchange, to do so. More than natural, it would only be proper. The wedding ring was concealed under his glove. Yet surely Miss Lucy knew him to be wedded; there was no need to establish a boundary both would, in common civility, abide. But he did not mention Florence.

With one hand Bram tapped the furled umbrella, in time with his step, to the chipped paving stones. The chilly fog was across them now, making unearthly the street. It was the hour most reminiscent of his childhood in Clontarf, when Queen Mab sang through the ivy, when the pixies flitted out of any shade-crowded wood. For a moment his mother's ghost walked with them.

I do not understand.

The seamstress looked at him questioningly again, a mixture of emotions contending on her face. She knew nothing of his hounded sense, his heart-sore nights. To her, he was only the Acting Manager, and his concern for a common worker's safety, like his willingness to allow her to remain in the Nook, was unaccountable.

What do you not understand, Miss Lucy?

She hesitated before breaking their glance, and his breath hitched a little.

The story… why it goes that way.

The play?

Yes. The O-phelia.

This, Miss Lucy, Bram said after a few steps, *is what is meant by* tragedy. *If you would learn dramatic art, you must first understand this.*

Perhaps, Bram thought—stray thought, almost poetic!—perhaps two invisible spirits, wandering together, might see each other. Perhaps magic worked like that.

Let us discuss it, shall we? As we walk.

Stepping over a puddle she reached out suddenly to clutch his elbow and Bram's heart took a jump. Lamplight, dropping in faint formless leafquivering shelves, sparkled along her shoulders and cheek. They were headed east, together, away from the sun.

Chapter 9

1.

HE CAME ACROSS MISS LUCY THE NEXT EVENING AFTER CURTAIN-DROP, accompanying her partway once more in the direction of her home. And then again, that Saturday, after Bram had finished snuffing the wicks in the great hall, he found her outside, simply waiting for him, as if a silent agreement had been reached.

He walked with her, that night, for almost an hour. Lost in a rewarding discussion of Polonius (he is quite pompous, indeed so, and yet he makes a deal of sense!) they proceeded along the rain-flecked bricks of Fleet Street, Ludgate Hill, all the way to Aldgate and the border of the original city. *Aldgate*, Bram mused, foolishly pleased at his own learning: the "Old Gate," the ancient boundary that delineated Imperial *Londinium* from all that stood outside. Once there had been an enormous wall here, a defensive centurion ring, built to protect the city. Beyond it might have been made out, reflected in the anxious night watchman's eye, the first, vague shapes of an elder earth, the primitive miles, unmapped by Rome, and defiant of all civilization. The howling, barbarian waste.

The East End was still, to Bram, such a wilderness, one whose conditions he had only partly glimpsed. As they walked farther into its littered boroughs, where the poor loitered on stoops and occasional sounds of drunkenness broke free, alarm began to whisper around Bram's taut senses, telling him he was beginning, now, to risk actual danger. They had been treading, with each journey, closer to some definitive threshold, one he obscurely felt he might regret having crossed. But he would not sacrifice the joy of these conversations, which were to him sunshine at midnight.

Sir, you must not come past here. For an instant the seamstress placed a small hand on Bram's chest, and his skin drew tight. He sought to feign a casual air.

No farther, this evening? I see, I see.

They were standing at the entry to a series of rather narrow walkways, down one of which shadowy figures leaned up against the brick. Bram had been in the midst of a long explanation of dramatic verse, and only at this moment had been made conscious of their actual surroundings. How late had it become? He was conspicuous in his bowler hat, gray Holland collar, expensive houndstooth coat. Near the end of the lane, a steel ashcan in which a fire had been lit was making the air cloudy. One or two of the figures turned in their direction, beginning to take notice of him. *Are we, then, comfortably near your destination?* He fought to keep his voice steady.

The seamstress' high cheeks were anxious with color. *You must go back.*

Very well, very well.

He nodded politely as she slipped off into the darkness, raising the shawl to conceal her head. Bram could feel his ears burning from the weird attempt to listen behind himself as he began retracing their steps, forcing his cloth-topped spats not to hurry, never hurry, for to do so would be to suggest one is conscious of threat. No one followed him, and after a few blocks his heart slowed its rhythm.

Yet somewhere even farther east, he reflected, with a thin breath—when he had made it home safely to Florence, his head still windy with all that might have happened, but did not—somewhere deeper in there, the most perilous boroughs of London, must be the place the too-sensitive creature called her home.

2.

WEEKS PASSED. IN THE PUBLIC EYE, ALL REMAINED AS IT HAD BEEN; NOTHing would seem to have changed, he felt reasonably certain, in the routines of the perpetually bustling Acting Manager of the Lyceum. His evenings away from Southampton Street were already frequent, the long hours hidden behind the office door no more numerous than before. Now, however, his professional burdens included an additional, secret labor, one that was in equal parts pleasurable and dangerous.

By the third week, Bram knew he was exposing himself to real jeopardy in strolling so frequently with the seamstress. Probably the greater risk was not even the garrotter's wire, but the gossip's tongue. How could he explain himself were they to be suddenly confronted, so far from house, or club, or his place of employment? There were plasterers, haulers, paper-hangers who knew his outline; some likely hailed from the poor wards. He imagined the pose he would strike. *It might not be considered outside the purview of Acting Manager,* he pictured himself huffing, *to see any of Lyceum's employees safely returned to her lodgings.* But such prevarication would be unlikely to succeed. The direction of their nighttime ambles was bending now, clearly, toward Whitechapel, and Whitechapel was home, as all knew, not only to the garment district. A gentleman risking its avenues by moonlight would be assumed, in the instant, to be animated by disreputable purpose.

Indeed, he reflected to his paused quill pen with some discomfort, might this be the very reason he had been able to pass into the shadowy region, thus far, unmolested? Those in search of lechery could go with a certain impunity. Such a figure was gold for the pimp—and bruisers might be set on any interloper who *interfered* with trade, rather than on those reprehensible types who paid for lust in the shadows. It was the economy of night. Picking his route hurriedly out of Aldgate after one of their evening walks, Bram had seen beggars, goitered women, filthy indigents huddled in stairwells for warmth. But, worse, he had made out also the shadows of other gentlemen, hat brims down, entering or returning from the Whitechapel district in silent circumspection. Would not the same conclusion be drawn of him as he drew of others, that they were one in a community of shame?

Yet when the opportunity emerged to go secretly, once more, with the brownhaired seamstress, he found he could not resist. He accused himself of betraying the trust of Mister Irving, even of inconstancy to Florence, and to the institution of marriage. But no, and a thousand times, no; he was not engaged in an illicit relationship. This was not a relationship of the *body* at all, but one of the mind. He was merely drawn to this strange woman's character, to the unusual combination of so lively an intellect in so lowly a vessel.

Surely this made a difference.

Despite her deep intuition, Miss Lucy had misunderstood *Hamlet* significantly, and much of their time was spent in basic correction. (No, no; Horatio is not his brother, merely a good friend. He has not many of those, does he?) Yet, for all that, what she had managed to accomplish merely by watching the play was remarkable. How would one know, Bram pondered in his more relaxed hours, if, through some humor of the gods, a woman were to be gifted with unusually high intelligence? It might go entirely unnoticed. No pork pie hats were to be seen at Cambridge, where it was assumed they would distract the dons with their irrelevant fancies. It had never occurred to Bram to question the general assumptions regarding the frailer sex and education. It did not occur to him now. But Miss Lucy's case might be singular, even extraordinary. Hers was like a man's mind inside a woman's body. Indeed, in some respects, her powers of apprehension could be said to surpass even those of some gentlemen he knew.

It struck him that his secret pupil might benefit from the written word, something in still worthy, but far simpler English. *Here you are, my dear. You might attempt, as best you can,* She Walks in Beauty. *If I have a moment, later this week, I shall be interested to see what you make of the lines.* Bram expected the process to take time. But she stopped him the following night, having devoured the whole, hungry still for more.

She was not always at the Lyceum; curtain-drop passed, here and again, with no sign of that face. Bram dared not inquire after her, not even to step through the wardrobe room more frequently than was dictated by need. Then he would spy her again, with two or three other seamstresses, her proud umber curls immediately distinguished from the circle of bowed heads. Well well, he grinned inwardly, the Spirit of the Lyceum is returned! And we shall see what she has made of *Hebrew Melodies*.

She was from a rural village, somewhere in the east of Europe. Her relations had conspired to come westward, with several others, across a great distance on wagon and foot. And then to the sea... but he had discovered no more. Of all that, she had no interest in speaking. Rather, she wanted to know poetry, to know about theatre, and how it was made. She wanted this magical power of art.

Part of him had quietly expected this situation to "run out its course," but the truth was that Bram found himself, as the weeks progressed, only increasingly delighted at their back-and-forth moments, snuck into the workday's bustle. It was wholly gratifying to have someone pendant on *his* word like this, someone eager to follow *his* thoughts. Once or twice he had jumped, thinking one of their discussions overseen by a passing set-man, but nothing had come of it. Would that he and Miss Lucy could sit, at their ease reclined, in some comfortable parlor; then he could better communicate to her the flavor of his most beloved passages from this poem or that play. She would bring him his tea, with a few of the pinwheel sandwiches he favored. He might make her a small present at Christmastime. Perhaps he would even share with her his own ambitions, the dream he still held of one day discovering "his book," the great, true thing he was destined to write. *Another sketch, my dear, from my own pen—but, I hope, leading toward something better. Will you honor me by reading it?* Certainly he was no longer invited to show his creative attempts to Mister Irving. The last time he tried, the actor had sighed heavily, tilting his Romanesque brow deeply into the fingers of one hand.

Which one of us is the artist, Stoker? Is it you, or I?

Of course, I wouldn't presume...

Will this... Irving had glanced coldly at the title. *Shall "The Mystery of the Windy Mine" allow you to occupy a position, one day, among the immortals? Will it, do you think? Then why must you write at all?*

The rebuff had wounded him—as had Florence's insistence that they attend a ball at Fitzsimmon's, on one of the few nights Bram had been able to conclude at a decent hour. Yet, even at the tedious soiree, he found himself newly intrigued, the social routine seen freshly, as if in a dawning light. Thanks to his familiarity with a seamstress (how unfavorably it sounded in those terms!), he had become conscious of the hurrying activity that ran, like a buried stream, underneath the West End social circuit. Everywhere he must go now was changed, so that a covert, amused part of his mind came to regard genteel society as little more than an exposition of women's dresses. Never before had he asked what it took to construct such orchid-like human display. Florence herself was mad to have the latest hue and cut; when they appeared, once, at the Argonauts Club in a gloss of stiff crinoline and whalebone that was thought (God alone knew how!) to be "out by a month," she had been unruly for the rest of the evening.

Yet behind it all, Bram mused: behind the Westminster stages and the Mayfair salons, those dual spaces devoted to human performance: behind all of this lay the needle-women, unknown Arachnes who wove up the dream.

3.

IT WAS THE END OF THE MONTH, A THURSDAY NIGHT—JUST AS MISS Lucy thanked him in her abrupt way, and disappeared once more into the fog—that Bram found himself, suddenly, in physical danger. Tonight had been their longest walk yet. So engrossed had he become with her company that he entirely failed to notice the badly declining character of the region through which she was leading him. Now, without warning, he was alone, well past ten o'clock at night, in one of the most threatening wards of all London.

Bram swallowed hard, finding his throat raspy. He believed he was somewhere quite near Whitechapel, perhaps within its precincts altogether. In front of him slumped a pile of old mortar and wood, all nails, fallen from an archway and left unattended. To its side, an emaciated woman clutched a baby wrapped in newspaper. It might have been past eleven o'clock, even; he dared not draw out his watch to check. The night was clouded. Spinning with what he hoped was a strong, unconcerned air he aimed his boots homeward, but must have taken a false turn; in under a minute he found himself horrifiedly pushing through crowds of besmirched indigents, beggars that had appeared from nowhere. The narrow buildings were a webwork of smashed windows, mice racing along their ledges. Where had he failed to retrace his steps? None of these streets were properly lit. How could he have been such a fool?

Stumbling across a cab stand Bram took hold of the painted pole and began waving strongly to attract a cabbie's attention.

Clean, a voice whispered at his side. A woman had emerged from the filthy alley behind him. *Clean*, she said again, hands lifting her small breasts, her voice a sad Irish brogue. *I am clean*. This was a threat of an entirely different nature. Her face was painted, an attempt to suggest knowing adulthood.

It was an appealing face, even in ruin. She had red Galway hair and wore a cheaply made bodice, and two sets of stockings, blue ones over white, the childish thighs held in their double embrace. He could smell perfume.

No... no.

Bram clambered frantically into the cab that had drawn up and hammered the roof, saying loudly the name of Covent Garden. As the midnight bells rang out once again he entered his own home safely, undressed in darkness, lay down beside Florence and stared at the dusty yellow ceiling.

Nothing untoward had taken place; there would be nothing to explain; he had neither compromised Lyceum's reputation nor sinned against his own character. He had never intended to be anywhere so indescribable, certainly not at such an hour. Florence stirred vaguely in her sleep and Bram wondered what in heaven's name he was doing. Why was he risking everything—absolutely everything—all that he had labored to create? Confusion and disquiet coursed through his blood. And yet, and yet... marriage had proved unrewarding, frustrating even. Why skirt the truth? The weird dreams, the anxieties he and Florence experienced in the bedroom, caused them both to suffer.

Clean, the voice whispered. It would have been so easy to touch female skin, just there, where it bulged above the tight band of the stockings... Bram almost whimpered in his bedclothes. In a terrible flood, he longed for what was bought and sold so easily under the cover of Whitechapel darkness.

But he did not, and would not. The frustrations of the flesh were a cross, but he would bear their heavy wood rather than unburden his need in perdition. Probity, integrity: these were the values by which all society stood, and if their maintenance required heroism, that served only to underscore their necessity.

Let the spell of the beguiling ghost, and her secret world, end. He would not go east again.

Chapter 10 (east)

1.

WHEN BRAM STOKER WAS A CHILD——THE MEMORY ENTERING HIS DREAM tonight, like a doorway leading to a doorway; by morning he will have forgotten once more——when he was a child, this had happened. In Clontarf, during the months and years of his long disability.

Late one night, he had flung down the covers and dragged his numb legs from the bed, sensing, in a child's intuitive way, that someone was underneath the window. The woman looking up at him was so thin as to be skeletal. Underneath one arm she held something in a blanket: an infant, its white head bobbing loosely. Bram realized it was dead.

Thornley. Thornley.
I was sleeping.
Look down there. There's a sad person.
Where?

Get away, get away, Abraham Senior, alive once more in the theatre of time, hissed over the front stoop. *You'll get no handouts here.*

Bram, appalled, watched the starving mother rejoin the other emigrants, scores, hundreds, how many. He would not remember this moment until decades later, kneeling in desperation in a Covent Garden chapel. Across the green at the docking slip his dying countrymen gathered around the ships, staring at the tied-up gangplanks as if at any moment one might turn into Jacob's ladder, some few easy steps between themselves and salvation.

2.

On a Sunday morning in early spring Bram left Florence at Lossiter Courts, where she and several acquaintances were hunting the new fashion in feather hats, and hired a cab to take him briefly 'round Hillcrest the back way to Lyceum. For the past several weeks Bram had been to Paris on legal business for Irving, with a long stopover in Wisborg, Germany, before returning finally to London—singularly refreshed, and free entirely of the weird sense of the sinister. Up from Waterloo Bridge, now, a group of bicyclists was squeaking, while at the busy corner a painter in a long frock worked on the "modern" style. Bram's indiscretions put well in the past, the blossoming city looked grand once more. He remembered the hurried, first days after debarking from Ireland, racing about this town with his new wife on his arm, both their chins hung at the enormity of the prize. Westminster Abbey, the Crystal Palace, the cavernous, echoing belly of St. Paul's. Nothing in either of their experiences had hinted that such structures might exist on the earth, filigreed from pavilion to spire with all the furbelows of Empire.

The very Lyceum had seemed to welcome Bram home, with its enormous stone edifice, proudly distinct from all other buildings on Wellington. Its front comprised four massive Corinthian pillars, exterior lamps hung on lengths of black chain, a bannered marquee depicting Miss Terry, arms upflung, in an operatic pose. Unlocking one entrance, Bram gathered some papers he had left absentmindedly on the edge of the stage, and turned to leave once more—but suddenly found his eye caught by the Nook of the Stair.

How that neither-here-nor-there space had once haunted him! As if in defiance he walked over to the Nook, laughing quietly, and, after a pause, headed down the stairway to the empty wardrobe room. For a moment he only stood, breathing the scent of raw cloth, surrounded by long streams of beige and pink satin. Slowly he put out a hand, running it along the curve of a dressmaker's dummy, feeling the softness from the hip to the gentle rise of the breast.

Stoker! Are you down there?

What is it, Henry. Bram hurried guiltily from the room, one hand clutching the inner lining of his pocket. There had been nothing inappropriate in his behavior, nothing he could not explain. Yet the unexpected voice caused his gullet to contract. *I hadn't realized you were in, this morning. I'm only stopping by, myself.*

My ink has come loose, Irving growled, throwing the defective cloak on the footstool. He was in a casual loose fitting shirt, his hair pushed back, as if still in his own house. *See the collar. The fools have done a botch job.*

I'm quite sure it's easily stitched. Silly nerves!

Bram stepped deferentially to the chair, picking up the jacket Irving referred to as his "ink" after Hamlet's own "inky cloak." Yes, the lining on the collar was showing a very small strip of white.

An omen, Irving sighed, touching the heavy, rose-colored cross he had taken to wearing under his shirt. *The show, too, may be growing worn.* Like most actors, Irving had a deeply superstitious vein, one that resulted in a series of idiosyncratic talismans: a St. Christopher medal, a cameo of the Queen, once a tiny silver spoon he sewed into his breast pocket. The cross, a silver outline with rosy glass interior, represented his latest indulgence, designed to keep his art strong as the run passed seventy-five nights. Bram had only ever seen the man take it off when undressing.

Nonsense. All are agreed it is a marvel, and tickets continue to sell. Your Hamlet will break one hundred performances, or I am a fool.

That may well be, Irving grinned, enjoying the ambiguity in his reply. Bram offered a compliant gesture.

It was ten in the morning, barely; the sky over Big Ben had been apricot when he rode past, a crowd of thrushes crossing noisily toward the river. Bram had not intended to do any business today. This morning, in fact, he had set aside as an opportunity to restart his own search for a suitable subject for a novel—he would of course say nothing of this—before Florence's luncheon. Then he had remembered that he needed the ledger. And then he had gone to stand in the wardrobe room, merely passing his fingers over the fabrics, gently, in recollection.

But Irving's mood had grown somber again.

It may be an omen. He fingered the cross, eyes burning into the lightly worn cloak as if a whole host of black cats vexed his path.

There now. Bram poured some tea from a fresh pot that steamed on the table. *This is your imagination.*

Ah, my mind has scorpions in it!

Irving ignored the proffered cup and rose instead, running a thumb along the edge of Lord Byron's dagger where it hung over his desk. The blade was curved in Turkish fashion, a figured wooden grip attached to a quillon for both ornament and stability. Lady Caroline Lamb, the story went, had used this very device to threaten suicide at a waltzing party in Switzerland. Lord Byron had been unmoved by her threats, only suggesting she step onto the verandah so as not to sully the furnishings.

For a time, Irving seemed lost in contemplation. Then his face turned severe. *Fix it, Stoker.*

The collar? This is Sunday.

Damn it, man! Did I ask for an opinion? I told you to fix this collar and you will fix it before the next curtain! Irving swooped into his greatcoat and cane, then stopped, tapping speculatively the door frame with his massive ring. *There is something different about you of late. What has changed?*

Bram set down the unloved cup, the heavy defective weight of the cloak slung across his free arm.

Nothing has changed, Henry.

His employer's eyes narrowed.

Truly, Bram added, reaching for casualness. *The ink will be mended by morning, just as you wish. I shall see to it myself.*

3.

OUT OF DOORS WAS LIGHTER THAN IN, SUNLIGHT PLAYING ACROSS WINDY rooftops streaked with the droppings of gulls. The unexpected task would keep him from Florence's luncheon entirely. It was a formal occasion, one at which he had not expected to see much of his wife, but he had promised to be on hand. Rapidly Bram sketched an explanation on the back of a card and paid an urchin to run it to her, lamenting how he had been detained once again "in the King's service" (their code) and saying that the guests should not wait to take refreshment. He hesitated at the note's end, feeling observed by the grubby boy in his cap, and winced before tearing off the section where he had written *Love* and signing instead *With sincerest apologies, B.*

Well, then—it would not be pleasant to travel into the garment district, and all unexpected, but now it had to be done. This was no clandestine stroll, skirting the edges of impropriety, but business. He should not be protected any more from seeing what lay beyond London Wall.

Bram hired a one-man hansom, folding closed the door. The shop from which the costumes were delivered was deep within Whitechapel itself, the very region wherein Miss Lucy had been leading him, though of course he had no expectations of seeing her. By his own decision, their paths had not crossed for a good stretch—over a month now, including the weeks in Paris—during which time he had avoided all situations in which the Acting Manager might, by chance, come across a seamstress in the hall, and had simply ceased their nightly rambles, leaving the theatre always by a different route. To come across her today would present difficulties: he had acted rudely, though out of necessity: but the likelihood of encountering one particular face in that mill of thousands was too small for concern. He planned to ride directly to the dressmaker's, demand his changes while the cabbie waited, and escape as expediently as possible. His fingers pressed down against the booklet in which the address was written. It would have been somehow odd, in any event, to encounter the seamstress by daylight; and it occurred to him, for the first time, that their entire, curious relationship had transpired after nightfall.

The wooden compartment swayed and Bram fisted one hand on the seat, where the cloth lining was coming away from the sash. There was an irony—was there not?—in his having walked almost to the rookeries several times behind Mister Irving's back, only to be ordered into them now. Vaguely a part of his speculation wondered again why the needle-woman had never allowed him to accompany her past Aldgate, but had darted off each night they were together, like a flitting shadow. It was, he had thought more than once, as if the solidity of his own social set vanished as they crossed from one end of London to the other, as if the city were two worlds side by side, each with its own distinct atmosphere. She had been of the immaterial side.

Well, Bram thought wryly (as the wheel knocked a quite material stone), he would, by close of day, have at least pierced one of the lingering mysteries of her world. Even if he wisely chose not to see her again, he would have seen where she passed her days.

Ere we are, gov'. Whitechapel, there.

My good man. I am bound for... Bram checked the address... *Goulston Street.*

The driver looked him over, eyeing uncomfortably his bowler, his gray gloves, the tailored coat.

Better you'll not be goin all tat fah, gov'nah. If you don' mind moy sayin, loik.

I ask you to continue on. I have business on Goulston.

Ere, no offense, gov'. The driver was not supercilious. He looked legitimately concerned. *Better back again, eh? Back again.*

Bram climbed angrily from the bouncing cab, causing the horse to snort. *I shall make note of your number.* Without paying, he continued on foot.

It was an appalling region; he had not understood. The discomfort he had experienced walking past Aldgate was nothing compared to this. Hurrying his pace Bram entered a tangle of decrepit brick courts, cut by dank, close, maze-like lanes. The true poverty of Whitechapel was worse than any he had seen in his life, and he pushed on, fingers pumping apprehensively the head of his cane. He was a large figure, broad-chested still, having kept much of the good muscle of his undergraduate days. Nonetheless he was glad to have taken the walking stick with the heavy goatshead tip.

Through a press of streets moved an immigrant sea, their faces made blue with ash. A rack of bottles, set out to dry; a refuse pile guarded over by a snarling cur; mounds and heaps and warrens of decayed housing. The footway itself on which he walked was no more than an earthen channel dug into the mud. Laborers' cottages, now, rot spreading in reeking patches right through their foundations. And everywhere, children. Their dirty smudged blotched faces stared up at him rudely, unwashed mouths turning over in amusement as he forced away their open hands. Trying to maintain a dignified posture Bram hurried under a railway arch, straining to find any indication of street names in the morass. A public soup kitchen; a black heap of building with painted-over windows, likely an opium den; part of a rail station, one that had never been connected to the main lines and so lay rusting like despair.

For your mama's sake, a dry voice hissed by his side. Bram twisted away. An old woman was holding out a necklace with a crucifix. Her face was scaly with lesions.

I do not wish to buy.

She was almost toothless, and he could see the brown tongue moving in there.

For your mama's sake.

Bram pushed through another series of warrens, locating, quite suddenly, the workshop by accident. It was a narrow brick building with two and a half floors, and, rising up a series of crumbling steps, he knocked sharply. The door was opened (he had the impression that his arrival had not been noted so much as that someone happened to have been standing on the other side) by a powerful looking, square-faced man in an unbuttoned vest. The man's sleeves were rolled over hairy forearms; on the back of each hand coiled a tattoo of a snake, one orange, the other green. A mane of hair, with freely growing, expansive muttonchops, surrounded his ill-mannered expression. For a minute he stood silently, regarding Bram's quality clothing.

This garment, Bram showed the faulty collar as fearlessly as he could, *has been supplied to the Lyceum Theatre. It is not acceptable. I will see it repaired, Sunday or no, at no charge.*

But the stocky man had left while Bram was still speaking; he knew no English. Bram waited, agog, on the cracked stoop. In the street, a small horse dragged forward a cart, its owner flogging the unhappy animal's sides. Figures in rags began gathering around the steps, watching him. To avoid them Bram went into the building, inside which visible pipework dripped down an interior wall, and closed the door as securely as he could. Awkward, then, in the gloomy hallway, he found a gas lamp and turned the little dial. No gas...

A second man, nodding but equally wordless, passed in suspenders and unfixed shirt. As Bram waited, this balding, rounder fellow ascended a series of wooden steps that occupied the majority of the front room with a heavy tread. Indeed, the space in which Bram was standing provided little more than a landing place for the questionable stair, which appeared to have been nailed in as an afterthought. Bram followed the man, placing his own weight carefully, and found on the building's second floor an entryway over which had been hung an improvised drape. The air up here was hot and close, the fact of his having risen even by the height of the rickety staircase compounding its oppressive swell. From beyond the curtain emanated the harsh sounds he had been hearing, he realized, since he stepped inside: mechanical, repetitive. Using his cane gingerly to lift away the cloth, he ducked through.

Inside was the sweatshop itself. It would have been cramped, were there only five persons in it, yet the immediate impression was of a crate jammed full to its edges. Perhaps two dozen women were seated within, bent low over rough wooden tables. The youngest ones appeared no older then twelve or thirteen. The uneven floor had been covered in newspaper sheets, with more sheets tacked to the walls in various orientations. A few green-hooded lamps stood about, but what actual illumination there was fell though a large opening that had been cut directly into the ceiling. Orange tints of sunlight, struggling to proceed through dirty glass, stained the mote-thick air.

Despite the uncomfortable press of workers, cloth lay everywhere. Tightly rolled bolts, fragments, stray pieces in dozens of shapes and hues, had all been preserved and stretched across thin wooden racks. If the costume shop at the Lyceum was a place for women's work, this room was its nightmarish apotheosis. Worst of all, the tumid air was full of a stink that leaped directly at his sinuses: harsh, vinegary, leaching up from steel pots in the corners, inside which stood open bottles of dye.

Merciful—! Bram gagged, fingers rising involuntarily to his nose.

The chattering sound that overwhelmed the room was proceeding from the operation of black enameled machines, underneath the snouts of which long stretches of fabric sailed like maniac spirits. The women crouched at machines, though, were outnumbered by those sewing by hand, each one's lap weighted down with a pile, giving a mocking resemblance to a salon full of new mothers. There was something Doré about the whole, as if he had entered on a scene of torment.

All the workers looked up—all save one, sewing busily still, in the corner—in unfeigned astonishment at his arrival. After a moment of abashed confusion, several stood from their labors, moving stools aside and turning toward him with hands and eyes down, as if accused. The rattling noises stopped. Before Bram could speak, the whole room of sweat-laborers was standing; one reached out to signal the sallow-cheeked girl near the wall, who rose uncertainly, her face pointing the wrong way.

I'm terribly sorry, Bram began, both fear and indignity flown. *My name is Bram Stoker. I represent the interests of Mister Henry Irving. At the Lyceum Theatre, on Wellington.*

The frightened women murmured hurriedly to each other in little bird noises. Bram was lost among the foreign, reduced to apologetic gestures. The mildly worn collar in his hands was farcical, the stench from the dye vats overwhelming. He wanted only to be gone from this building, from this entire borough, to be at Florence's luncheon, safely beyond the London Wall. By now she would be spreading the flowers in crystal vases, one to each table, tucking little pink cards beside each proper placemat... but as Bram backed away, the frightened needle-women began calling to each other, down a stubby hallway that nonetheless had a bend in it. One in a soiled headwrap signaled him, wordlessly, to remain. They were bringing someone into the room.

Miss Lucy. Bram felt a rush of confused emotion, part pity, part longing. *My Lord. Is this, then... that is...*

Come out of here, sir, Miss Lucy said. Her curling hair was not attended to now, only knotted functionally to keep it away. She was wearing the shapeless attire of a worker. She spoke to the others, quickly, in their own tongue, before taking him from the sweating area and through the narrow hallway to a side room with low, heavy beams. After what Bram had seen, even this mildewed interior was a relief.

Forgive the intrusion, I beg you. You work, all of you must work like this, he felt ridiculous in asking, *on a Sunday?*

Back here are the sleeping rooms, Miss Lucy answered, misunderstanding his question. Or has she answered him in a more expansive fashion than he realized? Sleeping rooms. Could it be that this place of affliction was her home? Was *this* what she had never wanted him to see?

Miss Lucy turned to the trivial burden, once so important, in Bram's hands. *Is the stitching come free, sir...*

The sewing machines clattered afresh in the next room and Bram peered almost unwillingly back into its hellish close. Mats rolled into one corner, a small potato pot, full of inky water. Wooden boxes full of pencils and screws. On a plate set directly on the floor, he spotted, to his horror, toast crumbs and a piece of actual potato skin, too green to be swallowed.

Miss Lucy... is this building also your dwelling?

He saw her lips draw tight with shame. *We fix this...*

Hang the stitching.

This I can mend.

Lucy, he said, breaking her from it. She would not meet his eye. *I am not concerned with the collar. This...* but how could he speak his emotion? All Londoners knew the conditions under which the East End sweatshops conducted business. Even he, always something of an outsider, was aware. It was denounced in the papers, talks were given at societies for the increase of proper sanitation and the alleviation of vice among the working poor. Everyone in London *knew,* but he had not *known.*

Miss Lucy. It is dismal, too dismal.

He was still looking back at the sweatroom. The purblind worker in the corner was not the only one whose eyes were failing. Several of the women used their hands to locate objects around them in the drifting, inquisitive way of those losing their discrimination of sight. Nor could breathing, all day, this rank mix of sulphurs be anything but withering to the lungs. All such environments were unwholesome, a breeding ground for consumption. As if to confirm his suspicion, the rattle of machinery was punctuated by a series of brittle coughs.

Yet beyond this physical toil, Bram thought amazedly, lay truer horror. For any sensitive person, such conditions would hardly have been tolerable. But for a mind such as he had found Miss Lucy to possess... for such a rare intelligence as hers, to be imprisoned here, like a dray-horse, a cog...

How long have you been employed in this shop? He was a bounder to have avoided her, to have cast their evenings aside without explanation. He attempted a muttered apology, but she deserved more. *Miss Lucy, look at me.*

This can be mended... I will take...

No more of that!

Bram pulled the cloak a second time from her shaking hands. And he saw: caught unprepared this morning, she was not wearing the cotton gloves that concealed her disfigurement. Every one of her little fingers was cracked and bleeding, one or two fingernails blackened almost to the cuticle. The backs of both hands were burned with dye.

But Miss Lucy, your poor fingers!

Bram took the tiny things in his own gloved hands. She would not look away from an empty patch on the wall.

How long have you lived in this sweatshop, my dear? Tell me, please.

Unhappily he looked around the sleeping room. It was nothing, hardly a lady's closet: four stained walls, bare wood floor spotted by candle wax, a mattress at one end next to a dressmaker's dummy that had evidently been moved in for storage. There was a single box on which was set a pitcher and cup, beside which rested—Bram spied it with a wince—his own copy of Byron's verses.

Stiffening suddenly, she pulled her hands away, her expression growing hard. *It is not right, sir.*

What is? That he had gone away, stopped speaking to her without explanation? That he had returned?

It is not right, the downcast eyes were adamantine. *You care.*

She did not mean that. Or, rather, she meant more; she was expressing that same incredulity she showed their first night together, when the great and artistic man offered to walk a mere needle-woman home safely.

I shall decide what is right, Bram retorted. *Tell me, please. How long?*

When she finally met his gaze, her expression was flaring, almost contemptuous. At him? Or the facts?

Since first I am to England.

And here—here—is where you have taught yourself to read our best language, to appreciate our arts, with such facility? With greater sensitivity than some proper ladies, even some gentlemen, of my acquaintance? Bram was stupefied, indignant with disbelief. The coping was damp, and probably full of insects. Jagged edges of metal, like treacherous serpents' teeth, could be seen emerging from spots. On one wall hung a crude violin, as if in mockery of the finer things. *To care, as you do, about theatre? With what power have you learned such delicate things… a broadside, a pamphlet? How have you come to…* his thought was: how have you come to be what you are?

Sir…

Answer me. I must know.

The sisters help each other.

The sisters… your fellow workers?

We read papers on the floors. Those who know, show the others.

It was too fantastical. Bram sighed, freeing a cloth from his sleeve to wipe at his forehead and neck. This heat was unrelenting, the only window nailed shut; and the miserable stench of dye. Under the bed frame he spotted another method, one she had not admitted: a small pile of what could only be stolen books.

And I had been giving you pages from George Gordon, Lord Byron. God in his heaven.

In the next room the machines were still at their clap-jawed clattering. It was as if they were having this discussion in the bowels of some infernal steam liner.

Miss Lucy, you have told me, I hope it is not impolite to recall, that you were barely nineteen when you arrived on our shores.

Her anger was done, but also her shame. There was solidity in her bearing, her brown eyes directly on his own.

Yes.

If I may be forgiven the impertinence...

I am twenty-four summers, in March.

And is this all you have known of London? These walls, this miserable locale? Have you never seen what is good and green?

Her silence was assent. The whole truth lit upon Bram at once: until Loveday made some arrangement—until she, and a few others, were sent by this shopmaster, like oxen carrying produce, across town to serve the Lyceum—this had been the perimeter of her cosmos. It was no wonder the plays had amazed her. Until now, England itself, beyond this squalor, had existed only in her imagination. On the first night she had dared to creep up from the wardrobe-room, she had forced her way out of Plato's cave and begun to witness the sun.

Two girls carrying baskets passed the open door, saw the well-dressed gentleman and retreated in astonishment. A third went by without noticing them, her young shoulders already bent like a coal miner's.

Come, Miss Lucy. It was unbearable. *Let me take you away from this.*

I cannot.

You shall, you must.

No, sir. Needle-women may not—the dresswork.

No work for today.

It is not...

Come. Is this your wrap? Come.

At the front steps, the balding man in suspenders blocked his way. His lined forehead was large and pinkish nearly to the top of his cranium, where the oiled black hair began all at once. Bram took him for an Italian. Miss Lucy stood unhappily by Bram's side, but by her clear deference (was it fear?) he recognized the shopmaster.

Sir. Bram, seeing how she evaded the Italian's ugly stare, felt anger in his heart. *You, sir. Do you speak English?*

... a leetle.

Bram felt his back teeth grit. The bounder could have greeted him properly from the first.

I am taking this seamstress.

I can see. Fingers arrogantly hooked in his high pockets, the shopmaster had spoken the words with an intonation of perfect ambiguity.

Miss Lucy waited in silent agony beside him. The other fellow, the larger, muttonchopped one, had come now to the head of the stair to watch over this proceeding, awaiting a signal. He massaged the colorful tattoos on the backs of both hands, as if the snakes were his pets. Bram gripped the goatshead cane more tightly; it occurred to him his bravado might have created a situation. Was actual violence a possibility?

He turned to leave, but the shopmaster stepped in front of him. The odious man's fingers wagged from his vest pockets, that falsely ingratiating face expecting something. Distastefully, Bram unwrapped his wallet.

Take this, Bram said, putting sovereigns in the shopmaster's palm. *I have need of Miss West-Ender for a while; she shall be returned. That is worth a dozen of whatever you might lose by her absence.*

When he saw coins in his hand the shopmaster retreated, his look of cunning replaced by the one men give fools who have parted with unnecessarily high sums. The muttonchops too on the stair had vanished. Transaction concluded. In a foul moment Bram wondered whether they believed he was purchasing Lucy altogether.

Miss West-Ender, Bram laughed suddenly, when he had secured a fast cab and the two of them were rattling and swinging north. *I did not know what else to call you.*

Suddenly the ridiculousness grew, and he belly-laughed loudly at his heroic moment. I am taking away Miss West-Ender! These were hardly the words of a rescuing knight. Miss Lucy, seeing his relief, broke into aghast helpless grinning as well, her fright and her tension mixing now with bewildered disbelief. Her red hands flew over her mouth.

I am taking her away! Bram cried happily. *Miss Lucy, of the West End! Oh, my heavens.*

Is it terrible?

No, no, I mean... It was incredible to be sitting here, in a creaking compartment, having done what he had just done. He was a gentleman, not a boxer; it was entirely unlike him. The day was bright again, the convulsing haunches of twin speckled horses hurrying them from all danger.

"*West-Ender*"... *I simply mean... Miss Lucy, what is your real name? You might tell me.*

She looked at him differently after his munificent act, something new coming to rest in those softening hazel eyes. Before, he had been the sage at the Lyceum who deigned, inexplicably, to explain Shakespeare. What was he now?

Lujzi Sido.

Say it again?

My family is from Szentgyörgy.

The name was all unknown to Bram, but evocative, as unvisited geography tends to be. He recognized none of the villages or towns she mentioned, though he did know of the mighty Carpathian Mountains, dragon's teeth of Eastern Europe. In his mind he saw stone towers, iceblue fastnesses.

Then 'West-Ender'...

Oh, this name they make me. The sisters.

Your fellow, the other seamstresses? He took it she did not mean actual relations.

Yes. They say I am—she laughed again, making a gesture with two fingers, nose in the air. Bram laughed, too.

It was the same, he thought, turning his flushed face toward the hurry of breeze, with women the world over. Her companions in that sweatshop had anointed her with a kind of pet name, for this one held her head higher than the others, this one carried herself with an air. "Little Miss West-Ender." She was the mistaken milliner, too intelligent by far, always dreaming of something past their general station.

He does not hurt you. Bram hesitated. *The Italian, I mean, or his companion. You are in no personal danger there.*

You are a good man, Miss Lujzi said quietly, looking out her side of the cab as if the words were confusing to her. Not the language, but the fact of what she was saying.

Bram had no words himself. He sensed he was a problem on which she was working, as intently, perhaps, as she had worked on understanding Ophelia. She held her raw hands in a bundle once more, and Bram wished he could unwrap them, salve the hurt skin, make it whole.

They exited at a green stretch near Highbury Fields, rolling out underneath an avenue of broad, decorous trees. The day had come clear once more, white, castle topped clouds, the copper factory smoke that proceeded always from the south blown into threads. With nothing—no context, no objective—they began to stroll, as if there were nothing else they might do than what they had always done: to speak to each other while walking. After a month apart, the pace of her feet seemed immediately natural, as if they had last been together only an hour before. Instinctively they followed the edge of the pond.

Tell me, Bram began. *Miss Lu—j-zi?*

Lujzi.

Tell me... well... your life. He wanted to say: your life before me.

It is only work.

No, I mean—that is how you have been living, I understand, in this country. Where were you, before?

She considered him again, her thick brow-line puzzling, as if she would crack the shell and examine the seed. For a space farther, they continued in silence. Then she said:

Your name is Abraham?

My Christian name? Bram was taken aback. *Yes. The actresses call me 'Uncle Bram'... I suppose I can be rather stuffy. But I hope it is said in affection.*

May I call you Abraham?

To do so would be wholly improper; on this, there could be no debate. But nothing Bram had done this day could be called proper.

I should like that, he said quietly.

Gradually, then, walking in time with their thoughts, she began. She spoke of her youth in the village of Szentgyörgy, in that alternately splintered and lambent version of English that defined her conversation, and which, part of Bram now felt, had always been the true location where they met. The fascinatingly incorrect language was itself a place, a retreat within which they might draw closer.

Grandmother... of the fever, I was very small... her skin I remember, how she smells always, like milk that is fresh. Icu, my brother, goes out to see fights, with three chickens. When one man lose, he beat Icu instead, they push him in the ring. Grandfather must come, and carry him home.

As they walked, the stories from this other world, this Eastern Europe she had known before Whitechapel, began to emerge in a deepening tide. Each came from her fully formed, without any wool-gathering; they were simply there, as if the forward motion of her life had been stopped all at once by sweatwork, and the leftover backed up to the dam. *Asleep in the lower field, covered all up in hay. Abraham, if you had see him! After this, Vilmos laughs, and says he will not drink again... agrees to take Samu, he is a little baby only, from snow until harvest... Vilmos sees the... the...*

She made a face.

Wolf? Bear.

Bear, it puts one foot through the ice, he runs here until his house, Samu is still inside his shirt. Do I say this right?

Bram had no conception of village life. He knew nothing of the exigencies of farming or husbandry, of those who cobbled, those who peddled wares on their backs, or those who sewed—the skill that would preserve her, this "Lujzi Sido," in a new land that must, still, have seemed as unreal to her as the Carpathians to a transplanted Irishman. *Caps and walking sticks they make to sell, mostly this. Grandfather, he makes always combs, out of sheep bones, the thin bones, here, in the side. No, first you must boil the skin. He, with Father, walks into eating places, selling the combs. My brother carries shoes.*

Is this Icu?

No, a different brother. Icu goes to Dunaszerdahely.

In a playful spirit, Bram purchased a Japanese fan from a cart. The salesman bowed significantly, making Miss Lujzi turn her head. The effect charmed him entirely.

Ah, dear—!

Her bearing was rough, yes, but hardly shameful. Once removed from the infernal Whitechapel, quite a different woman emerged. She had not only intelligence, but grace, a natural type of poise. It was an amusing conceit. Might a poor woman not, with instruction, pass unrecognized among her betters?

The fan could be opened on a sliding ring, with a peacock strutting plumage across white paper wings. *To shield you, Lady Luj-zi. I see you have arrived at today's outing* sans *bonnet.*

Taking the fan Miss Lujzi touched his wrist and Bram's blood began dancing. Oh, it was foolish, it was perhaps immoral even, but why not allow the feeling? His soul was at play for the first time in weeks. Then he saw her wince. She was hurt by sunlight, turning from the dappled reflections that came off the water. Should that surprise? The poor creature had been held captive in darkness; seven days of the week, evidently, must be spent in that vapor-filled chamber, straining her irises to the faint light from the panes overhead. Her teeth and skin were still healthy, her almond eyes not yet damaged beyond healing. But youth, Bram knew, was spent quickly under such conditions.

Let us walk this way.

The shopmaster was named Aiolfi, that muscular fellow, Bacco. Must they always work on the Sabbath?

Sabbath?

Sundays.

Oh, Sundays, yes: Aiolfi himself dressed for the church, his wife and his two sons went with him also, but the seamstresses must keep working. She turned the little Japanese fan against the light, shielding herself but enjoying the colored glow.

Does God hate the Szgany? she asked suddenly.

Gracious, Miss Lujzi. Bram stopped in his walk. *I hardly know how to answer such a question.*

Mister Aiolfi says he does, she said, *and the Mussle-man, and Jew, and so none of us may rest in England.*

Us... ?

Bram remained where he had stopped, pages turning in the book of his mind. Ahead of him, she was still playing with the little fan. On the pond, a squadron of brown ducks flapped about, making splashes.

Miss Lujzi. Are you... excuse me... are you a... he hesitated again, removing his hat and arranging it with the goatshead cane. Overhead, the white clouds; down here, where they stood, the pebbled walkway. Her dusky skin, her odd features. He had been quite stupid, quite unperceptive. *You belong to Europe, of course. In the conventional way.* How did one ask? *That is, your people accept God's son.*

Who is this?

I refer to the Savior. Christ Jesus.

Oh, him. She was untroubled by such talk, turning lightly her torso to consider its shadow. *At Szentgyörgy is a church for Jesus, very old. A thousand years. The church I think was very beautiful. The flowers I remember, under the priest's table.*

Oh?

At night, we go into the village and look through the tall windows. My brothers tell us, and always I picture what it is, inside.

Bram was stunned: he had been walking, arm in arm, with some kind of Gypsy. Of course Miss Lujzi must be of those ambiguous tribes. All frightful speeches on the garment district mentioned the mysterious *Roma*, unwelcome visitors here in the West. He himself had experienced some degree of the animus toward Irishmen that was common to society; his red hair and beard had drawn comments. Yet despite his own origins, somehow he had assumed Gypsies would be something—he was not certain. Not the horns and tail business, of course, but something... different. Not the same.

Much darker skin than hers. Shifty, suspicious eyes. Bundled sleeves, and dresses with colorful cross-stitching. Was none of that so?

Gathering himself, Bram resumed his walk. Jews, Gypsies, witches... he had a passing experience of Jewish persons, the occasional financier. Muslims he had never met. But the Roma were a different matter than even these outliers, different altogether, *no one* knew them, and it was to these mixed people that Bram had heard exception taken. Belonging to any state and none, strange speaking, Hungarian speaking—good heavens, was *that* Miss Lujzi's accent?—congregating outside all decent civilization, a shadowy presence whose growing number populated (infected, he had heard it said) the areas that huddled against the wharves. *The aristocracy holds nothing against races as a whole,* Bram recalled a tightly cravatted lord someone-or-other rumbling over his beef *tartare*. This particular lord was political favorite—Bram had forgotten the name—who attended Lyceum dinners. *But it cannot be denied, and it is known by those of us in the position of national responsibility, that the plague-bringer has been gaining ground. Rather like rats they continue to breed.*

Well, as for that, he had heard the same said of the Irish, those impoverished brethren who swarmed the East End. His people were depicted in cartoons as apes, hairy, hunched, poor because they were morally weak. Your proper Englishman had always been fixated by insiders and out, pureblood and mixed. There needs no ghost come from the grave, my lord, to tell us this.

Miss Lujzi was stepping lightly along the pond's edge. She seemed to have lost interest in the subject, but Bram must know. Were *all* the needle-women Szgany? No, but some, at least where she worked. And how had they come to be employed in the garment district? At the docks, when she arrived, a man had appeared, speaking quickly and pointing. No, not Aiolfi, no, but a different man, one she had not seen again. Another man translated, saying they had a place for her to live, she could go there right away, but only if she could sew.

But surely the Crown does not...

Wait, wait, it was Lord and Lady Boulstridge, walking this way, he was certain of it. They had just turned a corner where a great mass of briars had concealed them until this moment. The old fool with his "dashing" carnation, like a whole floral arrangement tied to his lapel; there was no mistaking that notoriously gaudy marker. Bram took Miss Lujzi's arm by the elbow and sharply led her down a side path. What had he done, what insanity had he allowed to close around himself? He was in public, spending the Lord's Day at liberty with a Gypsy! To be found out like this, doing what he was, meant destruction... Bram's heart was thunder as he signaled with his cane a line of waiting cabs, almost thrusting Miss Lujzi bodily into to the nearest one.

Drive on!

Where to, then, gov'nah?

Just drive, dash it!

No, no, all was well; the Boulstridges had passed without noticing. Though at the last minute, the damned graybeard turned his head, with a curious look...

North, driver. I will tell you where we alight.

4.

The afternoon, reversing itself, had returned to cooler breezes, in the passing way of London weather. Their second ride had been lengthy, almost outside the four-mile radius beyond which cabmen did not travel, but they were away from witnesses now. Bram apologized for having grasped her rather brusquely; and he felt, as he never had before, the burden of surrogate fame. His sketched likeness had appeared in the newspaper illustrations around Irving. Always in the background, of course, but he could not assume it was impossible that he might be "spotted." He was Henry Irving's shadow, never noticed until it detached itself from its owner.

The long second passage, at least, had allowed them to speak at more length. After a while, at his prompting, Miss Lujzi continued the tale of her earliest years. There had been an elder in the community whom she loved; this one used to carry children whenever he saw them. She remembered the stone buildings in the market square, horse officers who wore round, fur trimmed caps and braided uniforms. Of more specific tribal designations she seemed to have no clear idea, as if these were peculiar questions. Of religion, it was the same: not the atheism he expected, she indeed knew the name of Jesus and the prophets, and revered major figures from the Bible, but seemed to hold them all in equal regard alongside other beliefs: strange, folk conceptions, without any concern for proper ordering. All was an undefined mix.

What *did* concern her was the sweetness of certain flowering trees, silver and white, which had a name she repeated, looking intently into his eyes as if Bram might thereby recognize it. On a special night her family would gather the fallen blossoms for some purpose, involving heavy glass bottles that the children must carry. To her grandmother, or possibly the grandmother of another family, she had also been close. This grandmother would seat herself on a stump in fair weather, and smoke her pipe, and tell tales. These folktales (involving a magical boy called Cilka, whose companions were a deer and a mountain cat) Bram could not really understand, but, hearing them, he recalled Mrs. Kirwan, his Catholic housekeeper, telling him stories of Saint Kevin and the Devil, the cool embrasure of sheets pulled up to his chin.

Listening to Lujzi speak, Bram was embarrassed by his lack of worldly knowledge. Of Eastern Europe he was ignorant wholly. He had a vague sense that Gypsies must keep to their own.

May you, Miss Lujzi… that is… are you comfortable… he did not wish to say allowed. *Are you quite at ease with me? I am not of your community.*

At first I am worry, she answered, all bluntness. *Here I know only the butcher's wife, who teaches also England to me.* She thought for a bit, arranging her yellow wrap. *You have a good name.*

After a moment, she added, *Abraham, the Father.*

Yes—oh yes, I see.

Bram rode, marveling quietly at the thoughts she had spun on the loom of his imagination. How much there was of the greater world, beyond a few European capitals, of which he had no experience! The chill of the first snow, blowing lace into thatch rooftops; animal skins, hanging to dry inside rough, wooden sheds; the sable shapes of mountains, their forests carrying down the dusk. Vivid as these images were, though, they had the feel of selected things. More had passed in her adult life, of which she was not telling.

Curiosity moved inside him, but instead, he asked:

Is the violin on the wall yours?

Vio-lin?

Bram gestured with his hands.

Answering, however, Miss Lujzi's whole aspect turned dark, like a stream passing into an overhung region. The instrument was not hers, but belonged to another sweat-worker, Edwina, who shared her bed. When Aiolfi allowed it, that one would play melodies to beguile their famished hours. Recently, Edwina's hands had died—not her person entirely, but her hands—and the music fell silent. Aiolfi put the woman out, being no longer useful, and Lujzi had not seen her again.

Put her out. In the street?

At this, the abrupt, painful conclusion to all Miss Lujzi's memories, she grew silent, so that Bram regretted deeply his question. A crowd of shadows overcame her features, chapters in a book of what is unsaid, and he read their contents in sorrow.

This, then, was the secret. She had been hurt badly by Whitechapel, broken by it. The sweatshop was a suffering place, a prison in which her rare capacity and curious, open spirit had been ground flat like a cigar-ette end. Behind the sweating room's curtain all futures were lost, and Miss Lujzi's life there had become an un-life, a permanent waiting. Arrival on British shores must have been, to her, like premature burial, the Spirit for which Bram had originally mistaken her immured not in stones but in stay-making, shirt-making, baby linens for no one. It was not really Ophelia, Bram recognized in this moment, whose pointless engulfment in the garlanded brook made her weep.

5.

AT HIGHGATE, BRAM SUGGESTED THEY TAKE REFRESHMENT. MISS LUJZI was cautious on entering the three-penny ordinary, but on being presented with a dish full of carrot-raisin sandwiches she ate with a focus that was almost severe. Her motions were visibly taut as she forced herself to chew with dignity, the obvious hunger pushing against all restraint with an intensity that was almost animalistic. To provide for her need, he ordered extra bread and some candied orange rinds, which he feigned having changed his mind about, leaving the dish and yawning politely into space. An elderly couple by the door noticed Lujzi's behavior, the gentleman beginning to frown. He had a skeptical look, centered on thick, rheumy pupils that stared in unkind estimation. *Now Madam West*, Bram said aloud, patting her wrist to show that all was quite as it should be. Abruptly she appeared darker in feature than he had ever seen. *Do not overtax yourself. You shall be unwell.*

It is good bread, sir, she answered quietly, downcast eyes shining. She placed, with painful deliberation, an uneaten crust back in the plate.

Entering the cemetery they went more at their ease—for who, that either one of them might know, would be walking this early afternoon in a Camden boneyard?—among winding pathways that rose and fell as they passed among cedars, around hills dedicated to remembrance, through anonymous, dripping alcoves. A copper-haired fox, thin as sympathy, loped out from among the tombstones. Bram curved an arm across Lujzi's back, as if to shield her from the beast. He felt the little shoulder in his palm.

Be off there, Reynard! Shoo. Shoo.

Together they wandered the various sections dedicated to graves. Highgate Cemetery was magnificent, as justly celebrated as *Père Lachaise*, an ornate, multi-part burial ground larger than a city block. The trodden dirt pathway they had chosen led through a tunnel of yew trees to a silent, hilly region, overcrowded with carvings. This was the Egyptian Avenue, its columnar style made popular by British exploration. Beyond it, the "circle of Lebanon," a ring overhung by imported cedar, and a more classical feel. Only persons of real means could be enshrined in these tunnels of ivy; even in death, there was differentiation of rank.

Around them now was the smell of wet needles, softly compressed underfoot. At last Miss Lujzi and he might be relaxed; at last they had real privacy. A small, flowering bush cupped the light, and Bram dawdled on it with his thumb. Now and again he spied another couple arranging a wreath somewhere, a small, hunchback man who might be a groundskeeper, but it was easy enough to steer their path away. Increasingly their surroundings lent a reflective feel. He followed her into the shadow.

Tragedy, Bram said, gesturing toward a wall broken by a few doors, wherein lay a dozen ossuaries. *You wished to understand. Tragedy is the fall of what had promise. Loss, where there was potential. What you see around us here, in these silent communities of the dead, is tragedy.*

He was proud of his sensitivities, but she seemed unmoved.

You do not understand?

No, Abraham. These…

… sepulchers… loculi… the words are difficult.

These are lovely.

Of course she had never seen memorial carvings, or fine architecture of this sort. Before them in one direction stood a majestic family obelisk, taller than a man, of glossy bluish stone. In the other, a crowd of weeping figures, half-emerging from the front of a vault, their features discernible through cleverly suggested veils. Discoloration, accidental yet aesthetic, dripped greenly from an urn of oxidizing metal. What must a Szgany graveyard be in the wild hills of Styria, or Kingdom of Hungary? It would not even be that village church she had mentioned, with the tall windows. A level, dry patch, frozen most of the year, set off, perhaps, by some superstitious marker. Nothing more.

Lovely, she repeated, her features alight. *So many. Here I should like to stay forever.*

Do not say so, Miss Lujzi. You tempt the fates.

Bram stepped away for a while, sending his thought with his directionless heel. How pleasant to be able to share daylight with her, alone now, unmolested, where they could finally linger, at their ease. The air in these tree-lined passageways was moist and restorative, smelling of freshly turned earth. Here was a drift of leaves, fallen over a family stone and returning to skeletal paper. Each leaf had left its ruddy imprint, ghosts of the springtimes that had been. What courage was it that caused him to act so dashingly at the sweatshop in Whitechapel, so like the man he wished to be? In memory his deed became greater: he had stood toe to toe with a blackguard, keeping his level beard fixed. *Take this. The woman is worth a dozen of what you pay her.* Had those been his words? Something like.

The action itself, of course, had been madly incautious. Of all the risks he had undertaken so far, today's was by far the most reckless. Might word of his Acting-Manager's unusual interest in a seamstress reach Irving? And what would be the consequence? He must not deceive himself as to how, if word of it got out, this afternoon would be perceived. The Lyceum's public face had taken away one of its needle-women, after making a scene; he had been noticed strolling Highgate in this same surprising company, while his abandoned wife hosted an event by herself. It was *exactly* such scandal—precisely the appearance of moral corruption—that Irving had vowed to purge from his theatre. No one associated with the Lyceum (Irving had thundered over cast dinners, grinding his fist in the tablecloth), *no one* in his employment would be spoken of in a negative light. There was nothing the papers would enjoy more than a scandal, and the first transgression would merit reprisal.

And reprisal was in Irving's hand. Bram had seen him discharge a worker already, a cocksure fellow from Brighton who had spoken, in a lax moment, of the favors he enjoyed once of a certain front-row winger in a music hall. *That one, Stoker. Sever him.* Bram had been constrained to release the offender from all connection to the Lyceum in the instant; the gasping youth had found himself wholly unemployed, with neither recompense nor recommendation. And Bram had heard tales even more draconian than this. Rumor held it that Mister Irving had been riding home after a performance one night at Hyde Park when his own wife—his own wife!—risked a dismissive remark concerning actors. Irving had hammered the cabbie to halt, exited, and never spoken to the agape woman again.

Never.

Bram stopped in his tread, raising a gloved thumb to his brow. He felt like he was awakening from a daze. What softening of his self-preservation had allowed him to be here, walking these unauthorized trails? *Hunger, child,* Mrs. Kirwan's voice whispered across the years. *Hunger will make you do anything.* And it was true; this sad, lovely immigrant with the light step and the hazel eyes filled a hunger in him, something deep as his soul. But the longer he had persisted, the greater the likelihood of catastrophe. Conclude it then, have done! He had played the hero, had indulged some need in himself. Now, this risky thing must end. When Bram turned to look behind him, the pathway was empty.

Miss Lujzi?

Bram retraced his steps, but the seamstress was gone. Anxiety began to turn in his gut. He tried to recall whether he had passed a particular grave: this one, marked with a seaman's anchor, and surrounded by grey, draping chain... was it here, or another like it? *Miss Lujzi?* At the bend of the pathway a stone angel reclined luxuriously on an overgrown slab, wings in the dust, a crowd of crosses and headstones spreading along an ivy-covered hill. Overhead the clouds had once more begun to gather, casting their grayblue penumbrae. There were skulls, sleeping children, mourning cherubim, a menagerie all around him, but no living form. Bram tasted metal, looking left and right. Death was all encompassing, death extended mournfully in every direction. The world underneath these damp branches was nothing but a limitless expanse of graves.

Miss Lujzi? He felt awkward calling the foreign name aloud. *Lujzi...?*

Then he saw her, just as he had been preparing to run. She had left the path to ascend an embankment, and was pirouetting among the graves. Her delicate arms were raised lightly, holding in one hand the Japanese fan, in the other the material of her dress. She had removed, too, her tattered shoes, and her thin ankles were quite visible.

The act was fantastically forbidden, a violation of so many laws that Bram fell helpless before it. But he was captivated by the sight of her, and of her barefoot dance, as if it were a kind of vision. He remembered the first time he could walk on his own, the year the paralysis left him, standing outside his family home and spontaneously beginning an awkward, stumbling gambol of joy. He had fallen to the grass laughing and stared up at the world. Now again he stared, a pair of eyes hidden in the dripping. He was the spirit now, not she, he the watcher from the corner of the stage.

See her dance! She was so full of the wine of fresh beginnings.

Coughing loudly to give her a chance, Bram drew closer, pretending to examine a carving of veiled grief. But Miss Lujzi was indifferent to his cues, still turning herself, slow as a drifting leaf, among stones. A sepulcher watched over by a gryphon, another guarded forever by a loyal bloodhound. Shaking his head, Bram strode helplessly forward.

My dear, my dear. Do you not fear censure?

But she had climbed the embankment the rest of the way, setting herself by a tall, lamenting angel in white, as she had been when he first saw her.

Look at her, Abraham! Beautiful!

There is a certain glamour to the melancholic, he began, but this was neither the mode nor the place in which to give instruction. *Come away now. We must not be noticed.*

But Miss Lujzi was enthralled, her soul captured once more by beauty, and climbed with her bare feet the little grey pedestal. Reaching around the angel's robed torso she clasped its midriff, as if to breathe in the luscious mineral. Looking quickly around, hardly believing himself, Bram stepped off the dirt path as well, picking his way up the unclipped embankment until he stood at her side. Their faces were just level.

Now Miss Lujzi. We must not draw attention to ourselves in this way.

Sometimes…

Yes… ? He had not realized she was speaking. She had leaned her face against the moss-spotted surface, her eyes glassy. She could have been a sleepwalker, talking in a dream.

Did you say something?

Sometimes I think I belong dead.

Bram could feel the tapping in his ears, at his throat; he could feel his chest tighten. *Miss Lujzi, you, of all creatures, do not belong here. You are more alive than many, oh, than many I have known. More, even…* The firs overhead swayed secretly in a breeze, knowing his heart. *More, even, I fear, than myself.*

He could not help it: he was leaning his face toward hers. His hands too had found her hands, the little wounded fingers clasping him tightly. They were coming together, pulling their lips toward each other with between them the uncrossable stone, their arms in a ring now around the sad, lovely angel whose task it was to keep parted forever the living and the dead.

Part Three

Moonhour

Chapter 11

> Then, turning to my love, I said,
> 'The dead are dancing with the dead,
> The dust is whirling with the dust.'
>
> But she—she heard the violin,
> And left my side, and entered in:
> Love passed into the house of lust.
>   Oscar Wilde, *The Harlot's House*

> O, beware, my lord, of jealousy.
>   *The Tragedy of Othello, the Moor of Venice*

1.

ONE HUNDRED NIGHTS OF *HAMLET;* IRVING HAD ACHIEVED AN UNPRECedented success. But the past was prologue, he was a torrent, he must move from strength to strength. The long run had established his arrival in London. Now, even before the year was out, he would bring them *Merchant of Venice.*

    The mad machinery of production was once again set into whirl: the press, the pageantry, the endless correspondences Bram must write in Irving's name, the negotiation of dozens, hundreds of human working pieces. Loveday flitted about, squawking his upsets like a bird flapping plumage. The redecoration of the pit, long discussed, fell entirely to Bram, along with the slew of new musicians' contracts, a discrepancy in the gasworks, a certain dispute over the footmen's rates. Lyceum was a kraken, sunken in ooze at the bottom depth, and he must cause it to rise.

Following their stolen afternoon at Highgate, he had not seen Miss Lujzi again. This time, however, it was not his doing: along with the other needlewomen, she had vanished once the contracts for *Hamlet* expired. The wardrobe room, with its racks of frilled shirtfronts, dark purple vests, stood yawning and empty. When Loveday mentioned having succeeded in negotiating better prices for costume work at Harrod's, Bram only nodded, his gaze resting on the walnut table where they held business meetings until discussion moved to the next item of importance.

On that day in Highgate, he had inclined his head toward her until their lips brushed—but then pulled back, disengaging himself at the fatal moment. They had committed no true indiscretion, no crime; only, he had come close enough to smell her hair, its deep scent freshened by a sudden gust of rain. Only, the dazzling black of her pupils had met his—met them with a look of acknowledgement—and he had held her tiny fingers. Their lips had come touchingly close, close as two leaves on a single stem. But Bram had stepped forcibly away, pulse hammering in his throat, his whole person flushed with the wrongness of what he was doing. A moment later, the hunchback groundskeeper could be heard knocking toward their location and Bram, unable even to look, had hurried back onto the path.

Afterward, they came wordlessly from the cemetery. Miss Lujzi's hands had been folded on the Japanese fan, as if in penitence, while his own made tight, pocketed fists. He had sought, at one point, to suggest that aesthetics were still the chief subject between them, commenting academically on the merit of a certain *memento mori* near the gates. It was a child's grave, the dull stone smaller than its neighbors, as if a little body required only a little remembrance. On the marker's top had been cut what Bram had always felt to be the saddest icon of all: a cherubic baby face, surmounted by wings.

During the cab ride back, exhaustion from all that had transpired that day coursed suddenly through his chest, bringing a feeling of actual faintness. For a long time, the wordlessness between them had been ornamented only by the clopping of the horse, as if they had been headed toward, rather than away from, a place of lamentation. Then, quite softly, offset only by the shaking of the harness, Miss Lujzi said:

In Szentgyörgy, I have a husband.

Bram's breath had fallen away into whispers, completely caught out by this statement. His behavior with regard to her had been noxious. She must have felt this had been his real intention all along, his caddishness, his indecency. Was she demanding an apology?

You do, he said, as if agreeing. *Very good. And did he, did...*

Betl.

Did... Betl... not choose to travel to England with you? Or shall he be arriving later?

He dies.

Bram had swallowed, tasting ash.

I am with him one year.

I see. I see. It was the verbs, he realized, that difficulty she had with tenses. He should have understood.

Betl dreams, Miss Lujzi began again eventually, in that sententious precision born of grammatical inaccuracy. And she had told him, then, of her foreign husband's dream, how together they had planned out a life. While her own family had nothing, his ran a dry goods shop in the winter, only traveling half the year. These were not, then, Gypsies of which Bram had even a simple understanding. Betl had lived for a time in Vienna itself, where he apprenticed as a textile merchant. Thin and very tall, with a perfectly black beard, he succeeded always in the outside world, even where there was distrust. At first, their shared hope had been to relocate to Budapest. Betl had relatives there, one of whom assisted in a small school, while another had found work as a railroad porter. But Betl dreamed even farther than this. The journey he proposed to Lujzi one night—beginning from the cook stove around which they were seated, and ending at the Emigrant Landing Depot at Castle Island—would be long. They would travel with others of their kind, small pockets on the edges of communities often inimical. Rather than assay both Prussia and France (Betl had received letters of warning from others who had attempted the trek) they would take the short route, south, to the Mediterranean, reaching England, from there, by sail. Once they left land, he reasoned, they would be outside harassment. At London they would breathe, and when they could, find a second ship to undertake the greater passage toward America.

The Atlantic, she should understand, was vast: half a month, perhaps, with both of them pushed like cargo into the belly of a steamer. Little to eat, poor sanitation, nothing to see but an expanse of dark gray ocean, should they even be allowed on deck. Betl had said to her that if she did not wish to endure all this, if she was afraid, they would not go. They would remain in *Szentgyörgy*, and make do with this life. They had stood together as man and wife, and their union had been blessed by the whole people. As long as he and she were under one roof, he had already found his belonging.

Their first night on ship she had recognized Betl was going to die. The land passage had proven much harder than anticipated, and toward the end he had grown badly ill. Sweat covered his handsome features the night he went out, against her repeated pleas, and returned, exhausted but smiling, a few hours later with tickets of boarding; and the next evening, as the black hull rocked and sighed around the crowd of people among whom they were pressed, he kept asking Lujzi to comfort the child who was crying. Would she not give it the breast? She had told him hush, yes, be still, the child is well. Be still, my love. Only a little while now, and we will be home. The captain, on being alerted that an emigrant in steerage was refusing to surrender a corpse, instructed that her husband's body be taken from her and dropped over the side. He had no desire, he said, to be transporting a Jonah.

When Miss Lujzi concluded her tale, Bram had sat wordlessly as a new silence descended on the cab. It was of the sensible type, like a diaphanous, weightless fabric, of which each of them held gently a corner. Only the axel on the hansom creaked left and right to the horse's urging, the driver giving a small shake of the ribbons.

After Betl, Miss Lujzi finished softly, *I do not believe there are good men.*

Bram felt a heaviness, like a weight pressed to his sternum, as he comprehended the full meaning of her statement. *I am no different*, he said carefully to the long space of bench between his thigh and hers, *than other men.*

They had spoken no more for the remainder of the journey. Returning Miss Lujzi to her sweatshop in Whitechapel, after all that had passed, tasted bitterly of cruelty. But there was nothing he could do, nothing, other than fatuity, he could find within himself to say.

Good afternoon to you, Miss Lujzi. I wish—no, there he had blunted the dangerous words before they could not be retracted. *Good afternoon. Our time together has been pleasant.*

Had she expected him to alight, to assist her down from the cab? To do so would have suggested a proper relationship, one they could not have. The shop master must be near, too, and Bram very much wished to avoid a second scene. The heroic recklessness of this morning had left him. She opened, after a pause, the little swinging door with one hand, then turned unexpectedly.

I think of you, Abraham, she said. *Always I think of you.*

How Bram's spirit flared at these words, like some bright thing battering its cage! He had turned away in near panic, staring out his side of the cab where three or four urchins crouched in the gutter, playing a game with a beer bottle and sticks.

Miss Lujzi, please, let us say no more. Let—

Something wet touched the back of his wrist: she was holding her trembling cheek to the bare inch of skin between his glove and sleeve. Bram gasped, his whole being expanding at the sensation, as if he were a plucked string. Clutching the Japanese fan like a treasure, she hurried from the cab, running through the crowds, up the scarred wooden steps and into the shop. The door to the place closed behind her with a thump and he had felt it closing over his soul.

2.

So now she was gone, Bram thought hollowly from his work desk, gone back behind Aldgate, that divider of worlds. For him ever to revisit the shop was out of the question. Aiolfi knew too much, though, thank heavens, he had said nothing so far. Lujzi's fellow seamstresses would be aflutter for some time with the proper gentleman who had taken their "West-Ender" on the town, however, and Bram could not risk discovery further. Their long walks together discussing poetry after dark, their afternoon among the flower strewn mounds at Highgate. None of it could be repeated.

And the "ink," over which Mister Irving had made such a fuss? Bram had merely tucked in the offending strip with his thumbs and returned it to wardrobe, where evidently it passed muster—if it was even remembered. Now Irving's outrage was over a missing pair of gloves, of silver-gray kid, with a black pearl button. The *divo*!

Let it be, then, Bram counseled himself, let his mad moment pass, like the long line of days, and be relieved that nothing worse had come. The foreign woman had been exceptional, both in aesthetic sensibility and a strange, ethereal species of beauty. Had he thought her unhandsome when they met? Even peculiar looking? Hers had been a special kind of loveliness. But no matter, their almost-kiss had been the last of Bram's forbidden acts, dangerous as an icy trestle. As recklessly far as he had ventured against marriage, employer, even reputation—and, when he reflected on the hundreds of actors, supers, staff, any one of whom might have spotted them, it was madly far indeed—no disaster had occurred. *Hamlet* had finished its long run at last, and a new flock of needle-women had been commissioned. Let his guilty diversion serve as a lesson. Nothing in his life was to be feared more than scandal.

Florence, Bram sighed, one morning when he saw her arranging herself by her mirrors in her dressing gown of stern graygreen material, a servant holding the silver brushes. It was a Friday, a full house expected at Lyceum by nightfall, including a well-known Duke. For a moment he stood looking at his wife, as if at an acquaintance he used to know. How that beauty mark on her cheek had stirred him! He remembered how she caught the eyes of all young men in Dublin, remembered his own hothead pride taking her on carriage rides through Phoenix Park, where he surprised her with a gift of Tennyson's *Poems*. She had no true ear for poetry, it was clear even then, but a simple rhythm pleased her no end. As they walked, he had delivered verses from its onionskin pages. *The mirror crack'd from side to side,* Florence would repeat as she swayed through the lily beds, rocking her skirt to the sounds. *The curse has come upon me, cried... The La-dy of... Sha... lott!*

In the dying hours Bram returned home, finding his wife out. He sponged his face and neck and dressed in his new evening wear with the creamcolored cummerbund (a king's ransom had bought it; their financial situation was nowhere near as solid as he would have wished). Rather than dinner, he called at the Aerated Bread Company for a potion and biscuit and returned to the Lyceum to play host once more to the front-of-theatre. It was his duty to present a certain appearance to the public, that of genial host, overseeing not patrons, but welcome guests. At seven o'clock he took his usual position at the top of the carpeted stair. Beneath him, like an advancing army, the gathering crowd rose step by step.

A good evening, gentlemen. Good evening.

Yes, Madam. The Merchant of Venice tonight. Venice.

Bram raised his brow in politeness, shaking hands with a field officer who had distinguished himself among the Pakhtun, laughing warmly with one said to be headed for a government position, signaling a dull tawdry usher with a snap.

Good evening, ladies. A pleasure to have you at the Lyceum. Yes, the Duke is expected to grace us tonight with his company.

Good evening. I believe I can promise you a performance worth attending.

Gentlemen. Indeed, no, madam. We certainly should not have proceeded without you!

London—this press of middling aristocracy, these men in banded hats, women in pekin point and rich Ottoman satin, a shimmer of peacock feathers sewn at the bust, a ruby pin teasing the eye—for him to play his part here was the single, great accomplishment of his adulthood. All he had endured, the escape from muddy Dublin, the sacrificing of a solid career, had resulted in the shoes in which he now stood. This was the new life.

A heartfelt welcome to all. One and all.

This way. Allow me.

Threaten all this, for a forbidden kiss? No, and a hundred times no; he had been a fool to imperil so much. Mister Irving trusted him implicitly, and it was to that wonderful man, that bright star toward whom his professional sails were once again angled, that every—but Bram's breath caught in his throat. Lord Boulstridge was rising up the stair.

Their paths had not crossed since the fool almost discovered him strolling with Miss Lujzi near Highbury Fields. Bram's insides ran cold, as if a frigid gust had blown over the landing. To the left of him was the Green Room, already occupied; to the right, a closed corridor. There was no avenue of escape.

Lord and Lady Boulstridge! Now, that carnation is fetching.

Stoker, is it. Eh.

And with the Lowsleys, or I mistake myself, Bram hurried on, more loudly than necessary. The lady's ears were bad, and he leaned down as she put a finger to her jewel-pendant lobe. Was Boulstridge holding him with a critical eye? *We certainly should not have proceeded without you, Mrs. Lowsley. You know there is going to be light refreshment after the final act. After the final act. Indeed so. I think I can promise a performance worth attending. Allow me to show... this way.*

Wheezing like a kettle Boulstridge ascended the brief steps, gesturing his wife and companions to precede him into the box. At the last moment he turned and considered Bram, an unhappy look in his eye, just as the house lights were dimmed. Bram remained standing, pained smile frozen in place, lost in the balconied darkness.

3.

He has come home! Florence laughed. *The hunter returned from the hill.* And here she believed him abducted by brigands, never to be heard from again!

His wife settled herself under a complex tide of crinoline, dispensed with her packages and called for the tea. It had been so long, she had thought him abducted by highwaymen. Yes, highwaymen in robes and turbans, tying him up and threatening his life with flashing scimitars.

Very good, Bram conceded, bowing his head to the chiding. Yes, it had been a spell of long hours. How had she been keeping herself?

It was late afternoon, the end of another week. He took, for himself, the oval-backed chair by the window, the fingers of one hand playing absently over the tassel of the blind. Matters at Southampton Street, he found, were much as ever. The shade of the gas candle in the hallway had become cracked, and needed replacing; a delivery had been ordered of lovely throw-pillows, cleverly woven with puce beads and colored glass. Perhaps it was a touch *de trop*, but it was the best she could do, as the sitting room needed something, and after what *she* had been treated to at that Winnifred Learney's... the dilatory thread of his wife's commentary soon lost him. He could not have cared a tuppence for such trivial issues, but that was no matter; he knew that he was only being called upon to give occasional assent. If questioned, he had already mastered the husband's ability to reel in her most recent comment. There was no difficulty, really. Only he must sit here, and nod at his wife's monologue, and sip a little milky tea, and, when darkness came, have the servants draw the curtains in the front room. This was his lot.

... brought a libel suit, a mere painter against Ruskin, by your leave! Only the last laugh was his, wasn't it? And for a sentence Mister Ruskin must pay only a farthing. One might well say...

Again in his thoughts Bram breathed in the quick bright rain-freshed grasses of Highgate. Again he walked among the cool, somnolent stones. At the end of this memory—drawn out slowly, like a line of prose with delightful finish—came the crime he had almost committed, the closeness of strange female lips. Fresh lips, yearning to receive his, at the moment their eyes caught each other. I think of you, Abraham. Always I think of you.

... hasn't got the time for one, I told her, then one simply must say she hasn't time for his type...

She had been so lovely and sad. He had leaned his face close enough to feel the passage of female breath against his own. Her breath had been sweet, the smell of her hair dark and strange, like the mixed scent of a forest glade. Kissing her would have been like crushing his mouth against a just-opened blossom, still dew-wet and trembling on the branch. Her bottom lip especially had been tender, like the curve of a petal... like the rose he now held, gently running its velvet over his cheek... no, no. He must forget.

He must forget.

Weeks passed in this rhythm, their musical score the drone of his wife's voice. Slowly the earth began to change once more its character, Bram noting the arrival of summer as if from a distance. He had made few male acquaintances in London, but lunched with one or two. He tried to participate in a local men's club, where there was an amateur draughts league, with neither failure nor particular success. Eventually he found himself agreeing to an appearance, in a few days' time, at one of his wife's perpetual socials. Florence had invited a decorated officer from the Russo-Turkish engagement on whom she was currently doting, as well as a diplomat, and three couples whose significance he could not recall. When the evening arrived, he hurried about his own carpets like a butler, refilling glasses.

So, that Henry Irving has triumphed again, has he not?

I should say.

One doesn't know where he manages to find the energy.

One guest—dash it all, what was his name? A lardy fellow, they shook hands once at the gardens in Kew—was taken aback by Irving's portrayal of Shylock. Yes, yes, Bram understood perfectly; the role had traditionally been given quite a different interpretation. Well, after all, not *all* Jews are like that.

Are they not? the man chortled, his pink double-chin giving a hop.

Does the English God hate so many, Bram wondered sadly. And where, in all this life of his, was the elder who delighted in carrying children across the hayfields, or baby Samu, safe from the bear inside Vilmos' shirt? Where was the grandmother of a village, smoking on a stump?

I think of you, Abraham.

The next week, Bram had occasion to speak with the wardrobe man from Harrod's and turned the discussion casually to seamstresses. The sweating system was not of his making, but he felt almost as if he had abandoned Miss Lujzi to its jaws. He wanted to be told that he had misread his first encounter with the garment industry, that working conditions were nowhere as stark as appearance might suggest.

Needle-women? Yes, sir, we have plenty.

My good man, I inquire only out of curiosity. What...

How many would you like?

One day, at a particular intersection, a protester handed him a wide paper sheet on which was scrawled political agitation. *In our Christian land slop workers*, it cried in cheap burgundy ink, *live on nothing but tea.* An illustration depicted the evils of the shopmaster, a villain with feral pupils leaning over a crowd of lamenting females.

He was no social discontent. Society had its levels. Yes, the conditions he witnessed in Whitechapel speared his conscience, but then, protests of this type were socialist, anarchist; he really didn't know what they were. *Must a man be political?* How far was it from "workers' rights," as the overdrawn sheet phrased it, from "legislating conditions for laceworkers and sempstresses," to these New Women with their flat-heeled boots, women speaking out of turn, parading about in knickerbockers! All this contesting the order of things was the very definition of unnatural, *against the right way.*

And yet, he had regarded Miss Lujzi's case quite differently. The change that came over her face when she described how the violin on the wall had fallen silent, the woundedness written into her delicate mouth at the moment when, their afternoon ended, she had to return to that inferno of labor. These issues were not, in her, an abstraction.

Then once again his mind turned, like a restless sleeper. There were social ills in Britain, areas where prudence sought improvement. To deny it would be bootless. But Miss Lujzi's case had never been strictly political. She had stood out among her sex, and among the wandering tribes. She had been singular in her thoughts—singular, if he were frank, in a *passion* that mirrored his own. Yes, she had been passionate: so much more than the self-satisfied crowd of *poseurs* at Florence's fetes, or the mincing sycophants at Lyceum suppers: so much more than the hollering crowds around the newspaper vendors on Wicker Street, which even now he was trying to navigate, all of them mad to read the latest thing from the continent, type-writers and pneumatic tubes and a world made of steam. Pah! He had not created this world. To the Devil with it!

But purchasing his own *Dispatch* and escaping the noisy lane to sit over a potion and biscuit, all Bram saw was one face; all he read were the articles of remembrance.

4.

THE CLOSE OF THE MONTH BROUGHT THE LAST SOCIALS OF THE SEASON. OF course Florence must host, and one final time Bram endured the invasion. At its conclusion, the parlor maid delivered him the apricot-and-blue-ringed china cup in its little saucer and Bram sat, exhausted, only to rise again hurriedly and thank a few more of their guests, wishing them well into their waiting cabs. That was the last of them; some clever words at the door, and a good evening... it was done. When he ascended once more the stair, Florence, he found, had gone into the bedroom. Their rooms on Southampton Street were blissfully quiet once more, a broken yellow moon standing outside the parlor window. Bram relaxed fully at last, his gaze resting, as it had at several points this evening without his quite realizing it, on something soft and white lying under the sofa.

I do think the gold came off admirably, Florence's voice crooned from the far chamber. She had risked an expensive new dress with coral highlights, debating for days before being seen in the color. *Mister William Gilbert complimented me twice.*

Someone left something.

Bram rose tiredly from the chair, coming closer to the mysterious object, one corner of which was just visible beneath the sofa. Grunting, he reached two fingers down faintly and drew the thing free.

Silver-gray kid gloves. An expensive pair, with a wrist button made of black pearl.

Poor Wilde was the talk of the evening, Florence trilled with a pleased air, coming through the archway with some of her more constraining items removed. She had the appearance of a warrior unlacing soft armor. *He has grown into quite the dandy. I had to remind the ladies twice that he and I had a regular acquaintance, back in Dublin.* She saw what was in Bram's fingers and her expression fell. Then she quickly removed an earring.

He will be missing those. The tone was indecipherable. *You must return them in the morning.*

Florence...?

Yes, dear?

Mister Irving's gloves!

Bram stood ramrod straight.

These are his missing gloves! With the pearl button!

Quite, she said.

But... here? Mister Irving has come by here?

Yes, my dear, she said. *Were you not listening? I told you earlier, I'm sure.*

Florence was patronizing, her voice a little weary. Her face said, Who is this great child with whom I have been saddled? Bram tried to contain his mounting emotion.

But... when was he here?

Florence clattered her jewels on the tabletop stiffly, signaling this to be a matter of indifference. *Oh, the other day.*

The other day—!

Bram choked slightly to speak, as if inhaling cinders. He spread the gloves cautiously on the chair seat, plucked, for no reason at all, and twirled a deep red rose from a glass vase Florence had insisted he buy. *This is all quite astonishing. My employer, at my house, unknown to me.* But she would give nothing. *My dear... my dear... and I was not told?*

His wife's face was a Japanese mask.

Bram paced, not wanting to look at the gloves where they lay, as if they were the limp remains of some gruesome surgery.

Florence... but he veered madly off his intended question, unable even to think it. *Do look at me, dear. You must understand that Mr. Irving's business desires are of the greatest importance to us both. If he chooses to visit our home, it is absolutely necessary that you should inform me immediately.*

Uncommon is the day when I have seen you, she observed dryly.

Bram felt the sting.

That is of no consequence. If I have been removed, it is because my position at Lyceum requires as much. Our promotion in this city makes demands on my time... our good standing, everything we have... it all rides on my continuous and diligent application.

As you say.

Please alert me should Mister Irving ever grace our home in my absence again! Bram halted, uncertain. What was this warning note, sounding deep in his core—could it really be danger? Florence began examining her shoulders indifferently in the wall mirror, and something in her careful face made Bram ask: *How many times has he visited?*

I'm sorry?

How many times?

Oh... only the once, I'm sure.

I see—I see, yes. But to what purpose?

Really, dear, I am fatigued.

She left the parlor and Bram felt a new wave of astonishment rising. He followed her into the small sitting room.

Florence, you do recognize that we have put everything... our financial prospects, all the money you spend so freely... my reputation in society... everything is staked upon this association. I must never be left in the dark. He was flushed, hot with insistence, maddened that the face meeting his own remained cool and blank, almost uninterested. He could have been arguing some abstract definition in philosophy.

Bram came forward, taking his wife by the elbows. The housemaid stepped carefully into the kitchen.

Mrs. Stoker, I need you to understand how important...

Oh, Bram, Bram! she almost spat, throwing off his arms. The rose tumbled to the rug. *Are you a fool? Am I married to a complete fool, a child, a fool?*

And she hurried from the room, leaving a crushed, fallen flower at his feet.

Chapter 12

1.

INNOCENT, BRAM TOLD HIMSELF. THIS *COULD NOT* BE OTHER THAN INnocent.

Florence had only been visited by Irving in the manner of a professional man checking up on his property; the household of the Acting Manager of the Lyceum must, at all times, be presentable. Public image was paramount. In a certain sense, Bram's wife was within the scope of his employer's concern, just as his *taking* a wife had been. Or, perhaps, the visit had been no more than a passing fancy; the actor had spoken of requiring a female muse. Many did! Often Irving lamented his helplessness, save for the presence of a lady to inspire his craft. Bram had assumed Miss Terry fulfilled that particular function, but perhaps a second, or even a third, might be required. *But what did he want, coming here?* Bram had returned to the question over his tasteless breakfast dish. *Oh, what do they all want?* had come his wife's elliptical reply. Now she thought of it, there might have been a second visit, perhaps even more… really, she did not recall.

Well then, good! If his wife was to serve, for an occasional afternoon, as muse to the great man, so be it, jolly good. They should be flattered. Bram chewed his thumbnail, wincing as he tore a strip down painfully into the flesh.

And when he comes here, he… only for some light conversation, I assume.
Oh yes, that.

The suspicion that ate away at him was a mad inversion of the very guilt he felt. It was as if, in some twisted reality, the unacceptable feelings he had been indulging with the seamstress had turned against him now, threatened him with the jester face's mockery grin. He had been dissatisfied in Florence's company, even bitter at the prospect of a lifetime by her side. But this—this! Good God—was it even *possible*... ?

Something in Florence's pose was shut to him now, an inner door. Outwardly, there was no change, no special deed or intonation on which he might lay a questioning finger. Initially badly shocked (had she not seemed?) when he found the missing gloves, his wife was now quite composed. When precisely had been Mister Irving's last visit? Oh, perhaps a week ago, she allowed uninterestedly, perhaps a little longer. It was certainly before the evening with the Kensingtons, of that she was reasonably sure. Really, did it matter?

Of course it matters, Florence. It matters a great deal.
I don't see how.
Was it last week, or the week before? Tell me.
Oh, why don't you ask him? Am I your engagement calendar?
I certainly will not do that. Be reasonable.
He tells me to be reasonable!

A cryptic pattern began to coalesce before Bram's eye. In its center stood Henry Irving: the man who had swept him up in a tide of amazement, who had overwhelmed his impressionable nature with promises of a new and vibrant existence: the very man who had arranged, from the beginning, that Bram be so infernally occupied. It was undeniable that the actor's habit was to toss trivialities in Bram's lap, fix this, Stoker, attend to that, Stoker, and then immediately take himself away—Bram had never asked *where*.

But what followed? His arithmetically trained mind sought the sum. *What followed?*

The figure seemed denser now, more substantial, and Bram's soul quaked at the outline that threatened to reveal itself. The time he had been instructed to shore up the baize safety curtain, as if he were a rude mechanical? The nonsense with the "ink"? While he had believed himself, like a truant child, to be moving behind his employer's back, was it even conceivable the man himself had been moving, with far greater subtlety, behind his own?

No, and again no! Bram realized he had been pulling at his hair until his scalp was sore. Let not imaginings run madcap, dressed up as conclusions. Like tomorrow and tomorrow, it all signified nothing. Neither Florence nor Henry had mentioned these visits, these... *visits*, not because they had been furtive, but because they were of no significance. That Irving may have paid his compliments to the Stoker household, some unrecorded afternoon (or evening? Was it possible he had gone to her in the *evening*, and the servants out?) was quite within the bounds of honor. Anything else was the conjure-work of his own harrowing guilt. He was the one who had played loosely with the marriage bond.

Bram sought to calm his fraught thinking, entering a low, rather squalid public house in Charing Cross and sampling with his ale the sweet and salty wheels of cheese, each displayed on wooden pallets and still in their stained brown papers, delicacies that had come across the channel in the holds of steamships with a taste faintly reminiscent of tears.

Could such a world be dreamt (that unwanted thought again!) where word was so wretchedly far from deed, in which the great moralist of the public stage was in reality something quite animal? Could there be so berserk a landscape, in which all Bram's trust, and indeed all his livelihood, had been placed in the hooked fingers of a betrayer?

Never. He swung his fist at the uneven table. He would not, could not accept so demented a vision. If anything, this third party in the marriage (horrid accident of phrase! He thrust it from himself just as a cold drop of water fell from the ceiling, racing down the nape of his neck) might serve a beneficent purpose. Men had always shown an interest in Florence, with her thin, tight waist and patrician features; he saw them turn in the street, fingering their moustaches. This was nothing new, and in fact, a dignified attraction between adults might only fuse his family name to that of his employer. Was this not exactly the union he had sought?

Was it not?

Daylight passed in a mixed bustle, Bram forcing himself once more into the web of professional obligations. He returned the truant kid gloves to Irving's closet without comment. There would be an appropriate time to re-enter discussion with his wife, to pursue this event in more detail, but he must measure his position carefully. Surely this ugly suspicion (ugly! he could not even speak it) was born and lived only inside the guilt-ledger of his mind. Surely his own stolen hours with the needle-woman, so close to indecency, were reflected back at him in this whirlwind of distrust. Which of them, the self-accuser railed within his wits, had behaved in a way that should not enjoy scrutiny?

Bram went about his tasks, speaking to a designer who had been awaiting his return, arranging for some future food services. The leaks over the balcony had started again, and needed attending. But it would be too galling, to have been sneaking about like a schoolboy after dark... and all the while, in his home... under his own roof... what?

Good Lord. *What?*

But no, no! Once again his red brain had raked and caught fire from the smolder. It *could not* be that thing which he would not even allow to enter the arena of consideration. Let suspicion come and knock; he'd grant no entry. The demons, to make incursion on our souls, must bear warrant of our own invitation.

2.

THE FIFTH ACT WAS CONCLUDED. THE HOUSE—WHAT ELSE SHOULD THEY do?—rose to their well-shod feet. Irving's depiction of Shylock was the discussion of the town. Every silk lapel needed an opinion as much as a carnation, and the Lyceum's ticket-take had been vast, outshining even the Royal (Loveday informed him, having confederates in all the best playhouses). Good gossip, the dusty man chuckled, packed the aisles faster than good production.

A word, Henry.

Irving halted, his manicured nails on the office door handle. *Well?*

Bram would speak of the gloves, of where they had been found, of his employer's unacknowledged visits. Innocent it surely was, yet something must be said. But his heart quailed.

Let it pass. It can wait.

I shall be out several hours.

Very good, very well. Bram rattled his fingers against the cramped deal surface of his desk. *And where are you bound, this soggy afternoon?*

Why? Would you have me post your letters?

At their weekly meetings, he, Irving and Loveday took stock of the Lyceum's gains. The receipt was good, but Irving's spending had been lavish, especially the multi-course public dinners in which it was his habit to indulge. His employer, though, dismissed any suggestion of temperance. Flushed from his new diet of ovations, Irving was considering still greater conquests. *Othello* was currently the favorite. Edwin Booth had been touched—Bram was not consulted—on the subject of playing the horn-wearing Moor. Irving himself, of course, would play Iago: the false friend, worm in the rose, canker at the pith of love. *A sad demon,* Bram marked out slowly on his note sheets in pencil. *I go to hell, O.*

Seeking respite from his own mind he hurled himself at work. Entire days passed now in which he hardly left his office, entering the building before dawn and stepping out again only under the crystalline light of a clear London moon. He would be at Southampton Street, putting to bed all his suspicions—but he would *not*; was it worse never to taste certainty, or to risk witnessing the misty shape clothe itself in solidity? It was Wednesday, it was Friday already, the end of another week of managing crises whose character he could not even recall. He was standing on the unused porchway behind the theatre, having forced down a small supper in town and returned here, to the Lyceum, rather than going home. As he sucked the cold, smoking breaths of nine o'clock, the redhead trollop who had emerged from the alley suddenly entered into his consciousness. *Clean,* her voice purred in his memory's ear. *I am clean.* For many months now, his had been a celibate's bed, and his own body beat with frustrated pulses. He saw Covent Garden around him by moonshine, shadowy with recesses; in them, obscure figures making transactions. Bram turned away his head.

The situation was intolerable. Never had he and Florence spoken of what was happening to their marriage. Never of their ghost-haunted bed; never of the visits Irving had made; never of the dreams, whatever they were, in which Florence chuckled and whispered, and once, from the depth of her sleep, appeared to put a finger to her lip, as if enjoining someone to silence.

3.

AND THEN CAME THE TERRIBLE EVENING, A WEDNESDAY, WHEN HE HAD his first actual battle with his wife.

Well, how many visits? Three, or four?

Good lord, Bram. I feel I am placed in the Old Bailey.

Well?

Well, and well again! This is the little Dublin Castle clerk in you. You would send me to Australia for nicking a rasher of bacon.

Answer me! Bram shouted. He had never shouted at a woman before. Never in true heat, as a man. Florence's face turned gelid.

Mister Stoker, you shall not take that tone with me.

You are my wife! I shall speak to you as I damned... well... please!

Oh, it had been awful, simply awful! Florence stormed into the bedroom, clouds across her brow, and flung to the door. And Bram had struck his fist hard against the unyielding mantle, for the boom of that locking wood had echoed sharply through the years of his heart.

4.

WHAT HAD HE FOUND?

Here, in the pocket of Irving's greatcoat, the bear-brown one with the heavily furred collar. Bram was cleaning, as was his habit, their shared office; he had lifted the weighty garment from the chair where it had been flung, in order to hang it correctly on the rack. Now something square and hard had fallen to the floor. He picked up the item, then remained, staring.

A small, rose-colored book, with cloth cover. The flat edge of the pages, when closed, made a watery blue. It was a fine piece of binding, a collection on which someone spent at least a guinea. Embossed on the spine: *Poems. Alfred, Lord Tennyson.*

I'm off, then.

It was mid-afternoon only, but Loveday was traveling to the Scottish highlands for a stay, and had a train. The stage manager gathered his satchel and case and exited into the hall, raising one burdened hand in salute. *Until next week, Stoker. Don't forget the business with the register.*

Until then, Harry.

Ad astra per aspera.

Yes.

Loveday's boots tramped unpleasantly the hall and Bram was alone once more in the low-ceilinged chamber.

This *could not* be the copy of *Poems* he gave to Florence when they first were romancing. *The mirror crack'd from side to side*—this could not be *that* book. Yet it had been just such a singular piece, bound in cherry cloth, with watery blue edge when closed, that attracted his eye at Trubner's. Bram had inscribed the dedication page. He knew by heart the phrases, over which he labored the entirety of a Sunday afternoon before marking so expensive a gift: *To Miss Balcombe, on the occasion of her nineteenth birthday, with fond hopes that many more shall be observed in his grateful company, Abraham Stoker.* In a daring moment, he had drawn a little vase of roses (embarrassing sketch), intending it as a secret tussie-mussie. If she had given something so personal away… he turned over the small volume, began to lift the cover.

But stopped again, slapping it fiercely closed before allowing himself to see. He pocketed the book and walked expressionlessly, with neither coat nor hat, rapidly into the worrying street.

5.

Where is the Lady of the House?

Bram found he had walked entirely home, bypassing crowds, arriving there all unexpected in the middle of the day. In his trouser pocket hung the offending volume, still unexamined. The astounded housemaid stared at the throw rug she had been beating on the bricks.

I'm sure I don't know, sir.

Do you not. Do you not, indeed.

It was too terrible, too disgraceful… his own confused nerves, he could not even think… he had been working for their good, their very survival in London. And his young wife, at the same hour… if this thing, in his pocket, was *their* book, then betrayal cut deep, as deep as the life. His own small dalliance was without any real significance; he was calm enough now to distinguish the two. He had behaved like a child, but done no actual harm. But if it had come to such an intimacy between Florence and another man—*that* man, above all others!—if it had come to such disregard for Bram's status as husband, anything might have passed between them.

Anything at all.

Bram explained to the startled servants that he was not feeling well, and would retire to the bedroom. They curtsied quickly and made their exits.

Door closed, seated rigidly on the mattress edge, slowly he withdrew the cloth book and rested it in his lap. With fingers of ice, he dared to lift the cover; turned, after two tries, the first few papers to expose the dedication page. It was unmarked, pure as a field of snow. This was not the same collection.

The blood uprushed into Bram's head, making his senses tumble. He felt almost delirious with relief. He gasped, double and triple checking, and giggled aloud. Nothing: all imagined. He had shouted at Florence cruelly, for no reason. He had engaged in a wicked fantasy about his employer, the man whom he admired most in this world. He had played the part of jealousy too well. Too well!

Bram danced foolishly about the bedroom, holding the volume to his chest. It was nothing, a coincidence. He had pilfered from the greatcoat unforgivably, and must return this false flag before Mister Irving returned. He stood in front of Florence's silkwood dressing table, with its half-score of ornate little nooks. In each of a dozen secret spaces were her bedroom items, bonewhite cameos and brooches, her glass disk of powder puff, tangy perfumes, a locket necklace with no picture. The original gift of *Poems*, so similar to the volume he now held, must be here somewhere. He slid open and closed tiny drawers, their pearl knobs no larger than his thumb, with the pleasant sensation of cloth casters slipping over wood. Where would she keep it? His eye caught on a glint.

Bram's pulse slowed. Slowly he put a finger deep into the back of the drawer and drew out a long, thin, silver chain. At its end, a cross, made of rose-colored glass.

6.

A MADMAN, RUMOR SAID, WAS PACING THE MARKET STALLS OF COVENT Garden today, peddlers dodging him as they would a rough animal loosed in a public place. Rain streaked the grubby amber panes of the roof overhead as Bram pushed his way through the crowd. The centerpiece of Covent Garden was a neoclassical building of chipped orange stone, constructed to replace the ancient mélange of wooden vendors and open on both ends, but the overall feel was still of a vegetable market from the previous century. Around him pressed the afternoon mob, their noisome melee bringing the scents of ginger beer and animal dung, grease and woodsmoke, vegetable crates and spilled vinegar. The vendor of geese was suspending three fleshy, plucked bodies on a pole, his companion waving off flies. Some indigents singing a chaunting lay held out the hat as Bram passed, but withdrew quickly when they caught sight of his expression.

He purchased, smoked a Turkish cigar, which tasted foul, and he hurled the unfinished thing at a green pile of droppings. What should he do? What do? His heart began to gallop in his ribs, out of all rhythm. Florence! Henry! His head was rolling; all at once he must escape the market congestion, and began forcing his way around shocked-looking carters and belled horses, the crying sellers, the stink of animal urine. The whole street whirled about him, a flaring chaos of sensations. Bram panted like the runner he once had been; he pulled fiercely at his beard with both hands until russet threads sprinkled his shirtfront. Seeing a small chapel he pushed toward it, finding it blessedly unoccupied. Purple mosaics, a marble font surrounded by a wreath of candles, the hushed gloom of the sacred. He fell into a waxy pew, gasping. The air in here was sweet with lamentation.

For a time he did nothing, only staring at the tiled floor between his shoes. Eventually a groan rose, a pain from the very nucleus of his being. Henry, Florence... Henry! He took the rosy cross from his trouser pocket, clutching it like burning iron. His torso sagged, he leaned forward, sliding first to one, then both knees, a penitent sinner. On the stone wall before him glittered an ornately wrought series of mosaics, Abraham and Isaac, the rejection of Hagar. Beyond and above them all, whispering to him a recollection from youth, Jacob's ladder: that childhood dream of escape, from this suffering earth.

7.

BRAM RETURNED TO THE THEATRE. NOT HERE, THEN, AND NOT SEEN since morning? The great Mister Irving had chosen to pass his afternoon hours elsewhere? He laughed loudly, once, a sour, barking noise that caused two haulers coming up from the property room to catch each other's eyes.

In the office, Bram slammed closed the door. He drew the terrible cross out once more. Abruptly, staring at the hammered silver frame, he wept; then he laughed, holding painfully his own teeth. King Laugh and Queen Cry came when they would, and each would be served. And again his exhausted brain went blank, his whole overwrought mentality an unmarked sheet.

Am I any better than he? he thought. I too have been unfaithful; in my heart, I have desired another woman. I desired her terribly, I dreamed of her kiss.

But the answer dashed out with unexpected violence: *True, too true. But he has been lying not to a woman... but to me!*

And this was the real crux of it, the masterpiece of pain. Bram had placed, in Henry Irving, every fiber of his belief. What had he not sacrificed, in order only to serve him? Shall he dismiss a prudent career in Ireland? Irving had no more than to command it. Shall he marry, with improper haste, a flirtatious child whom he hardly knew? It was done. Shall he take all the labor, shall he receive none of the credit, shall he live maddened by a loveless bed, month upon desiccated month? Done, all done. And if, all this time, his assigned wife had been enjoying the attentions *of the very man...*

Sudden fury blasted inside him, volcanic in its heat. Bram flung the serpentine chain across the room.

Stopped. Looked again.

There, on the office wall. Hanging above Irving's desk, by his piles of books, by his button-eyed rook under glass. His most precious memento, inherited from Lord Byron's own hand.

The dagger.

8.

BREATHING SOFTLY, BRAM STEPPED CLOSER. THE BLADE'S LETHAL ELegance spoke of Eastern cultures and their disregard for life, of that passionate savagery that was theirs. Circassian women were the most voluptuous of all, their beauties so fabled that invaders from other lands could be overthrown by a whisper. Only men of the steeliest temper, men of pure and steady power, wore the name of Circassian. Perhaps such a being had fashioned this very killing edge.

A drop of sweat inched its way down Bram's spine, neatly between shoulder blades, a chill finger delimiting each vertebra. Carefully he lifted free the weapon, feeling its antique weight in his hand. Many in the street were back from service in Khushab, in Zululand. Many whom one strode past in Hyde Park with a curt *fair morning* had committed such acts as he was contemplating. The blood, hot and running, was sprinkled generally about London. If all crimes were to be seen, there was not a finger in a thousand but was deep-dipped in slaughterhouse hues.

His sweating fingers gripped and regripped the dagger by the pommel. What would emerge (something inside him speculated in jolly, evil tones) were he to slash this across Irving's throat, thrust the relic deep into his black heart? He suffered a weird vision of *money*: gold coin, silver sovereigns, spangling and tinkling across the floor: all the coinblood Irving had drunk up from overflow houses, all the surrogate life he had drained from the mob. The monster would bleed applause.

So neither Florence nor Henry were to be found? He knew, he knew, where they took their afternoon ease. And from that place, there was no escape.

Like a winged vengeance, the hired brougham crashed toward Mayfair, Bram perched ferociously in its box. His skin burned, enlivened by the smoky congestion through which the driver whipped the horses. Henry Irving's personal chambers were on New Bond Street; the actor would go there to conduct his secret affairs. That was where Bram would find him out. That was where, at knife's end, he would demand a final accounting of the fiend. He *too* was a man.

Bram leaped from the cab the moment he spied Irving's terraced home. He ran to the door, taking the stairs two by three, found the front salon unoccupied, flew directly to the bedroom. Closed, always closed! But no more—! Brandishing the dagger high, its edge catching the light, with a shoulder-thrust Bram blasted open the wood. Inside were Irving and Florence, naked on the four poster, holding between them a twitching thing. Their laughing faces were smeared with red. Bram looked down: his own chest had been torn open. The heart was gone, and in its place, a black cavity...

Mister Stoker? Mister Stoker.

Bram sat helplessly on the floor of the Lyceum Office, a hesitant knocking on the panel directly above his head. His back was against the shut door, his cheeks wet to the line of his beard.

Are you in there, sir? We're shutting off the gas for the evening, sir. It's that pipe again.

The gas room keeper, a decent chap. Bram lifted his leaden brow. Was there truly a dagger in his hand? How grotesque.

Very good, Simon. You go ahead. I shall be leaving presently.

Very good, sir. A pleasant evening to you, sir.

And to you, Simon.

It was all too ridiculous, too jejune. Bram Stoker, the red-faced avenger! Like something out of Dion Boucicault.

Bram rose creakily, settled the Lord Byron knife back in its holder, straightening some papers on Henry's desk. He retrieved the cross, replaced the ink blotter in its drawer, found his own coat and muffler. One early star was just visible in the blue as, hands in their quiet pockets, he carried his grief into the streets.

9.

AT THE NINE O'CLOCK BELL HE WAS SQUATTING IN A SMOKE-THICK LUSHE-rie, far from the world. His big body, so strong and so weak, was pressed into a corner where the stucco walls made an uneven surface that dug at his back.

So this was the feeling of drunkenness, true drunkenness! Well, it was expected of the Irish. And in the end, despite all his attempts, he was inescapably Celt: a service-man, like his father before him. The Stokers provided for the aristocracy without belonging to it; their true nature was that of footmen, effective but expendable, a whole family to be fed off by superior English. That fellow Conan Doyle had been by the theatre again. He fancied himself a writer, had been bothering Bram to look over his sotted plays. *Galway?* Doyle had asked out of nowhere, as if making a medical diagnosis.

Dublin, Bram managed, startled by the densely mustachioed youth, both his prescience and presumption. *How did you know? Have I an accent?*

One can always tell the Irish, Doyle had grinned across papers, huffing his pipe in a self-satisfied cloud. *That hungry look.*

When he was certain he could stand, Bram rose, paying his tab with careful deliberation. He would not go home tonight, would not lie in a cuckold's bed. He left the pub—a "paddy club," as its type was known—just as the unkempt crowd of whiskey bibbers was growing boisterous. Bram adjusted himself in the deepening cold, underneath the hanging sign with its crude depiction of a golden harp. How much liquor had he taken? He found he could not perfectly recall. When he closed his eyes, little blue lights flickered behind the lids.

The air, he quoted Prince Hamlet to the black street, *bites shrewdly.* He headed east, into the night.

10.

AT ALDGATE, BRAM CROSSED THE IMAGINED BARRIER BETWEEN WORLDS with a little hop. Mindlessly he followed the same route he recalled from his private, late walks, not asking where his unfocussed boot soles were tending. Immediately on passing London Wall he was enveloped in a wet, chilly fog.

A crowd of rowdies appeared from behind a corner, harassing a Malay. In his current, emboldened state they were amusing; they had the appearance of children wearing naval costumes. A distant bell in Bram's mind sounded alarm, even panic, but through the whiskey he paid it no heed. The sailors passed by, more concerned with the frightened Malay than the stumbling toff with the thick reddish beard. If he could only disappear completely into this sea of particles, Bram thought, ducking almost too late under a dripping stone arch: this mudflat-scented nothingness, where men struck other men for entertainment and the voices of mockery and abuse echoed meaninglessly. If only one could enter a fog and not return.

How far had he come? This could even be Whitechapel now, slum lanes and doorways, undisposed refuse. The whore in her doubled-up stockings had presented herself in just such an alley. *Clean?* Bram inquired of the vapors, he could not tell how loudly. *Still clean, are you, girlie? I... am... ready!* Ocherous candles hovered like bogies in the mist. An unpainted window, the glass cracked all over: a taper burned in the third pane, the obvious signal. What a fool he had been to think that London society would ever accept him. He had always been a Moor among Venetians, a creature of the outer darkness.

In here.

Bram halted, heels scraping brick. The voice had come from a glow that appeared unexpectedly alongside him, lighter than the surrounding cloudy blankets.

In here.

The glow became a yellow luminance, within it a female figure, hovering a foot or more above the street. The effect was visionary. Had he not taken strong drink, he would no doubt have reacted with shock. Instead, the warning signs in his stunned brain were like the distant moan of the foghorn, only faintly discernable from the docks.

Bram drew closer. No, she was not floating, but standing on a small rise—at the top of three stone steps, the deep white cushion of fog covering all but the open door behind her.

Come on, then, love, come on.

Bram mumbled excuses, but was it not for this very reason his inebriated legs had carried him east? Was this not exactly the comfort he sought? Female hands took his fingers, his sleeves.

There were two of them, their faces eggwhite in the lamplight. The makeup was so poorly done it appeared comical. He knew the device from his theatre work: burnt hairpins for drawing the line of the brows, belladonna for opening pupils. The room he stood in was warm and smelled of mold, its close atmosphere heated by a sputtering coal. Wires and hooks hung on the bare walls, rectangular patches showing where pictures had been taken off.

She's waitin for you, sir. She is. Now go ahead.

Bram attempted a dignified expression. Whenever he closed his eyes, he found, his eyeballs attempted to roll gently backward in his skull.

She? Is she, now.

Go ahead in.

Taking his hands the two women led him stooping through a narrow tight hallway to a back room. It was a cramped space, hardly enough for the bed with its filmy drapes, hardly enough for the oversize mirror or the plate of scooped oyster shells from some previous client's meal, taken to sustain him, no doubt, in the heroic act. Feigning a look of hesitant naughtiness the girls unbuttoned their blouses, revealing beryl satin corsets, the boning decorated with ribbon. One had almond eyes; the other was taller, with a French look. She had a faint odor, as if she were nearing her time. Bram gazed fascinated at the exposed female flesh, but both women were waiting for something else, smiling expectantly toward the dark end of the room. With a rustle of curtain material she came to him.

Her face was golden, the paint on it so thick it created a silky, unreal mask. The mouth was a bright crimson moue, a single rose in a goldenrod field. Each eye had been outlined in jet, forming sharp, Oriental slants.

Ere she is now, sir.

Et voila.

The three women eased Bram onto the bed. His blood thundered, his unrestrained breaths starting to deepen. Unfamiliar fingers passed inside his vest, trailing his sensitive ribs. The golden one crawled on top of him like a cat. She was wearing a patterned chemise that hung down at the neckline, revealing the inverted U between breasts. Beneath the chemise, he realized with a gasp, was nothing at all. The golden face that leaned over his own was ceramic.

Wait... wait... this is wrong.

The sparkling mask tilted in a voiceless question. The other women's fingers had not ceased exploring.

What are your names? Bram whispered, trying vaguely to sit up. *Can we at least not...*

The faces gives no sign. The golden one was unbuttoning his shirt, her painted flesh coruscating weirdly in the candlelight. Small insistent fingernails pushed him down. He retreated, more than lay back, on the lumpy stuffed mattress.

Please, Bram said, as if to the dirty ceiling. *Please... you at least must have a name.*

The golden woman crawled higher until her red lips were sliding along one supersensitive cheek, touching the rim of his earlobe.

Tell me, the painted mouth whispered. Her voice was Oriental silk. *What iss my name.*

Bram pressed closed his eyelids in shame. He heard his own voice, featherfaint.

... Lujzi.

Lucy Lucy Lucy, the smiling mouth sang into the burning cup of his ear. She was unfastening his trousers. *Lucy Lucy Lucy.*

The door flew open with a thunderous bang and the three women scrambled off him at once. A man was there, short but absurdly musclebound. His skull was straightrazored down to the skin, the mashed ears swollen into cauliflower shapes. Spastically Bram pulled his knees up, terrified and ridiculous with his trousers at his knees. He looked like a turtle flipped onto its shell.

Easy now, gov'. Don' kick up a shine. Dinna mean t' give the fright.

Slipping a plug of tobacco to the other side of his mouth, the man gestured with a thumb. The painted women scurried from the room.

They'll be back 'n I say, gov'. I'm let ye have all three, I am. There's a noice catch. 'Specially that goldface quim. She's me special luv, ain't she.

Let me go.

Nah, nah, gov', ye got it wrong. Stay a bit. We're just decidin' fair price, haint we? Three fillies fer one rider, that's a noice bite. An me goldie, she's a proper bit of frock. She come dear.

You are mistaken. These women... I did not understand... I sought only lodging for the evening. This is a house of ill repute. I have been taken unawares.

The ugly mouth began to turn down, the black pupils shrinking as if receding into their sockets.

Bit of a fancy man fer these parts, aincha? Ye'll ave a go at me chickens, but ye won't pay, is that the way?

Unhand me, Bram managed, but this was wrong. The man had not touched him. *You shall not... have... a farthing.*

Bram struggled to maintain himself while frantically fumbling with his trouser catch. The pimp mouthed his wet green tobacco, his thick lips turning to full grimace. When Bram tried to stand, the man thrust him back down on the bed.

How much ye carryin tonight, squire? Pocket full, I'm guessin.

I shall summon the authorities!

Bram rose a second time and forced his terrified way past the pimp but in the hallway another man appeared and punched him in the head. Bram stumbled crazily backward, catching his fall on one knee, and enormous hands dragged him out a back way. He landed in an alley, struggling, trying to adopt a boxing stance as the bruiser punched him repeatedly. Bram's sporting trophies from youth were without meaning; the bruiser was fast and relentless and without the slightest misgiving about his work. The pimp had removed Bram's billfold and was unwrapping it at ease. Bram swung at nothing, his fist painfully hitting brick, and fell to the cobbles. The bruiser aimed a kick at his gut, his shoulder, his head. Bram's consciousness swam, and the dreamworld took him.

11.

WHEN HE CAME TO MORE FULLY—HAD HE BEEN DOZING?—IT WAS TO the coppery taste of blood under his gums. He struggled to focus. Miss Lujzi was wiping his forehead, as she had been for some time; but this was more dreamwork, surely; had he not, moments ago, been in a vague, rainy place where a supple form was dancing among gravestones?

Sir. Do not touch it.

She wrung the cloth in a bucket and the falling water needled his ears.

Ah, Miss... West-Ender, I believe.

Her expression was a mixture of anger and heartrend. And something else—she looked frequently behind herself, as if expecting someone—was it anxiety? His presence was a danger to her, wherever they now were, one she had undertaken at risk. She spoke quickly and quietly to other women, who then hurried from the room. She was wearing some shapeless gown, the hair pinned back in disheveled masses. Her unhappy hands, red-skinned, twisted and untwisted the cloth.

Why do you scowl, my dear? I'm afraid Mister Loveday has made new arrangements for the costumes. All the contracts have been filled. Quite beyond my powers to object.

Be still, Abraham.

Was I asleep?

You have been fighting.

Bram's hurt body brought his mind into focus. Suddenly he comprehended his situation. He began to rise, but his ribs hurt badly, and his head was still clouded. When he tried to speak, his tongue had trouble with the syllables.

Miss Lujzi, is it you, truly? Where am I?

Lie down.

Where—

Some of the sisters, they see you in Goulston. She examined the rim of the dirty cloth. *You say my name.*

Did I? Was I.

Slowly Bram raised a trembling hand to his nose, his eyelids. The left one felt fat, though not enormously so. The blow he had received there made contact with the orbital bone more than the eyeball itself. The nose had been bleeding, from both sides, but was not broken. He remembered raising himself from the alleyway, staggering on. There had been crowds in the street. A woman had come up to him, speaking a language he did not know. Now, evidently, he had been sleeping on this low bed, or something like it: thick headed, his addled brain meandering dreamily between alcohol and bruises.

Trying again to achieve some kind of focus, Bram began the careful lie.

Business… business reasons required I find myself in Whitechapel this evening, Miss Lujzi, and I seem to have fallen among thieves. I came here… I came…

Oh, what use? Sweatworkers had rescued him from the pit of dishonor, drunken, robbed, humiliated in a den of vice. She had mopped his cut face while he dozed, reeking, no doubt, from a disgusting partaking of whiskey. Whatever mask of stiff china he habitually wore had been dashed.

That is a lie, Bram admitted quietly. It was as if he were speaking to the subtle glow behind his own eyelids. *You see me, Miss Lujzi, as I am. I can say nothing in my own defense, save that I am a ruined man.*

He had hoped at least for the dignity of defeat, but the whiskey still in his gut propelled him quickly forward into sobbing.

Do not, sir.

You have told me that I am good, Miss Lujzi, but you are wrong. I am fallen, completely fallen.

No, Abraham.

I am not a writer, nor an artist. I play no part at Lyceum, beyond Irving's drudge. I am nothing, a terrible, empty nothing, and a bad man, a bad wicked sinful sinful man.

Stop this, she said firmly, coming close to grasp him. The pink cloth in her hand dampened his shoulder. *You must listen, Abraham. Do you listen? You are strong. Always you must stand again, always. I know you are good.*

You do not know me. I am so weak…

You are in pain only. Pain is not you.

She took his hand, placing the hurt fingers against her own. Now, he thought, their hands were alike: his large and hers small, both reddened and torn. Gently she rocked his hands by her cheek, stroking with her fingertips the back of his wrist.

It is pain only, Abraham. Only pain. I understand this. You know I understand this.

The side of her face touched his damaged skin, the raw and weeping scratches where the knuckles had collided with brick. When she stopped, when she would replace his hand on the mattress, Bram gripped her palms.

Lujzi, he whispered, pulling her toward himself.

The first kiss shocked her. *O* she said, and something in her own language. At the second kiss, Bram felt her hesitating, then responding, answering with her own lips, warm and alive against his mouth. He moved his other arm around her shoulders and the taste of her was as he had dreamed, the smell and the closeness of her deep as foreign earth, a distant and shadowy forest full of whispering life.

Why do you do this. She bent down her face, pulling back harshly. *Why do you come to me.*

I cannot forget you.

Sir, she whispered, as if she did not know him, as if they had only just met. *It is trouble, it is great trouble.*

Kiss me again.

You are not you. This is not yourself.

Bram took and kissed her blistered fingers. She turned almost painfully away, amazed eyes shining, as if this were too great an intimacy to bear. But she did not stop him.

Your little hands, he said, sobbing over the rough skin. *Your poor little hands.*

Pulling the hair pin he drowned his breath in auburn waves. He kissed her cheeks, her neck, and slowly he felt her yielding to him. Hesitantly, then with increasing welcome, she began to explore his beard, his bruised face, the backs of his shoulders. In the faint light Bram could make out bare plaster walls around them, the low timbers, a dressmaker's dummy with a carved wooden head. On a wooden peg the violin hung suspended, like a spiritual sign under which they lay.

12.

IN THE EARLIEST BLUSH OF MORNING BRAM AWAKENED, SOBER, WITH NO knowledge of where he was. Miniscule rays of lavender were touching the nail-studded beams. Dawn was perhaps an hour away. It was a secret, unrecorded time, the hesitation between night's last breath and morning's first.

He came to full consciousness of these sensations, and of what he had done. His trousers were flung to the edge of the mattress. There was no sound, yet, from the street below, or the sweatshop around him. But this was a place of business; it was already another day. To be here, as he was, was unthinkable.

Bram sat partially up, flinching suddenly from the bruised rib. Miss Lujzi was standing in front of the window, he realized, her form silhouetted by the approaching sun. She was wearing the sleeping gown only, hair tumbled loose to her shoulders. Through the translucent fabric Bram could distinguish the outline of her slender body. Her arms were at her sides, the hands just faintly raised, in the same awestruck, receiving posture he had seen her adopt when she first appeared in the Nook. He had the impression she had been by the window, watching the minute changes spread their silks across the atmosphere, for some time.

Lujzi, Bram whispered, dolor and longing mixing.

God sees me. Her voice was no louder than the turning of a Bible sheaf. He could see the wetness on her cheek. *He sees.*

Bram looked guiltily around the brightening room. No one but the dressmaker's dummy, its painted eyes blue and astonished. But there was no mouth: it could not tell. Only the blue, stupefied eyes. Only the cloth hide, all scattered with needles.

Chapter 13

1.

ONCE, WHEN BRAM WAS STILL AT TRINITY, A PROFESSOR NAMED DOWDEN had invited him for an evening of discussion with a number of other Third Years. When he arrived at the Georgian house the group inside was already laughing chummily, sipping their mulled heated cider. This was the semi-annual meeting of the literary club, but Dowden's invitations were more than an academic event. Turning the invitation over in his hands, Bram had felt a paternal inclusion in this world.

It will have blood, they say, the scholar began. *Blood will have blood.*
Sir?
Go ahead.
Macbeth, sir. He is saying that secrets will come out.
More than this, Dowden mused, nursing the hearth logs with a blackened prod. He had good skin and hair, with an open, pleased looking face. When discussing literature his habit was to travel gradually about the room, drifting his fingers through the flamelit air as if coaxing his ambulatory thought.
The Bard is telling us… with the choice itself… no more tea, thank you… at the moment of choosing… therein lies the consequence. The two, in reality, are one.

At seven on the small chiming mantle clock the congregation moved to the sitting room, the students who were familiar with proceedings arranging their chairs in a rough circle. An oil portrait of the Viscount Melbourne looked over the scene, near a dancing Pan wrought cleverly in marble. The whole comfortable house had been paneled in Brazilwood and cherry, its glossy surfaces yielding lampglow from a half dozen changing angles.

Very good. Are we all settled? Master Lane?
Sir?
If you would grace us with that baritone of yours.

> O what can ail thee, knight-at-arms,
> Alone and palely loitering?
> The sedge has wither'd from the lake,
> And no birds sing.
>
> I see a lily on thy brow
> With anguish moist and fever dew,
> And on thy cheeks a fading rose
> Fast withereth too.

The poem was passed from hand to hand, each student delivering his best under the Lecturer's watchful eye.

Fast withereth too.

Master Stoker, Professor Dowden interrupted, stopping the book in its progress and delivering it directly to Bram's lap. *A new voice amongst us tonight.*

Professor.

If you would.

How Bram had swelled at that moment of recognition! With what caution, what careful enunciation, he let drop each resonant syllable:

> *And there she lulled me asleep.*
> *And there I dream'd—Ah! Woe betide!*
> *The latest dream I ever dream'd*
> *On the cold hill's side.*

The dinner afterward had been memorable, oysters with soda bread and cabbage. The sharp edge of vinegar heightened each gustatory sensation, like the trilling of a lady's maid's bell. At the evening's close, Dowden had smiled, patting coat shoulders as the scholars filed once more into the night.

Evans. Kells.

Sir.

Master Stoker.

Sir?

It was a good bit of reading we had from you tonight. You seem to have a poetical ear.

Thank you, sir.

Dowden laid a finger at the thick of his moustache. *I wonder,* he mused, examining the great book-stuffed antechamber by the door. His silk vest, opened after the evening meal, flamed glossily in the candleshine. *Songs Before Parting. Are you familiar…?*

Bram had struggled with the title, searching his mental accounts. *To be sure. Are they popular airs?*

Dear, no, Dowden laughed, making a decision and slipping a small leatherbound edition from a nook. Bram had noticed that, among the variety of thin and thick tomes, some with scalloped edges, some with hasps, this text was the only that looked actively used. He read the inverted title: *Leaves of Grass.*

An American—poet, sir?

Don't give credence to the naysayers. Read the poems, and let me know your mind. I shan't play games. I fear they may be great.

Fear?

Dowden fixed him there. *It isn't often a living writer finds immortality. There is something fearsome in the event.*

Keats is certainly timeless.

What did you make of La Belle Dame? *Of course she is not a person, but an ideal figure.*

Yes sir, Bram said strongly, *I also read her that way. A dream of love.*

A dream of love, Dowden had echoed him, approving. *Very good. But the lady is dangerous, as well. You agree?*

Bram had stepped out to the lightly raining night with spine tucked smartly under cloak. *Thank you, sir. Until next week.*

Dangerous, yes, the old scholar pondered, already returned to his solitary thought. *But then, actual love so often is…*

2.

IT WAS ALMOST ELEVEN AT NIGHT, FIVE DAYS LATER, BEFORE BRAM STEPPED, cautiously as he could, onto the landing in front of his home.

Abraham, his wife began quietly.

Bram stood frozen before her, his fingers grasping fiercely the leather satchel. A small eternity passed in which he remained at the threshold of his own residence, bound there as if by force. It was the latest in a series of cold, creaky nights that followed on rainswept days, the windows of the late avenue all tied in place, candles in their tin hog scrapers sensibly snuffed.

For almost a week he had avoided even brief interactions with Florence. Henry Irving was away, drawing inspiration from a train journey through Wales and sparing Bram the necessity of looking at the man, and time and again Bram had manufactured reasons for not returning to Southampton Street until the latest possible hour, whereon he would sleep in the parlor chair or, if need be, the extra bedroom. One long, wind-bothered Sunday he passed entirely at the British Library, exiting his home with no word of explanation. Among the rows of old books he had tried desperately to comprehend his situation, but time and again his shocked mind refused to comply. For almost an hour he had sat staring at a yellow Roman vase that had been smashed and repaired, its once-pristine surface a maze of faults.

Bram's feelings, after his night in Whitechapel, had swirled and re-swirled into a foul witches' brew. Periods of intemperate, knee-gripping rage mixed in his mind with stretches of almost ruinous shame. The back of his throat burned, as if he were mouthing vinegar from the sponge, when he thought of the deception that had been played on him: the lies Florence had told, the mockery Henry Irving had made of his entire life. And yet his own act, undertaken against all respectability in a filthy East End sweatshop, with a Gypsy maid—a night from which he had not returned at all, taking himself directly to Lyceum the following morning—could it ever be forgiven? The events of a single day had shattered both his sense of himself, and of his world, as completely as the blasted vase.

Come inside, Bram.

He had had no intention of seeing Florence tonight, nor, in fact, any specific night or day to come. All week long he had had no intention that he could name, waiting numbly through the hours like a fire victim at Barts Infirmary. But Florence had surprised him on the stoop. She turned and rustled, without further comment, up the stair.

Reluctantly he followed her, viewing his own domicile as if for the first time. The gas candle that had been poorly installed, and about which Florence threw such an upset; the oval portraits, all dusted; a colored shade with little nubbins along the bottom, giving the hallway a warming cheer. Here was a sampler his sister Matilda had sewn as a girl; here, a sketched likeness of Florrie, surrounded by four preserved loops of her jetty hair. What noble souls, he thought bitterly, what admirable beings, must reside in so upright a space?

The servants have been sent home, Florence instructed his silence. *Come, I had them build us a fire before retiring. It is a dreadful chill at this hour.*

Bram's jaw was so tight that, when he tried to speak, the bone produced a loud clicking sound in one ear.

I had thought... you would be... abed, as usual, and would not wish to be disturbed.

You see I have been waiting, she answered. *For you.*

Bram removed his damp coat, set his umbrella numbly in the brass stand. The resonance of their last, hollered words in this room still shimmered in the captured air. Yet the motions of casual domesticity—simply drawing off his muffler and slapping it against his wet shoes, as if nothing were amiss—precipitated his next meaningless comment.

And you are well, tonight?

I shall be well, Florence responded, fixing his eye carefully, *before this hour is done.*

The outrage he felt at seeing her curdled and died inside him. Somehow— oh, it did not matter how!—somehow his *own* disloyal act had become known to her already. There would be no uncrossing Aldgate, no unmaking the stroke of the past. It would be of no moment to insist that his shame was not wholly of his choosing, that his native moral sense had been occluded by a flood of intemperate and disordered fury at her scalding betrayal. No use at all. Like the Thane of Cawdor and his wife, they were both steeped in the same crimson river.

Come, Abraham.

She led him into the parlor, where she arranged herself by a weeping fire. Bram, his mind a hot flux, lowered himself carefully to the grate. His breath was thin and small.

No, no. Over here.

She had settled on the walnut sofa, and indicated the pillow beside her. Beside her on the sofa!

As—as you wish.

Now then.

What purpose was she after, why this pretense of amity? Florence knew her own webwork of lies, had known it for weeks, perhaps months. Nothing but spite could exist between them now. But what should be the final line in the ledger? Mulling his situation over the past few days in endless repetitive loops, Bram had found he could not say. The knot was complex. He could not seek legal redress against Florence without bringing ruin on himself. Everything he had, everything, was predicated on the good will of an actor. He would be a fool to name Irving in a suit; no man in London had a greater power to sway public opinion. Nor would Dublin offer him shelter in the event of a scandal. Colonel Balcombe held him in contempt, and any accusation against his daughter would mean social opprobrium before Bram's luggage had even been unwrapped. The Colonel might even place a proceeding against *him* for befouling the family name. Yet he could not live, he would not live, with a woman who had humiliated him, in the employ of a monster who had visited his bed.

Our last words, in this house, were severe, Florence said, and raised two fingers, as if to block his responding. The nails had been cleaned and shaped. *And I am grieved that this should be so.*

A pause. Bram had to force himself to stop blinking.

Madam, he replied heavily, *I too regret this change in our state.*

Florence's mood was all softness. Was it only duplicitous, this pretend civility between them? But she was looking on him with strange soft kind eyes, stranger and softer than he had seen in her, ever.

Bram waited, on the edge of speech. Behind the dip in his throat, his blood beat in unresolved tremors.

Florence began again, *And I fear I have been the cause of our distance.*

Madam. We must both accept that—but she silenced him, now with a touch to his wrist. Florence was holding his wrist!

Bram, she said. You are too good. Since you adventurously brought me to London, yours has been entirely the risk. I have enjoyed here the pleasure of a more prominent circle of acquaintance than I should ever have hoped to discover in the unassuming precincts of St. Stephen's Green. I recognize too that, poor as I am, I brought but little to this union of ours, and for your condescension in having me, I am profoundly grateful.

He was nothing but astonishment. A whitened chunk of ash fell in the grate, letting off a long, sighing sound.

I... have no words.

Then let mine speak a while. Florence rose with a look of intention, and it was only now that Bram noticed she had dressed herself in her finest crinoline, the robin's egg-paneled dress in which she had met him on the day of his proposal. Her form, open to his view in a way it had not been since courtship, was displayed to advantage.

I see you recognize this dress.

I... yes...

I must confess it was not all coincidence that I should have donned it on the afternoon you offered that our fortunes should be joined. Shall I share with you a secret of women's craft? The language was strange. And her look... was it possible?... had turned almost coy. She would let him in on hidden things. *When I saw you emerge from the hansom that morning, I instructed father to delay you at all costs, while the housemaid arranged me in this! The housemaid!* Her mood was unreadable.

Florence, you... Again the fury rose in him, boiling hot. Did she taunt him with triviality, having ruined his life? Did she dare?

You were thought by many the great beauty of Dublin, Bram concluded stiffly. But his voice cracked slightly with the honesty of it. *The day we wed... the day we wed, I believed you the finest woman I had ever seen.*

You are kind, she replied simply. *And because you are also good, I must now speak on a subject in which there shall be, for us both, a certain measure of pain. But if our union as partners... do not turn away, Abraham. Be strong, as I am strong... if our union is to continue, there can be no deception.*

His whole torso clenching, Bram stood.

Madam. We—

But his words failed in astonishment: she had thrown herself at his feet. Her expensive dress crumpled about her like a crushed blossom.

Florence! You must not kneel—!

I insist it, Florence cried, refusing his attempts to lift her. *And I insist you hear me out. My connection to your employer, Mister Henry Irving, has been nothing other than innocence.*

Bram recoiled, steadying himself on the mantle ledge. The attempt at ingenuousness sounded pathetic even in his own ears.

You say… Mister Irving… ?

Bram, you seek to spare my feeling, but I shall—I must!—refuse even this. I know you have discovered the ruby cross.

The… the…

Do not gainsay it. Mister Irving offered it to me, and I, child that I am, took it in flattery. You were right to remove it from my dresser! But Mister Stoker, Mister Stoker, do not mistake it for the species of gift a man may give to an unattached woman. He and I had been speaking of the dangers that London presents to the unwary, and he suggested the necklace as a charm against evil. You know he is quite superstitious.

Yes, Bram stumbled. *That is so.*

It was inappropriate of me to entertain my husband's employer in his absence, she lamented to his shirt. *Your anger was justified, wholly justified. I recognize now, as a better wife might have then, that all of these actions might cause a terrible misunderstanding.*

Bram felt as if he were tottering, his feet on a windy ledge.

You mean—

You have been tolerant, too tolerant, but as a wife I must censure myself. I should have recognized that such actions might leave a false impression in my true partner, the man whom I love. It is this impression that I want you to forgive.

Florence, then you didn't… you haven't been…

Can you forgive me?

But you haven't…

Bram was awhirl. He felt his brain opening in wonderment, reaching madly for this offered straw—but then stopped, staring hard, at the woman prostrated before him.

Could he be understanding right? Was this not simply another Persona Mask in the Greek tragedy of their matrimony? Still he stared, jaw partway open, helpless.

Bram, hear me, please. I confess I was seduced, for a time, by the London social life, delighted by its glittering scenes. The speech sounded prepared, that was what was so odd about it; Florence was not one for eloquence. She had spent time, careful time, designing these words. But did they not carry, also, the signet of her sincerity? *And a little bit, I think, I may blame you. For was it not you who plucked me from my native soil, naïve as I am, and insinuated me into the larger world?*

I... Florence, I... let me think.

He was overawed by her female speech, sundered wholly. If this be true, if this be so, then there had been no betrayal. Nothing was as it seemed. The full import of her confession came over him in a rush. The nightmare of suspicion in which he had been living was just that, a dream, another ephemera of his mind. The man he loved—yes, the man he *loved* like a father, and to whom he owed all—that man had not played him like a chess piece, had not revealed himself as a species of devil. Despite his confusion, this was a joyous balm, honey to his soul. But dared he believe?

Florence. It was indeed as you say. Mine was the hand that so... the niceties of language, so critical to the Victorian social life, evaded him. *I hurried us both into marriage, yes, and brought you here, still quite young, and left you unattended in this place. It is true, I confess it, I have done all these things. But you never... that is, you never...?*

I swear innocence, Bram.

It was too terrible to say aloud, but he had to speak the words, once. Bram closed tightly his eyes.

Florence... you and... Mister Irving...

Never. I swear it.

Staggering, unable to find phrases, Bram got down on the vine-patterned rug.

Madam, if you will not stand, then I kneel.

He moved to embrace her. The repentant flesh felt warm underneath the fabric of her sleeves.

Bram, she whispered to his buttons. *Bram, I beg you, I truly beg you, to return home. To sleep once more at my side. Do not disown me.*

Disown her! So that was her great fear—and for nothing, a trifle. Joy began to well in his hurt stomach. He had behaved like a cad, he had frightened the poor woman terribly. She was not dissembling, he could see the truth in her face. Yes, this was grace from heaven, an unmerited dropping off of the albatross…

… but then Bram's pulses slowed as a second, more profound horror moved toward his mind. Its black enormity was like the hull of a ship whose full dimensions he only now conceived. Florence knew nothing of his own wicked fall. While she had retained her purity, only indulging at worst in flirtation, his own record was fouler than pitch. If her story be true, if he had been so utterly mistaken, then the act he had committed was beyond forgiveness.

Bram turned away, his face wrenched.

Oh Bram, she said in a wounded tone. *In your expression I see, now, how my girlish vanity has made you suffer.*

Not you, he whispered, cold lips moving toward confession.

Florence hesitated.

Then…

Oh, but go not there yet, Bram's agony cried, not yet! The ship of his guilt was too massive, its black prow driving him under the waves. He could not tell her, not now, not if she had been steadfast all along.

I mean to say, Florence, only that I, myself, have been the author of half our distress. You and I are husband and wife. We must keep each other, always, in the utmost security of trust.

The rest of the night passed vaguely. His conscience paced the perimeter of his skull like an animal, the machinery working harder than it had done since his degree in Pure Mathematics. To outward appearance he maintained a steady demeanor, while inwardly he labored with his problem, and retreated; advanced, and drew back; was overmastered, finally, by simple exhaustion. Her own trivial sin purged, Florence chatted in a more familiar vein. But that Henry Irving was a tedious fellow, was he not? She had been captured a bit, it was true, by his charms, but now saw him rather more clearly. No man so intolerably promotes himself who is not in the end rather dull.

You need tell me no more about it, Bram insisted, taking the cup of warmed cinnamon milk. How long had it been since he ate a full meal? For days he had not been able to taste his tea, and this milk—fortified by her, he realized on sipping, with a thimble of scotch—entered sweetly his mouth. He found some bread and thick cheese, cut and gnawed it like a convict only narrowly escaped from the gallows. Laughing, Florence must continue. *You know Mister Irving was sent away when he was still very young, some kind of heartless aunt in Cornwall. It's all very Dickens.*

Well, well. The food gave him nourishment, a simple, animal need, while the scotch eased his brain. *I am relieved… Florence, I am greatly relieved.*

The funny way he walks, of course, is in the family. His father, he says, had it as well. When he isn't paying attention, he almost lopes around the room.

Irving's bent spine was a congenital condition, something he labored diligently to conceal. Bram had frequently seen him go through a series of spine-strengthening exercises before walking onstage. Low witticism in the press, now and again, had suggested the actor might try his skill at the hunchbacked Richard III, a tease that Bram had seen draw the man's brows almost to the point of touching.

Yes, he managed. *The limp is a problem for him.*

Bram tried to steer her to other topics, but having confessed, she would expunge all. *Sometimes, you know, a man may wish for the ear of a woman, and of course not that dreadful Ellen Terry. With her, poor Mister Irving must be as much 'on stage' as with the rest. Yes, he is 'poor' Mister Irving. I know he has been a perfect ogre to you, but we must both be sorry for him as well…*

Mister Irving this, and that, and the other thing, and never had it occurred to her that Bram was not aware of his visits, though really she had not given the matter much thought, occupied as she was with so many social engagements. It was true, Bram thought distantly; an outsider would no doubt say Irving had treated him callously, making Bram's continued feelings of devotion difficult to explain. Perhaps this very contradiction in their relationship accounted for his leap to wild suspicion. But his wife was still running on, something about how Irving made her listen to a long and, she thought, rather wordy monologue he was rehearsing, and of course he paced abominably all the while, loping about, and smoking that frightful clay pipe. Had Bram not smelled it?

Indeed, Florence, no. Well, indeed. I have been quite unperceptive.
How did you hurt your eye? Oh, my poor dear.
Nothing…

Again his uncertain mind turned, seeking to view this reversal from differing angles. He wanted, with profound urgency now, to believe: to accept that this dark passage in their marriage had all been confusion, the foppery of an Italian opera. Ridiculous as that made him, it meant salvation from ruin, and the keeping of this life he had built.

D'you know, Florence warbled, bringing him back. Her diction had returned to its norm, the other voice retired upstage. *Do you know, I do not believe I ever felt alone in the room with the fussy gentleman, only with a rather large child. But still, a child, an infant in need of nursing. And any lady may comfort a child without fault, may she not?*

Madam, yes. Indeed she may.

You men.

It was over. Some hours had passed, crossing midnight. Florence turned abruptly playful. It was a side of her person he did not recognize; perhaps he had never seen it. She swatted teasingly at Bram with her removed stocking, as if he were representative of the breed. *You turn to women to be your mothers, not for anything else. It's why you hate us in the end.*

Bram was standing by his bedside table once more, shirt unbuttoned, pressed trousers pendant in the closet like half a hanged man. The fire was declined in the grate. There had been a second cup of milk, again with addition. He hardly knew how it all had happened, how long she had been explaining. It was a dizzy, almost drugged feeling.

Oh Bram, I am so glad we have cleared this darkness away, Florence concluded, her body reclining by sections on the turned-down bed. *I have missed my husband.* Her pupils became steady.

It was an invitation, one meant to seal their renewed pact. She was summoning him in a way he had never known.

Kiss me, Bram.

To do this would be to accept her word, and to stand, hereafter, by that decision. It would be to confirm his choice. This life, and no other.

Perhaps tomorrow, my dear, he attempted. *We are both…*

Now. I insist.

Bram lay next to her after it was done. For the first time, he felt, he was in the marriage bed, truly in it: next to his wife, his legally betrothed, in a state of mutual possession. Her body, wrapped in her triumphant sleeping gown, was curled up and sated. On her sleeping face, a slight smile.

The ceiling at which he had so often stared, with its painted border of dusty yellow scrollwork, held no terrors tonight. They had come together, man and wife—come together, finally, in triumph. The dream of betrayal, the image of the leech bowl, were as fevers forgotten. His spouse was a Penelope, Henry Irving a trusted benefactor. Bram's extreme relief at having his life given back, at his standing made sure, pulsed over him in incredible waves. How the past few months had conspired to remove utterly and then to restore a horizon of possibility must, like the teeth of the horse, not be closely examined. All was rubbed out, redacted. Fantastically... impossibly... all was well.

Only as sleep approached him did a second face come and hang over the bed, eyes like glittering marbles. *No more*, Bram prayed, half aware of his praying. *Any gentleman may sin, as indeed I have sinned. But let that be forgotten.*

Does he sleep? Does he dream? It is deepest night, what his mother Charlotte called *moonhour*, a hidden time not contained on any clock. Outside their window casing, the secret fog swirls and turns. From the distance, a voice of nightbirds. It sounds like someone calling him.

Chapter 14

Camden, *N. Jersey*,
431 Stevens St
U.S. America,
Cor. West

My Dear Young Man,
Pleased I am, and proud as well, you have chosen to write. You should never have hesitated. Such correspondence as I receive from readers across the broad atlantic brings with it the joy of a new tide, all unexpected, &replete as with treasures from the sea. Let us be companion'd!
You ask me what I think of the artists of our age. Who among them sings with that clear, that lusty innocence that men call Great? Of England's palmiest minds, I cannot speak (as I know not.) But I say to you no man is the American Bard, or takes the laurel here. For every American is both poet and poem — every Soul that works this land, sees the sun setting mellow'd on its hills & rising, richly renew'd ; lies down in amity & good conscience ; every such a one is great poet and great poem, the seeming-smallest citizen an unending Iliad and Aneid [sic] of himself.
The Pow-Wow sitting cross-legg'd at his morning fire, grasping his painted cohort ; the three mates starving in a boat, cast from the schooner sinking and cracked ; the youthful virgin frighted by the bridal bed ; I see her in the Territories, in the Slave States, at Washington City itself ; aye she is both singer &song, she delivers the great opus of America.
The Pow-Wow sings it ; the minister on his way to revival, carrying the sacred blood of his God, sings it ; the pioner sawing great slabs of oak &white pine, fell'd also by his hand sings it ; the dying soldier in the clinique, dying with his free brothers in the Union war (I call them free men all.)
The washer-woman in Louisiana carrying her lode ; the negro children in their plantation shacks, along the dark & silent river ; the negress mother

screaming as she goes to labor, bringing all her womanhood to task ; I see them, common people, they are all great poets, greater than the greatest.

And let us not forget the old man sitting in Camden by a small coal fire, dipping his quill (as now I do) to write this, a letter to you—Mister Abraham Stoker of Westminster London!

Also I like Mr Hawthorne, esp Blithedale Romance, some of the Twice-Told Tales.

Walt Whitman.

Camden, N. Jersey
U.S. AMERICA,
431 Stevens St
Cor. West

BRAM, as you bid me call you—

In receipt of your latest to-day by mail boat. Huzzah!

I retrieve &deliver them direct, not waiting for the land service. This saves always on time.

You ask me regarding Mr E. A. Poe. No, I do not like him. I grant his work was strong while he liv'd and in areas he wrote well as a man might. There is lustiness & feeling at times but too often he was fatigu'd, without manliness &seemed positively to dwell upon unhealthful thought………the leaving of vitality was his theme, as if all the world were Convalescent Camp. Such things as decrepitude seemed to him worth endless meditation, while the new growth, flow'ring daily, he valued at a pin.

His characters I find are not men but little jack-straws, panick struck at fancies (I commenc'd to re-reading his Tales of Mystery this past Spring, and have taken in some half a score; for I would not judge a workman's labours lightly. Though we differ on all points of substance I will hear a man until he has finish'd, and beckon him then to more, that I may sound him well.) His characters read not as hotblood peoples, the kind I like &love, but weak-will'd, brooding, nay abysmic……… and [ILLEGIBLE] the national cemeteries.

Mr E. A. Poe's mind was in large part fasten'd to sickly, wasting women, & this is very unhealthful &very much against me. I laugh with death—not at, but with Death — I cast athwart a thousand pricks and stingers of age ;— tomb and wreath have to me no significance ;—to the coffin-springer I toss his coin (for his trade is good) but offer no business ;—I have liv'd a thousand centuries before and will be here, vital and amative, a thousand centuries hence...

I am told there is about Mr E. A. Poe's works a 'pleasure in the dreadful.' Very good! Tho' why is the body done such pitiable disservice? Have you read his 'Man Who Was Used Up' — the poor fellow finds an eyeball behind the couch — 'Berenice' is too terrible .... not for its command of a certain murky speech but as a story great God.

Only sometimes his comedic sketches are delightful. The 'camel-leopard,' I think, which I encounter'd in my Evening Star— "Loss of Voice"; a bit of merry fluff—&c.—

one I found in Southern Literary Messenger in which the little Frenchman quite gets his cummupence.

The man fell terribly of drink [ILLEGIBLE] only real sin is that against the body.

His entries on landscaping are fine. He may I think have been a fine Naturalist, & shaper of landscapes. This was perhaps his proper occupation, had he but found it ; and would have done some good to his countrymen.

BRAM, do you think to journey ever to our Democratic shores?

Your letters give me great joy, &I would love to dine with you some day & learn from you, all that you have to give.

I waft affectionate salutation.
     Walt Whitman.

# # #

Camden, N. J. U.S. AMERICA
[UNDATED]

Dear Abraham (you should use the fullest version of your name—ABRAHAM—That is a name brim-full of hist'ry),

How pleased I am to learn of your recent success! The theatre goes well, under the famous name of those actors, Mister Henry Irving and Miss Ellen Terry. And now you are to be a father!

In fatherhood lies greatness; you shall be, I have no doubt, the progenitor [sic] of nations. I send heart-swelling congratulations.

You say America is young. Here I answer in the negative. America is old, old ; it is older far than England &France, exactly because it is new. It has the wisdom that is only found in novelty& [ILLEGIBLE] wash-kettle [?] countries of the "elder world" have taken for granted and so lost.

Infirmity be damn'd! Rode out to Timber Creek this morning in the [THE REST OF THIS CORRESPONDENCE MISSING.]

Camden, *New Jersey*,
U.S. *AMERICA*,

Bram,
Yours receiv'd.
Thank you for the story, which I have read with pleasure. Hm-m!

Your work is indeed like that of Mr. E. A. Poe tho' writ in a simpler style. Frightful stuff &a good "page-turner."

But you have not yet writ yet [sic rep] of your own life, only of your imaginings. Write only of that you truly love ; in love alone be fearless. When you tell the tale of yourself, you will know inspiration.

You think my tastes perhaps, infirm and airish, owing to my age & to your own good star, which is just approaching its zenith & must rise swiftly, out-shining all others. It
[PAGE MISSING]

Across the wide desert ATLANTIC — [ILLEGIBLE] Free States, and with this our [ILLEGIBLE] sentimentalism [?] to [ILLEGIBLE] ad libitum. I have din'd regularly at the Metropolitan Hotel, where telegrams may be both sent and receiv'd.

We
[THE REST OF THIS CORRESPONDENCE MISSING]

\# \# \#

328 Mickle Street
Camden *New Jersey*
U.S. *AMERICA*

BRAM—
Thank you for your concern. The flux is well pass'd (except in my stomachic areas). In its wake I feel the warm sun of recovery. I take in nutriment and chile, I reform &improve myself.

Claudet I do not know (Did you mean Claudel? I knew a Frenchman of the name fighting in the Union war, I do not know what hap'd him). To-day spent several hours wandering the dock at Delaware river. Distinctly impress'd by
[SIGNIFICANT WATER DAMAGE]

How feel you at approaching parenthood? I turned my calendar this morn, calculating when the first child of my Irish friend's loins shall spring free, &he enter a new phase of living
[DAMAGE]
Post Scriptum:
Not the interminable rows of your houses, nor the ships rocking in the wharves,
Nor the long silence of your dead, in their coffins, &c. &c.
— can you divine my feeling?

W. W.

\# \# \#

328 Mickle Street
Camden, *New Jersey,*

My Dear Young Man—
The missives of these past few months have been, to me, a season of joy. I thank you for them, from the deep of this heart.

Bram, I beckon you to your own special future. Whatever life hails you, embrace it. Be a writer, as you dream—be a father of tribes. Everything in this grand green world has been prepared for you, and awaits your pleasure.

You ask me, at last, about Emerson.

About him I will tell you this........ . one felt the heaviness of his greatness. I first read him sermonizing, and in every line found my soul rous'd—he summoned me even to a boil—no other man was so much with me. In old age I prefer both women and men swifter on their feet than even when I was young, less absorbed & sooner to laugh , to take up ax or adze & join a comrade at his tasks. Emerson was a fine one for thinking, & at his best went to it like work. He never was a grand one for laughter—which is so much finer than thinking....... .

Tho' there was once I traveled once [sic] to hear him on a lecture tour [?] saw him choke upon a fly &afterward commence a spell of [ILLEGIBLE] frightened by this as by a thunder-clap [ILLEGIBLE] ran up the inside of her skirts — the dear woman shriek'd as if the Devil pinch'd her privates — stuffy Emerson grew red with chuckles& quite lost his place. If

[MISSING]

Shake-spear

[MISSING]

Old Waldo, as you say, was my father, & I his son. Truly I lov'd him if I lov'd any man. Yet we each must do to death our parents, or they bury us.

          Walt Whitman

Chapter 15

1.

SPRING HAD COME IN ONCE MORE WITH ITS MARVELOUS PARADE. BRAM'S labors—amusing word—at the Lyceum had long since ceased to be oppressive as new hope for the future blossomed in his heart. Even his own attempts at literature, so long pushed aside, had met with their first success.

The letters from Whitman, arriving in mailships over the past few months, he cherished immensely. His desire, since Trinity, to share himself openly with his literary hero, to send a yawp of camaraderie across the Atlantic, he had finally risked, never expecting a reply. But the elderly gentleman, like his verses, had been more than generous. And the wonderful night that had brought him and Florence back together had likewise allowed his creative energies to flow. It was as if these forces were bound in some arcane manner: the marriage bed, production, imagination—in the past few months he had both completed and sold his first story collection, *Under the Sunset*, a group of unusual children's fables. And why not? He was going to be a father!

For several months now Florence had possessed a matronly air. The new life was not yet visible, though it could be recognized by way of (how should a gentleman phrase it) certain changes in her relationship to the moon. The black-spotted cloth Bram had noticed being removed to the washrooms was no longer in service. Like that same all-feminine orb, his wife was hiddenly waxing; yet, had she not told him of it, he might not have realized the almost immediate effect of their night together. What a mystery, after all, were women! Without their admission, how long would it be before most young husbands suspected the great change had taken place? Nothing showed it at all, save, perhaps, a morning pallor on Florence's cheek, followed by times of flushed over-fullness, as if two natures within her were at battle, which shall preside.

Her revels now were ended. The teas and *soirees* had been brought to a close while her more basic, female nature asserted its prerogative. And if she spoke rudely to the servant girl with regard to a stained apron, if there had been one or two "tiffs" over how to prepare a simple kipper dish, such was to be expected of the brooding hen. The physical closeness of their own night of confession (as he thought of it) had not been repeated, but Bram was content. The most fearful ordeal of his life was a chapter closed, and his manhood to be furnished, now, with sequel.

The triumphant Stokers moved to a house in Chelsea, nestling into a more dignified area whose residents included Whistler, Rossetti, his old friend Hall Caine. Oscar Wilde himself kept house nearby, and Bram had encountered him once already, with his preposterous velvet cape and ribbons, leaving the cane-makers.

Well then, Oscar, shall we be seeing you in society?

My dear Abraham, nothing could be worse luck, for either of us.

The expense of living in Chelsea was great, but Bram would find some means of satisfying his creditors in time. His was a tall, brick, connected building looking out on an orderly expanse of the same, flanked dramatically by the embankment gardens. In nearby Burton Court stood the ornate and sunwashed Royal Hospital, where troops of uniformed soldiers might be seen any afternoon tramping the enormous green. There was convalescence to be had for those returned from spreading Victoria's good influence about the globe. Not infrequently one passed men on long wooden crutches, or with wrapped heads: not infrequently, the empty sleeve of an amputee.

Cheyne Walk, on the Stoker side, was leaf-happy, a brisk amble to the embankment, where he caught a steamer upriver each morning. A father! *And* a published author! Blessed season. Some time later this year, *both* of his progeny should be revealed.

#

In a lighthearted moment Bram purchased a large glass bowl for the front hallway and filled it conspicuously with fruit. He had found himself eating more these days in general, as if, pelican-like, he were feeding his wife through his own gullet. Fruit of his vine, fruit of their nuptial hour. How much more bonded he felt to Florence—bonded in a fundamental, almost mystical way. Just recently they had begun to discuss names. If it was a boy (let it be so!) he preferred Noel, or perhaps Thornley, after his older brother. *Noel Thornley Stoker. N. T. Stoker.* Checking the day's post, pinching with his thumbnail the leaf from a red ripe apple and taking it to the kitchen to peel, it seemed to him that it was a different man who occupied his skin this season. *Mister* Bram Stoker, by your leave, newly residing within the old one's mossgreen vest.

As Florence's body had grown in its secret ways, so too had his imagination. As a younger man, he had published a number of stories—well, three— in *The Shamrock*, and also in *London Society*, but more significant work was sure to come now. He had always believed he had a *novel* inside him. Where, though, to find inspiration? He had started reading again for pleasure, a thing almost forgotten, and quite enjoyed *Lady Audley's Secret*. Old Whitman had told him to look at his own life, to "tell the tale of himself," but this he found uniquely unsuited to drama. There were several cracking ideas that had scurried away at his call, including one about cowboys; others that had sat unloved in the bottom drawer, functionally assembled but lifeless, like the creature in Mary Shelley's horror. How droll to muse on the connection between author and mother; both labored to bring some uncreated entity to light. He remembered arguing the merits of Mrs. Shelley's book in a formal debate, once, at Trinity. He had been Auditor for the evening, intent on proving himself to the chamber full of Third Years. His opponent had been a Scotch fellow named McGinnis, beefy and scarlet, a favorite among the crowd.

Squaring his young jaw, Bram had held forth on certain alarming trends in contemporary fiction, summoning up for inspection the popular productions of Ellen Wood, Mary Elizabeth Braddon, some other scribblers whose names he had now forgotten. His thesis, though, he recalled perfectly: that the modern novel was *less moral* than its predecessors.

All its predecessors? McGinnis, from the podium opposite, gripped his lapel like a barrister.

I confine my observation to the English novel. Though my essential...
You include Frankenstein? *That is a deeply impure creation.*

Not so, Bram had responded, taken off his stride. It was an amateur's mistake; in the fluster of the moment, he had been turned to a debating point for which he was unprepared. *Mrs. Shelley's novel is certainly frightful, but it shows, at its core, an ethical conscience...*

Gentlemen. The work of a young woman in a state of mental exaltation, no doubt aided by laudanum.

McGinnis leaned into his syllables like a man prying open a cellar door on the unspeakable. In his delivery, *lau-DAN-um* became a trisyllabic invocation of all acts corrosive of the social order, almost pellucid in its putrefaction. The student assembly rewarded him with moist laughter.

Very good. Bram stumbled. *But to the point...*

Imagine them: the notorious Lord Byron, culpable already of the most heinous acts of license, an incestor, a man excoriated by every respectable institution of his day!

Now as to that, Bram tried, but his opponent's tactic was working. The cheering crowd hammered their seats.

Poor Mary! Victim, at once, of William Godwin's distorted societal vision and Bysshe Shelley's Satanic lust. This is the species of writer whom our new Auditor, young Mr. Stoker, would have us believe represents moral conviction!

It was an all-round rout, as sound a drubbing as Bram had received. *D'you think he means what he said?* he asked his friend Dillon in the paneled recesses of the Morrison, where they had slunk off to drink. *Mary was a dissolute, to be sure, but the scene...* he searched for one, his mind thickening over with Guinness. *The moment, you know, where Victor has created a being, and flees from it, taking no responsibility for his actions. It feels like abandonment.*

Percy Shelley destroyed women for inspiration, Dillon sighed. *'s what makes him an artist.* Dillon had always taken alcohol poorly, making it difficult for Bram to know when his comments were insightful and when merely spongy.

D'you think?

Anyone can have readers, Dillon declared to his froth. *True artists have victims.*

2.

The Lyceum would produce *Romeo and Juliet*. The same astonishing tasks must be met, but Bram rose to them, this season, with a welcoming laugh. News of Florence's condition had spread, solidifying his position as the public face of Irving's project. There was, he thought, a certain light of respect in the eyes of persons who before had regarded him with a rather more conditional nod; he had entered an important social structure.

It was odd for Irving to choose Romeo, of course, a role for unshaven youth. He had become known in the papers for his uncanny ability to wind back the timepiece on his own appearance, but the art of stage makeup would be stretched, by this, to its very limit. Even Loveday expressed concern. Irving's silver-gray temples could be blackened with raven's wing, his costume done up in vibrant colors. That troubling stoop of his spine, of course, would be harder to conceal.

Good evening, Commander and Lady Meath! And with the Simsburys, or I mistake myself!

Well, well, stage magic was Irving's business. If any man could play Romeo past forty, it was he. On opening night Bram stood, happily for once, at the front-of-house, greeting ladies overwhelmed by their furs, their husbands in tow like leashed pets.

Yes, madam. A love story tonight, but you know, with a bit of a twist.

All tragedies ended in death, Bram thought freely, directing a lost couple to the ticket taker, while all comedies ended in birth. If comedy, progeny; it really was that simple. Perhaps he would write a treatise. *A Key to Understanding Shakespearean Drama*. No: *A Guide to the Proper Comprehension of Dramatic Form, Using My Experience As Acting Manager Under Mister Henry Irving and Miss Ellen Terry, by Bram Stoker*. Well, well... it was piquant, the way art and life had a tendency to enfold each other, like dancers at a ball. Florence would not have cared. But then, thanks to her, an actual being was coming their way. And, if life truly imitated art, the omens, in his house, were bright.

Adieu... adieu...

Chapter 16

1.

IN THE MORNING BRAM RODE THE STEAMER *TWILIGHT* ALONG THE RIVER that snaked across London, passing through dense white fog like the crossing of the Styx. The earlier parts of the year had seen the first "killer smogs," low-hung clouds of ash and coal smoke so thick that, for days, the long brick lanes and dockyards had become ghostly, evanescent. In the worst of it, livestock had been sickened to immobility, lowing in terror with a pitiable sound.

Left wrist crooked on her cane, a portly woman with warts on her neck made her way to the unoccupied bench at his side. Her companion was hirsute, sporting carrotcolored moustaches that blossomed across either cheek. Even the knuckles, Bram noted with distaste, were lightly haired. He suspected some degeneracy.

The poorhome, the man pointed eagerly toward the passing bank.

I can't see.

Just past the horse guards, plum. It's where the indigents are whipped.

The fog opened, revealing a clutter of black masts, but Bram could not find the asylum. Then again the smoky billows closed down across the Thames, again the weirdly changing light, neither night nor day. Terrible stuff, this, like the damning of a city.

Bram thought to make a comment, but the strange couple had vanished, their seats occupied now only by tendrils of wet mist. He started a little, looking in both directions. The new fog was disorienting, obscuring both sight and sound. London had always been a liminal region, seen in part, but never whole; one became used to the rising and falling of veils, but this was unnerving. One might almost—as cool mist closed around the steamer once more—one might almost imagine one was alone on this vessel, cast into rocking nothingness. A prisoner of the Flying Dutchman, making its gossamer and insubstantial route around Hope, forever. Bram pulled his overcoat tighter. Was he alone on a steamer piloted by dead men? Shall slimy things crawl with legs upon the slimy sea? But no, he was not *quite* alone. The degenerate couple had vanished, somehow, but there was that other figure, standing at the far end of the prow. Only half-seen in the haze, how spectral: only standing motionlessly, a woman dressed all in white, facing this way. Looking at him, as if with intention.

No, Bram said aloud.

He did not know what he wished to say—only that the monosyllable *no* had leapt from his core, a blunt, unalterable rejection. She was standing mutely, one hand on the brass rail to support herself. And he knew what was coming, of course he knew; before he had even seen the face, his ill-divining soul foresaw all. In the instant, he felt quite certain they would both cry, and he knew also that this was his personal damnation. He and she would merely stand there, in wet river fog, tears dropping from both their faces, looking at each other's pain, forever.

But the words that came from him were calm, almost measured in their cadence.

Miss Lujzi.

I cannot be let go.

Her voice was low, hollow, made more so by the echoless character of the mist. She had bypassed the whole of whatever empty pleasantry he might have been tempted to conjure. To discuss other things—his new lodging in Chelsea, the Lyceum's latest production; to ask after her "sisters," and lightly to inquire how she had been keeping—would be insulting to them both. Her lovely hair had been cut away to only an inch's length, and the expression underneath the worn bonnet was difficult to see. The white clothing suggested, even more so than the first time she had dared to appear in his office, a sad attempt at presentability in this culture. She had been thin, but was now unwholesome, hungry to faintness, though she labored to hold herself with dignity. Her hand on the rail was perhaps more a necessity than he had, at first, thought. And her eyes—

My dear, it is clear you are not well.

I cannot be let go from the shop.

She did not respond any more than this. Perhaps his comment did not merit it. Looking quickly up and down the deck, he continued hurriedly:

I trust your ailment, whatever it may be, is nothing serious. And, in that same trust, I cannot believe Mister Aiolfi... if I recall the name... would consider a passing spell, as must be common for women in your line, any reason to cancel their employment.

I am with child.

That certainly... that certainly, if Mister Aiolfi has any traits of a gentleman, or even sound business sense... I confess that I have been so preoccupied with professional tasks, since the close of last season... months, I now recognize... really, I assure you that I would have been pleased indeed for our paths to cross. Yet you must grant how changeable has been my...

Bram stopped the meaningless patter, his breath rising and falling in low, solid pulses. They only remained where they stood, he dressed for work, she as if for a wedding that never happened: she watching him, his head turned to seek desperately confirmation of the riverbank, a lantern in a tower, anything. But the cosmos beyond the steamer's deck was reduced to unknowable fog.

I... now, Miss Lujzi, I...

Despite the cold condensation Bram could feel a heat swelling from his collar up to his tight forehead, drumming behind the eyeballs. His fingers on the umbrella handle had gripped it hard enough to dent the leather.

No one knows, Abraham, she said quietly. *Not even the sisters. But Mister Bacco, he has suspicion. He watches me. In not many weeks now, he sees. And then Mister Aiolfi puts me out.*

I... I...

The heat boiled over into full-bodied panic, Bram's tissues arrested in a way he had not experienced since the Shelbourne. Every direction his frantic thoughts turned was blocked; he was a prisoner in a castle with no avenue of escape. Irving's public pronouncements that he would sweep immorality from his theatre; his punishment of subordinates for even minor offenses. Bram's awful guilt over what he had done—the hushed, almost desperate hours he had spent trying to make concord of his behavior and his former self-image. And throughout, hardest to bear of all, the rush of lamenting desire with which this woman did not cease, even now, to inspire him. Even in this moment he felt a strong drive to hold her, to feel her body pressed tightly against his breast.

But he could not allow that feeling, he must not. Beyond *that* door in particular, baying and hungry, man-eating hounds snarled and leapt.

Excuse me. Bram stared blankly into the mist. Each lying syllable was a cinder on his tongue. *Excuse me, miss. But you seem to have mistaken me for some other.*

One ungloved hand rose gradually to her mouth, the sad eyes widening in disbelief. Shaking slightly, she turned to go.

Lujzi, Bram almost cried, dropping his belongings and taking her forcibly in his arms. Then he did cry; the unmanly tears dropped free, wetting his face and hers, wetting his tousled beard. *O Miss Lujzi. We have done such wrong!*

She too wept, but tearlessly. Thank the mercies that yellowwhite clouds still washed the deck, so that while voices of the other passengers rose and fell, no one could see them distinctly. She clutched his coat and he squeezed eagerly her whole hand—how thin it was, with its scars, how fragile the little bones!—as she trembled against him. Her body was so frail, so wasted away from even its former state; but a double-life was beating inside these ruins, a secret part of himself.

Forgive me what I just said, Lujzi, forgive me, I beg it. I am amazed, undone. I thought never to see you again, never.

I did not know your words, Abraham. But I know your meaning.

As ever, her mis-phrasing, agonizingly precise. *No, no, I deny it, I spoke only out of dreadful... but never, Miss Lujzi, I could never reject you, pretend that we had not...*

Other passengers appeared and they pulled frantically apart, waiting while the steamer docked. Like strangers he and Miss Lujzi exited the gangplank separately, then found each other in an anonymous brick shelter on the other bank, dripping with weeds. They had not done it, yet; they had not spoken the word, not struck the great unbearable gong that needed be sounded. Bram tried, but found he could not. To say it would be to cast himself onto a second voyage, one whose end he could not foresee.

But in this one moment he ungloved his own palm and put it to her icy face. *Ah, your poor white cheek! And your eyes, dear Lujzi, your eyes!*

It was true: when sunbeams broke through the fog she winced painfully. Light was no longer just unfamiliar, but a needle to her senses. She was becoming the dressmaker's torso, every inch stabbed.

Abraham, I have no way to live. I cannot be let go.
Have you saved nothing?
We are not allowed money.
Not a farthing?

Aiolfi had outdone himself in fiscal prudence; the shopmaster had told his needle-women that sweat labor was learning a trade, and that education in any trade was its own pay. He had cut off her hair, she whispered from trembling lips, as punishment for not finishing a basket load on time, saying he would sell it for hair sieves to make up the difference.

The beast. Indignity twisted inside Bram's gut, hot and real. But the other thought took precedence. *And*—*you are certain, Miss Lujzi*—the words burned as Bram mouthed them out, closing his eyes. *What you said, on the steamer.*

Yes.

There, they were discussing it, and before Bram spread out the ocean of infinity.

And you have had no—*no other. Perhaps, from your own… kind…*

So shocked, so offended was her expression that for a second time he detested himself utterly.

I am sorry. Lujzi, I am—*so sorry.*

No one was looking. Bram hesitated, after a moment lifting a defeated arm gently to her back. She stiffened, then accepted what became their embrace. For a time they only held each other. Despite what he knew, despite the double-life growing inside her, this woman felt to him less of a body, not more, as if she were disappearing.

I have no money, Abraham, nowhere to go. If the shop…

Tosh, tosh. I can find you a place, we shall make a way.

Where? Where make a way?

There are workhouses. Yes, that is a difficult word, but necessary. These institutions exist, by our Queen's wisdom, to nurture those—

Stop this, she said to his eyes. *Stop this saying.* She pulled away from his arms. It was as if she did not know who he was, as if she were staring, incredulously, to find the man behind the mask of the cruelly respectable gentleman.

Bram felt his shoulders sag. *No, you are right. No more of that. And yet, you are quite certain.* How he hated himself! A cad! *You know, the female body* gives strange signs. Often it is difficult... even with one's wife, one can hardly be definite, until...

Our child is coming, Abraham.

A minute, then another. Our child. *Our child.*

It had been clear what she was saying, had it not? Clear enough. Had he indeed held out hope this might be some bizarre misunderstanding, a little women's blood missed, nothing more, but no; there would be no flight from the prison he had built for himself, stone upon massy stone. Its walls were thick now as Dublin Castle, its hidden rooms as dank and inescapable. Bram felt the irony of it all. Miss Lujzi had been with him on the very week he and Florence had lain together, and conceived their own, proper child. The two acts were entwined, commingled in nature. He had given himself to both women, and now both had returned.

That night, she began, then faltered.

I know—I know, he said, cringing. *I came to you. The sin is my own.*

But she stoppered his too-easy castigation. *Listen, Abraham. Listen now. That night, everything changes.*

It was the same phrase she used when he met her, to describe her first experience of artistic beauty. Everything changes.

Betl... my Betl...

Your husband, yes, I remember. In the other country. Something closed inside him at the name. Could this truly be jealousy, or was he a stranger, simply, to his own gradations of feeling? What evil demiurge had created humanity, such that our most precious truths were like diamonds in a mine shaft, the hardest of all to expose?

Always, as a girl, I see God, she said painfully, struggling to be understood. *Always, as a girl, I feel God. He sees me, always he watches over. When Betl dies, Abraham—when my Betl dies—no one sees me.*

He understood her meaning; they were close enough in mind, even now, that the enormity of what she was saying came clear.

After Betl, never does God see me. She waited, the length of several breaths. *Not in this country. Not even in the sky. Until you come.*

Lujzi, this is too... but she was ill, and his earlier suggestion of the workhouse obscene. This was not an "offender against marriage," as the broadsides would call her, but a mother in need of rest. Abruptly the poor girl began a series of racking coughs, painful to watch. Whereas Florence had grown fuller and more luminous with her motherly change, Miss Lujzi's life-force had been diminished. Hers was the battered look of a voyager constrained to navigate her way, unaided, through a midnight and sooty passage.

Bram peered frightenedly out of the shelter as a loaded wagon rumbled past, porting barrels under a tarp. When he returned again Miss Lujzi was bent forward, trying to recover her hitching breath.

O, Abraham, she whispered, her face blanched. *Help us.*

Slowly, almost ashamedly, she reached out until she had his lapel pinched between her fingers. The full implication of what she had actually said—how not only she, but *they*, both Lujzi and the child of their union, had come begging into his hands—filled him with unimpeachable terror.

Miss Lujzi. Miss Lujzi.

Shall he say it? Shall he confess that she still populated his waking thought, still made regular appearances in his dreams? Shall he tell her that in joining with his wife, in the moment of crisis when all nature quaked and stirred, he had to stifle his lips from crying *her* name? Florence was his betrothed, but it was Lujzi who had raised him from the wheelchair of his haunted past.

A group of sightseers passed by and Bram lowered the rim of his bowler. The mist on the sidewalks was beginning to blow off into pockets and streams, burned away by the sunlight's increase.

Lujzi... he began again, when the crowd was safely passed. He paused, began to speak. Paused again.

Lujzi, he said finally, mournfully. *Lujzi, my dear... it is quite... impossible.*

He meant: everything she had said, all that she might be asking. Surely she must see how impossible it was.

If you say this, she responded in a low broken tone, *it is true. Only if you say.*

And because she had answered him in this way, because she had neither raged against his character nor made demands, Bram's gut turned to sour ice. He had wished to believe there was not any decision for him to make, had tried to hand back to her the suggestion of choice. Her perspicacious mind, though, would bear none of his illusions. The only choice there could possibly *be*, in this situation, lay with him. She was powerless, absolutely without purchase. English law would not recognize her claim, no jury of first-circle gentlemen pay a

Gypsy girl any heed at all. Bram knew something of the Bastardy Clause and the New Poor Laws; he had read fervent broadsides against "vicious mothers" in the *London Times*. The accused male, in nature's game, was always only putative, while the female carried the consequence. The outsider's status as a seducer of *someone* would be without question; let her come forward, and all of outraged gentility would fall howling about her shoulders. Nor could she remain where she was. She had seen, already, the way workers were discarded when their usefulness was at an end.

And therefore, all she had given herself—this innocent who, in the soft vulnerability of her person, was carrying a part of his life—was this chance to place her bowed head under the possibility of his clemency. All she had hoped, with this fog-locked meeting on the edge of day, was to discover whether the quality of mercy was not strained.

I cannot. Bram turned away, his back teeth almost shivering. *I cannot...*

He had to wait until the words would form themselves.

I have a wife, Miss Lujzi, and since you and I were together, she has also come to harbor certain expectations. I intend to labor the rest of my days to deserve the faithful woman to whom, in the eyes of our creator, I am permanently wedded. All this talk meant nothing. The red fingers still held his lapel, waiting to hear something else, and he could not bring himself to disengage them by force. *There is no way, my dear, simply no way. Please, have pity. I must not be associated with this, in any measure. Can't you see that.* Slowly the fingers opened, and he could not bear to look at the sad little hand. *Please understand. I would not wish you to think me unkind... I am in an important position at the Lyceum. I am the Acting Manager, mine is a public role.* Then, absurdly: *Mister Henry Irving himself relies upon me.*

Those subtle eyes, having risked all, were down. With one hand she adjusted the little shameful ribbon under her chin. Her lower lip was tight.

I thought... Bram hurried on, despising the note of self-exoneration in his own voice. *Please understand the state I was in that night. I had lost all hope... of honor, of goodness itself...* No; she was turning away, viewing only the milling street. He felt with increasing desperation that she must come around. *Virtue, affectionate trust, seemed to me merely an evil jest. Now my hope has been restored. You do understand. I know that you do.*

Did she not say something there, did she not speak? No, no: she was silence itself; he could have been petitioning an alabaster in the British Museum. Only he saw her breaths coming and going, raising the dull fabric at her chest. Abruptly he wanted to take her by her tiny shoulders and make her accept reason.

Don't you see, Lujzi? I have put everything I have into my position. Everything—my life entire. I must not. I cannot. What do you wish me to do, what would you have me do? Do you wish me to take you in, to give a home to your child, to offer the three of us some kind of life together?

Yes, she whispered.

You want—?

I want... Abraham... in extremity, her command of the language was failing her. Each phrase took longer to appear, like a parade of limping things. *I want you... with us. I want you... you love... our child.*

To be with you, to live somehow with you, raise a child with you? To sacrifice my legal wife, my employment, my reputation in decent society, forever? Don't you see that such a thing cannot be?

This was unbearable.

Miss Lujzi, I am beginning a family of my own. I am to be a family man. All my dreams—the things I have longed for, since youth—all of them are coming, at last. He added, ridiculously, *I have published a book.*

It was this damnable fog, this acrid, tarry lingering in the air. He had not meant to spend this much time breathing its evil perfumes. And now a second crowd of commuters was coming, a belled line of horses; strong morning was dawning all around the congestion of buildings, brightening the streaked windows and the enormous colored advertisements pasted everywhere for *Bentley's Water Cures* and *Reed & Co. Printing at Cost* and *The Mighty Raja's Wonderful Healing Powders!* The city stirred, the time for secrecy reaching a close. The glow-worm 'gan to pale his ineffectual fire, and like the haunt in the drama, he must be gone.

I must now leave you here, Miss Lujzi. Please understand. If there were any way, any possible way.

Her weak eyes were brimming, but as before, she did not conceal them. He turned to go and she grasped his arm frantically.

Do you know what happens to us, Abraham, if you leave? Do you understand this?

But the worst of it was that her complex expression contained, within its multitude, shame *for him* as well, shame on his behalf, an appalled suffering for what he was going to do. Bram pulled away, his heart tearing like a book from its spine.

I have tried to be a good man.

He turned, he walked quickly. Around him the busy crowd's heels made a clapping against stones, the noise following him like slow, mocking applause.

Chapter 17

1.

Since Florence announced her change, they had kept separate beds. The physicians concurred: no contaminants—their word—must be allowed to interfere with the child's development. Even the Mrs. Stoker's *thoughts* must be monitored, for a wife's mind was not to be conceived of as a sovereign estate, but one over which the husband had to keep careful watch. There had been cases in which women (the head physician would not say ladies, exactly, but let that pass) who had mused too long on intemperate acts, often through the reading of novels, had given birth to misshapen things. Others had spawned offspring normal in appearance but with criminal minds, some of whom later met their ends in the gibbet. In such cases, society suffered; and was not a case to be made, too, against the male actor, through whose inattention some avoidable thing had been born to perdition? Keep the expectant mother, too, in all material comfort; anything she desired, he should supply in generosity. Now was not a time to stint. Did he understand?

The head physician patted Bram's chest, smiling conspiratorially under his moustache. *Congratulations to you, sir. The missus is a lovely specimen.* Bram only nodded blankly. He had already moved into the spare bedroom.

#

For once, the dull oppressive weather suited Bram's heart. He wanted clouds, the far-off muttering of thunder, which he heard. In a kind of fury he attacked, once more, the slew of unsolicited submissions from Londoners hoping to "break in" to the Lyceum's off-season, when lighter fare than Shakespeare was enjoyed. In the same sip of cold tea he flung aside two scripts while beginning a third: one more wronged lover, some ham-fisted turn-about in the last act. Disgust rose hotly in him, making his temples beat. Only wheelwrights could craft wheels. Why the devil did every Jack-the-Lad think he knew how to write? His forearms cramped, his own spine suffered from an excess of slouching. In the glass bowl at home, the fruit smelled faintly of decay.

2.

ONCE (HE REMEMBERED THIS, OUT OF NOWHERE AT ALL, HE REMEMBERED what he had not recalled in years; his past was re-emerging faster now, hidden things seeking light), on Castle business, Bram and another clerk had visited a Traveler camp—Irish Travelers, in the West Country, where a mystical Seer told fortunes from a cowhide tent. How could he have forgotten? The other man had suggested the visit partly in jest, when they spotted the bowed wagons and horses, the long smudge of smoke above the willows, but Bram's curiosity had been piqued. They had been required to enter the tent singly, his companion crouching with the dark-skinned men around a central campfire while Bram stooped under the tent flap. Once inside, he had recoiled at the smell— drying herbs, everywhere, though with an unpleasant undertone of something else. He had been put in mind of bringing a piece of uncooked chicken closely to the nostrils to check it for rot.

The Seer was two: an old woman and a child, their bodies so close that in a shocked moment Bram feared they were some kind of conjoined twins. Looking closer, he realized they were bound tightly at one wrist. The child itself was a starveling, naked, apparently demented. Its head was only a mass of unclipped hair. The old woman grasped Bram's hand with surprising strength and leaned over it, so closely that he could feel her breath against his palm, but had given him, for his coins, only an elliptical warning: *I see a man with no face.*

Bram's scalp had contracted terribly and he hurried from the meeting, seeking to make light of the event so that the real depth of his disturbance would not be seen. But the Seer's words had remained with him, only the more alarming for their aspect of unreality. He thought he had forgotten that event, forgotten completely. And yet some other part of him had been watching, ever since, for the spectre of the faceless man.

It was dusk, a low cloudbank gathering over London. Instead of ferrying home to Chelsea after work, as was his habit, Bram hired a hansom to ride him through Whitechapel once more. He was driven by guilt he could not shake away, a perverse need to endure the dreadful sights. It was as if by punishing himself sufficiently he might burn off the responsibility, make it so that Lujzi and he were equal partners in what was coming.

At a rapid clip they swung past a seller of pork, the odor of singed fat bittering up the air; past boarded and chained entryways; past a group of unfortunates angling their hands over a spitting blaze. On the corner, three smutty youths were playing with a rag. No, it had moved: a rat. Deep in an ashcan, bitten with rust, a human skeleton searched out its dinner. Chimneysweeps went by on both sides, among them one of the little boys who must squeeze naked into the smallest openings, his nose and chin rubbed permanently blue. A gathering of soldiers in long coats now, circling a Match Girl like predatory things. Billing takers; cheap lodging for sailors; shipping offices; rope merchants. In the distance, a child crying.

It was all the same, perhaps even worse than those dens he had already seen. Abandon hope, all ye who enter here, for the whole of East London was a people lost. From the safety of the cab Bram tried to imagine a child of his own abandoned in these streets, left without any family or recourse, but the thought made him physically ill. He thumped the roof angrily with his cane.

To Chelsea again, cabbie. Stay at this quick pace.

Very good, sah.

The poorhouse was a death sentence. He had been monstrous to suggest it. Workhouses, little different, existed to accommodate exactly such cases as Miss Lujzi's... but Bram groaned deeply in himself, arresting his own line of thought. Such talk, the very mention of social institutions and the kindness of the Sovereign, was without any real meaning. For a penniless female in this Stygian morass—a fallen woman with a bastard child—there was only one real destination.

The doors of the brothels whispered open around them, dropping long squares of ashamed light. Bram saw the first customers already entering. Through the soiled windows, their passing shapes: sinuous, strange.

3.

THE DECISION TORE AT HIS SOUL. THE WOMAN WITH WHOM HE HAD EXPErienced such passion; his child now inside her, his own flesh; how could he condemn them both to ruin? Another few weeks, at the most, and Miss Lujzi's condition would become clear. She would be bereft then, utterly cast out. How could he proceed with his life, sipping wine at luncheons, drawing up bills of lading for wardrobe, knowing that in the worst pit of London his unacknowledged family was abused?

And yet, his daylight world blossomed! Florence clucked about her little dissatisfactions, basking in the expenses he laid at her feet. Wooden high chair, embroidered bonnet, baby shoes, a clever little rattle done in silver. Her relatives congratulated Bram on the news, one brother who had become a somewhat influential barrister staying at their home for an agonizing string of days. Bram found himself walking about in a trance, coming to with a startled, guilty gesture. His dreams were a parade of horribles. In one, he was tallying up costs on an endless roll sheet with Henry Irving when the man's clothes began twitching; the actor's shirtfront was boiling over with rats. In another he was at the brothel again, passing through a curtain. He could hear the rhythmic driving of Singer machines. On the other side lay a half-dozen prostitutes, naked in a pile, wiping each other's bodies with pig fat. *You never loved,* one of them teased, red eyes sparkling. *You never love.* His male member throbbed with desire. But his brother Thornley was there, holding a bone saw. Looking down, Bram realized he was sitting once more in the wheelchair. His manhood was stiff, but both his legs had been sawn off.

Tonight's dream, by contrast—the one he was having right now—was of a gentler sort. In it, he was abed, in his Chelsea home, as, presumably, he must still be. In this one, he suspected he was dreaming, though the situation was unclear. His dreams had become, lately, the kind he used to experience as a child, hard to distinguish from waking thought. Was he lying, now, on the feather-lumpy mattress they had moved to the spare room by the landing? Or had he indeed risen silently, as it seemed? Was he crossing now this rugless floor, his bare feet registering its uneven surface, entering the master bedroom where Florence slept, to stand at this window, and look over moonlit grass?

Bram rested a palm on the casement. The wood grain was chilled, and spoke of windswept miles, of Carpathian mountain reaches, pine forested, heavy with dripping shadow. He seemed to see all these things, peering sleepily through the night-misted glass. But was it all a dream within a dream?

He woke a bit more. There was no wilderness, no moonlit reaches. Outside was Cheyne Walk once again, all its linked residences orderly and controlled, every holly bush pruned. The tall terraced houses on both sides were fronted by black gates, matching the grillwork that ornamented their second floors. But there, in the street below. A figure in white, standing in the shadows, looking up at him.

She came into the moonlight from under the linden trees, her gesture one of faint supplication. Though no candle was lit, she had seen him there. And he wanted to go to her. He longed to.

Bram. What are you doing in here?
I didn't mean to wake you, my dear.

Florence was astir in the bed, making his heart double over. *Come away from the window.*

In the frosty street below, the figure waited. Bram pulled his silk bedrobe closer.

What hour is it, Bram?
Quite late, my dear. I only found it difficult to rest... go back to sleep.

It's the moonlight, Florence sighed, stretching. *So bright.* Bram rubbed harshly at his face. Was this really happening? What if she were to look outside? Would all his secrets be exposed?

I didn't mean to come in unannounced, he apologized quickly. He wished there were a curtain to draw. *I shall return, now, to the husband's banishment.*

Well, you have made me awake. She began to lift the covers.
No, no, my dear! You must not get up. Shall—shall I read to you?
Read...?
To relax you again.

Oh, tell me a poem, Florence conceded, settling back. *You used to tell me poems.*

It was true, of course, in the early days. The Tennyson, the very book over which he had felt such terrible suspicion.

Perhaps you should just rest. The doctors will say I am remiss even to visit a lady in your condition by night.

I want a poem. This moonlight makes me want it. She bundled the heavy wool under her chin, making an indentation. *About the weaver. The girl, up in a tower.*

I don't believe I recall...

Oh, tosh. You do.

Sadly Bram sat at the corner of the blue and white counterpane. Florence, one hand on her filling waist, closed again her pleased eyelids.

But in her web she still delights, he began softly, his gaze on the beckoning window glass,

> *To weave the mirror's magic sights,*
> *For often thro' the silent nights*
> *A funeral, with plumes and lights*
> *And music, went to Camelot:*
>
> *Or when the moon was overhead,*
> *Came two young lovers lately wed;*
> *"I am half-sick of shadows," said*
> *The Lady of Shalott.*

Florence slept. Bram rose, pulse working in his throat. The street below was empty.

The mirror crack'd from side to side, his wife's voice sing-songed behind him, faintly from the dimness. *The curse has come upon me, cried.* Her dreamy face was closed, complacent.

Chapter 18

1.

AT DAWN HEAVY CLOUDS MOVED IN FROM THE SEA; BY LATE MORNING, waiting in a tram shelter, Bram stared blankly at spitting rain. The modern tram was an ungainly contraption, resembling a bread box surmounted by advertising plaques, the largest capable of holding a dozen riders at once. Drawn by snorting horses, trams could achieve speeds significant enough to require those adventurous souls who were willing to stand on top to grasp their fellows on occasion for support. The whole bagatelle was being outlawed in the West End, in fact, and a segment of respectable opinion thought the very notion of "public transportation" somewhat distasteful.

A beet-red, muttonchopped man entered the brick enclosure and seated himself. He wore a suit of dull green checks and a dirty, tight-fitting cap. The hair stuck out around his large ears as if it were of a piece with the cap, like some element in a child's pantomime. He was eating walnuts out of a rumpled paper bag, compacting the shapes loudly with his molars while keeping his lips open so that noises were projected. Bram, in his lap the *London Dispatch*, inched surreptitiously away.

You know me? Maybe you no like me.

The brawny man had not turned toward Bram; his thickly veined neck was still angled forward. Bram caught an unpleasant whiff of lime cologne. Those wondrous muttonchops attached to a full moustache in front, forming a single, strap-like adornment that had become sprinkled in crumbs. Slowly the man positioned another walnut deep in his back teeth and compressed it, like breaking a spine.

Brought abruptly out of his stupor, Bram shook the paper, hoping to appear occupied with it. Aside from the two of them, the stand was empty. Lupus Street itself was largely untraveled at this pre-dinner hour, and the sudden, rude comment from the stranger had startled him.

You know me? the man asked again, still not looking.

Excuse me, I rather... but he did know this person; the memory connected. The backs of both the man's hands sported ugly tattoos in the likeness of snakes, one orange, one green. This was Aiolfi's muscle man, the one who had waited patiently on the stair while Bram took out Miss Lujzi. Waited, he had thought, for instructions.

Bram folded carefully his *Dispatch*. NIGHTLY HORSES. A TIME FOR HONOR. The graphically complex, 30-point headlines swam before him, suddenly absurd. CAIRO MUMMY FOUND STILL MOVING!

Aiolfi, he no gets contract. No business.

I have nothing to do with that decision, Bram said to the turned-down page. To leave the enclosure would be to admit he was feeling confined, that his breath was beginning to come more shallowly. Irving expected him back at the Lyceum some time ago. He had only journeyed to this part of town to speak with a service man in the Equitable Gas Works, but remained wandering about afterward, lost in his turbulent thoughts. POLYGAMY OUTLAWED IN STATES. NELLY & NELLY'S PHOSPHATE SOAP.

No more contract, the bewhiskered breath continued, as if Bram had not spoken. *Aiolfi, he loses money. You see? Money.*

This is not my concern.

Eh, mebbe no. The man's thick fingers broke a walnut, one bushy eye examining each half carefully before casting them both away. *But mebbe, sì.*

Bram labored to keep his voice steady. All that was within view across Lupus Street was a painted iron fence and the backs of several anonymous, plastered buildings, one utilizing the newly covered surface to advertise itself as a hotel with an entrance on the side. In the distance, a series of raised flags set along a bridge—was it Vauxhall?—were just visible. He tried to gird himself. The courage he had shown before this brigand, that long-ago day in the sweatshop, was nowhere.

I'm sorry... Mister... Bacon, is it? I do not know how you have found me, but I must say that I do not appreciate your manner of address. Now, I have made it clear that business relations between the Lyceum and Mister Aiolfi's garment shop are not...

Tha girl, she don' look good.

Excuse me?

Not so good... no well... needle-girl. You know this girl? No well.

Here Bacco wiped his grand moustache and turned sidelong to examine Bram closely. His eyes were thoughtful. He could have been offering counsel to an equal.

Mebbe, na, somethin there no good. Mebbe somethin bad. Mebbe, you see na, I talk 'bout it. Talk some people. You understan? Whas you, you... in a shuddersome gesture he stabbed at Bram's chest with the crumpled lip of the bag. *Stoker, thas you? Mebbe Aiolfi, eh, he gets contract again. You see? Or Aiolfi, he say me, Mister Bacco, he say, you go talk Stoker again.*

I don't... I certainly will not...

Or, na, mebbe Aiolfi, he say, Mister Bacco, you leave Stoker alone. Na, you go talk some other people.

Bacco returned to staring, only speculatively, out of the too-tight enclosure. It was a difficulty, his expression said; how would he discover the right people to tell? This was work, work he would rather not undertake. His direct brain preferred uncomplicated matters: the boxing of ears, the quick twist of the thumb out of its socket. But, either way, the shop needed a contract. So Bacco goes out, and gets a contract. It was as simple as walnuts.

Abruptly he plucked the *Dispatch* from Bram's hands. Bram remained staring, jaw clenched, at his empty fingers. His heart slammed in his chest.

Newspaper, eh, he said, enjoying the headlines. *Mebbe newspaper people—mebbe they want know 'bout Stoker. Henry Irving, Stoker, an needle-girl. You think so?*

This, Bram whispered. *This is blackmail.*

Na, na. Jus good story.

A presentable lady in a walking suit and a gentleman in a gray frock entered the enclosure and nodded, Bram returning the gesture woodenly. He labored to maintain his composed expression, panic-struck for fear he might vomit. Bacco offered walnuts to the couple, who looked away. Taking back the bag with a hurt expression he rose, still gnawing, and, as if quite alone with his new copy of *London Dispatch*, strolled lazily into the rain.

2.

BEFORE BRAM HAD EVEN REMOVED HIS COAT, LOVEDAY SIGNALED HIM aside. His bristling eyebrows disagreeing vehemently with the rest of his features, the stage manager wished to alert him to several matters of urgency. Both he and Mister Irving had been trying to find Bram for several hours. Nor was this the first time he had been strangely absent when needed.

I have been somewhat… distracted… of late, Bram said. His throat, becoming suddenly dry as sand, gave his last word an embarrassing hitch.

Loveday examined him with one unhappy eye, propping open the doors to the foyer. Item: There would be no more smoking of "cigar-ettes" by patrons in the lobby, as the paper in which these were wrapped had been increasingly found littering the grounds. Item: Arrangements were being made for the affixing of the novel marquee, in expectation of reliable electrical fluid by season's end. The *Alhambra* and the *Adelphi* already had such, and were drawing nightly attention. Item… well, there were several more items, but these should be addressed in proper fashion at the next business meeting. Go see Irving now, go: he has been calling for you, and you have been dashedly hard to find.

Bram asked of Loveday's retreating back:

Will the Harrod's seamstresses continue on?

Seamstresses…?

The folds of sagged flesh that framed Loveday's lips wrinkled into frank displeasure. The Harrod's contract had been extended for the length of *Romeo*, and beyond. Why the devil was he asking that?

Oh, certain minor issues. Could you be persuaded, do you think, to return the contract to the previous house?

Certainly not, Loveday huffed. His eyes grew indignant. The pricing at Harrod's was superior, their needle-women's work both more rapid and more detailed, and, if it came to it, he had extended himself greatly in securing an official Harrod's connection. No, sir, he would not. What was the purpose of this question?

Curiosity, merely. Bram lifted a tired hand. *It is no matter.*

For a moment longer after Loveday was gone, Bram only breathed. In, out. In, out again. Then, pulling straight his spine, setting his shoulders back, he proceeded down the purple midline carpet and through the vast open space of the majestic London theatre that he managed, against all likelihood, passing row upon row of unoccupied seats. He spoke briefly to various employees who were engaged in their tasks, including a common sweeper, on whose shoulder Bram laid a hand with compassion. At two or three painters he nodded, grateful for their labors; one man on the balcony he brightened with a raised salute. Then he ascended the smaller stair, straightening his tie and making his way along the hallway that led to the office he shared with the famous Henry Irving. Before arriving, ten paces from the door, he clutched his spasming heart and fell in a heap.

Let me die, Bram prayed earnestly from the floor, his nose bone pressed against boards. *Let this be my hour.* But no, his heart did not cease its thankless work. Gradually he sat up, found himself able to draw breath. The hallway where he had collapsed was empty, and no one had heard the noise. Bram remained where he was, waiting for the spinning sensation to recede. He resembled a wet leaf blown against a trunk.

This was the end, then, the end of all; confusion had made its masterpiece. The final door had closed on him, the final turn of the screw pressing down the lid. Even before Bacco had found him, he had made his decision. He could not allow Miss Lujzi to be ruined, could not accept so utter a destruction of her very life. He could not condemn her, through his own moral failure, to the begging streets of Whitechapel, to the life of a bordello nightflower, prey to every Gouty Jack who paid tuppence to abuse her. It was too obscene. He could not live knowing, while he sat at his biscuits and wine, that the child she would bring to light—his own child!—was writhing in starvation, or had been imprisoned in a squalid home for bastards; or, if it was a girl, had entered herself, in a scant twelve or thirteen years, in the ranks of the child prostitutes. He could not.

But of what use were these fine protestations at the eleventh hour? Even were he cruel—even were he to sanction monstrosity, and refuse to help Lujzi in any way—even *that* would no longer be an end. Aiolfi knew whose child she was carrying, and if he did not get his contract, he would advertise. Was this why the shopmaster had said nothing, months ago, about Bram's strange behavior with one of his needle-girls? It was likely. Bram had probably offended whatever sense of honor the low man possessed, but the villain's retribution had been calculated, rather than impulsive. *Blood will have blood,* Professor

Dowden had once explained. The crime contained the seed of its punishment, and Bram's secret life was finding its way out.

Achingly he stood again, arranging his twisted shirt as best he might. With both hands he pushed back his hair. This was endgame on the chessboard whereon he had played his professional life. The last moves were easy to predict. Irving would run him from London completely. Florence would file for divorce, and be granted as much; the notorious nature of Bram's misdeed would force her into public court. Colonel Balcombe, with all the furies behind him, would attend to Bram's ruin in Dublin. The rest was silence.

Outside the oak door he paused, noting a disarranged cufflink. He adjusted it, taking a moment to detach the sleeve ring, watching his own fingers operate the task. Detach: polish: re-attach. Here was one small activity he could accomplish, one thing that was still under his control. Detach: polish: re-attach. It was a kind of consolation.

Stoker! Is that you lurking?

Mister Irving. Good morning.

Good afternoon, I think.

Irving was spread out in the Louis XVI like a judge at tribunal, white thin hands gripping arm rests. The expression on that sharp face, though, held not anger, but unexpected good will. The clay pipe he was smoking assaulted the room, happy streams huffed from each side of his nose. Around Irving's silvery head a brume of tobacco was hanging, giving him the air of some infernal grinning host.

With playful insouciance, Irving half-tossed the *Saturday Review* on the stool.

Behold. Therein is a critic who feels my Romeo superior to Edmund Kean's.

No! Bram blinked, at a loss. *That is… unprecedented.*

Irving added nothing but his grin, and Bram, stooping to retrieve the publication, perused briefly the section thrice circled in blue pencil. It was, indeed, flattering language. The tendency to hunch, as Bram predicted, had been regarded by many as an impediment; Irving's walk had too much of the elder statesman in it. Yet somehow he had been able to conceal his infirmity. It only occurred to Bram in this moment that he, himself, had not yet seen the show.

Ha! You might well say so, Stoker, so you might. Here is another.

Again the triumphant hand proffered a paper, this one the *West London Advertiser.*

How proud you must be. Bram, blinking now convulsively, took the pages in hand.

You would not know, you would not know. Irving turned inward, conversing with his ego. *Ladies have been sending boxed hothouse flowers all week.*

Bravo.

Do not sit.

Bram straightened himself, halfway to his chair. He tapped, rather pointlessly, his broken watch chain with the twin papers' folded edges. The watch, a silver piece he had inherited from his uncle William, had disappeared during his fight—or, rather, his beating—in the alleyway, no doubt clipped by the bruiser while Bram pulled himself into a ball. With all that had happened, it was not until the following day that he had realized the added theft.

He took a breath. The office around them felt close, tight.

I am told you have been looking for me, Bram coughed. *With apologies, I should confess that I have been not entirely myself of late. Certain—*

Bram, Irving interrupted softly, and the use of his Christian name was so unexpected that Bram dropped one of the papers he had been holding. Irving's face had alighted on him, impossibly, with a look of compassion. The sight was so unexpected Bram only stared, as if distrustful of his senses.

Bram, Irving said again, genially. He set aside the clay pipe, arranging its neat bowl in a tray of amber glass. *Perhaps you have heard it said—or if not, I am well aware that so perceptive an eye as yours must have gleaned—that Romeo was, to me, a particular challenge. I admit, to you alone, that I entertained the notion of performing a much younger man's role with an element uncharacteristic of my nature: the element of fear. Yes, I too have felt stage fright, and not a little. Once, though, when hesitation would have impeded me, I found myself reflecting that Bram Stoker, my lieutenant, had diligently assembled all the pieces necessary for me to achieve my greatest triumph. What had I to fear? Mine was simply to tread the carpet laid out by my all-too-capable Acting Manager.*

In short, Bram, you have been an engine of unceasing industry. For your dedication... thank you.

Henry, Bram tried, when he was able to speak. His left knee buckled and he had to place a quick hand on the seatback.

What was happening here? This was a shining fleck of his dream, a piece of the great Henry Irving as he had first known him, on that original, sublime evening, at the glittering Shelbourne—the man who withdrew his elegant fingers and touched Bram's heart directly. Out of nowhere, he felt the arc of their relationship completing itself. Could it be that he was seen by Irving, finally seen; could it be that he was known, finally known? Had his ardor, his great admiration of the man been requited at last? Overcome, mind racing, Bram opened his lips.

Help me, is what came out.

Irving froze, taken aback. The look of paternal kindliness still hung on his face, like stage makeup he had forgotten to remove. Bram tried to continue but his Adam's apple merely rode up and down, all his emotion centering inside his throat, a whirl of unleaked admissions he fought painfully to swallow. He lowered himself, literally, to one knee, great segments of his musculature trembling against the bone. Were he not to do so, he realized, his watery joints might not hold him. *Henry, I have done something so terrible ... so ruinous for us both...* The strange position, with eyes averted, made him feel as if he were genuflecting. *If I have done you some service, let me beg you to look on me, now, as the friend I have always hoped to be. I am*—*Henry, I am quite desperate, and have nowhere else to turn.*

Irving's eyes widened until the complete rounds of his irises had become visible. Like a geriatric, Bram struggled into his chair.

I... need... to tell you a story, he began.

And he did. The story, he discovered in speaking it, was one on which he had labored for many years; one that might truly be called his own story, the only legitimate tale any author had to tell. It was about a child born midway between worlds: Irish, but of Tory parentage; adored, then abandoned; a dreamer neither in this world nor out of it, entirely. Like the caricature of the foppish Celt, this fellow came bravely to London. Here he would work for a certain proud Englishman, a true artist, one whose visionary spirit was profoundly inspiring.

Bram told his tale, leaving nothing aside. He related the hero's marriage to a beautiful if uncultured lady; his dawning awareness of how this new world of London had dazzled his bride, causing her to undergo particular changes in character—though it was as much true to say that certain elements of her person that had been present all along only grew to occupy a dominant position. He told of how the Great Man and the hero's wife were found to enjoy one another's company, outside all observation; he related what pangs our hero conceived at this discovery, what unthinkable avenues of despondent imagining. Through the entirety of this recital, Irving never blinked. A white line of smoke, from a reignited bit of leaf, rose straightly from his bowl.

This particular melodrama, however, did not conclude with the happy revelation of the hero's mistake. Rather, Bram's story continued on, with his adding in, as story-tellers must, details of time and place, particulars to give layering, all in the service of a mounting conflict. The secondary tale wound cleverly about the first; it surprised; it was full of dark discoveries and arcane unveilings. With the mention of a shocking impropriety between our hero and one of the seamstresses in the costume shop, an abandoned Gypsy no less, Irving's static features drew heavily downward. By the time Bram, having inserted so unlikely a device as blackmail, and the threat of public exposure, reached his final, unwritten chapter, Irving was a basilisk, the core of each cheek gone an ominous scarlet.

You see, Henry, Bram concluded, *how exquisite a dagger my hero has fashioned, only to aim it at himself.*

A single tear stained his lap. Bram rubbed both his sore eyeballs, watching the patterns of light. He slumped back heavily into the chair.

Henry, Henry, if only you hadn't been so good. You have quite put yourself in the public way as a moralist; your speeches, your dinners, the editorials you had me write, have all bent to this recurring theme. Other men would have been content with applause, but you, you must be a Father Matthew of the stage, the one man who would lift English theatre from the brothels. And here I have undone it all.

Irving was stone. Bram sighed long, picking up the *Daily* from the floor. His trembling fingers, he noticed as if from some distance, were those of an octogenarian.

News of my behavior… of your Acting-Manager's relations with a needle-woman… a filthy Gypsy woman, Henry, in your very employ!… cannot fail to get out. This fellow Bacco is only the first of his kind. Any man may threaten violence, and be arrested... but the Baccos of London perceive where the real power lies. They have seen you, Henry, and Miss Terry, night after night, clamoring for the attention of journalists. They understand ours is the great age of newspapers. We are captured between ink and paper, Henry, and it is there that they shall convict us.

There was a time that passed, marked only by the sounds of the set-men making changes and an occasional tired creaking that Bram realized, with a dim curiosity, was his bones. From the street outside came the book vendor's cry. A little girl, barefoot, certainly illiterate, she pushed her cart up and down Wellington each afternoon, calling with enthusiasm *come read, come read*, as if she recognized the preciousness of the very words she was denied. Not a flinch had played across Irving's graven features. Those mighty brows, which Bram had never known to be immobile, were finally fixed.

Eventually, the thespian rose. His long pace took the carpet in three steady motions, setting him by the turned-out window. With one large-knuckled finger he delimited the line of his jaw, coming to its end after several seconds and tapping, once, at the chin. When he spoke, his tone was utterly blank.

You are indeed a fool, Stoker.

Henry—

Be silent.

Bram waited, minutes passing. Irving's physical person appeared, it seemed to him, compressed, as if all the disparate energies that normally animated his tissues were focused on mentation, the way a magnifying glass may bring ambient sunlight to a single, burning point. Eventually he spoke again.

I would destroy you, Irving observed flatly. *Only my purpose in London is not yet complete. Understand that, were you not so necessary to my theatre, this conversation would already have concluded.*

Bram closed his numb lips in a swallow, only to let them drift open again when he found he could not breathe through his nose. He had known this about Henry, all along he had understood. Had he not? Father had been just this way, giving such wonderful love at first, then never again showing that side of himself. Had a simple mistaking of the two men been what had driven his relationship with Irving from the start?

Yet still Bram's aching mind, like a child used to its beatings, searched out for the gentleman who had spoken to him, however fleetingly, with such nuances of kindness.

Help me, Henry, please. I beg you.

You have the effrontery to hold up your red face to me and say that. Irving paced the room's length twice, eyes inward and fixed, before caustically shutting the door.

I know you are angry. I have let you down utterly, I have disappointed your trust. But what can I do, Henry, what can I do? It came out before he could consider it: *I love the woman.*

The actor flinched, as if scalded.

Do not use the word 'love' again, Stoker. Your mouth does not deserve it.

Bram fell silent. His employer stalked the chamber in meditation, eventually running his fingers a second time down his long, well-proportioned jaw. *Very well.* He addressed his large desk, plucking buff cards and papers from a ceramic holder. With his free hand he stuffed and relit the dead pipe, drawing his smoke loudly.

I have an acquaintance. Someone who relieves fools of their indelicacies.

Irving was holding something in his long fingers. Bram only waited, blinking.

Leaning forward, Irving intoned each syllable with the precision of a diamond cutter. *Still you sit there, with your imbecile expression.* Every third consonant, hissing around the clay stem, popped out a small gust of smoke. *Let us be clear, Stoker—you tread very close to the edge. Take it.*

Bram examined the narrow, cream-colored card.

>Dr. Jack Seward
>Hanbury Street
>Spitalfields

There was a house number, nothing else.

I will alert the surgeon named there that you and the unfortunate wretch—whom I need hardly say will never be seen by you again, either working in my Lyceum, or attached to any aspect of your personal life, whatsoever—shall be appearing. Aiolfi shall have the contract for one season, after which, when it is clear the seamstress in question has no bastard to conceal, I will ruin him. You will attend to this matter tomorrow evening, at an exact hour of which you shall be informed. Irving drew and exhaled his smoke. *Do not be seen by the police. There will be no mention of this event, or of the present discussion, at any time.*

Bram turned around the small card, as if it might say more, before letting it drop in his lap.

Henry, for pity's sake. This woman is carrying my child.

Irving's visage snapped wildly up, Bram's whole person freezing. He recognized the face that had appeared in his dream, grimacing out of his father's coffin.

The Mrs. Stoker, I am given to understand, lives, at the moment, in hope of just such a blessed arrival. Irving's hatebrimming eyes regarded him like something distasteful discovered under his nail. *On your delusions with regard to her constancy, I will not lower myself to comment. Except to say that while you, sir, have been gallivanting in the pit-holes of whoredom, that charming lady has evidently been home, devoted to the purpose for which God fashioned women of distinction. You hardly deserve her, but that is not my concern. This other—thing—you describe is no gentleman's relation, and very much my concern. It is an abomination. You will kill it.*

Henry—

Irving slammed down his pipe, shattering the stem, hot ash launching across the floor.

Man, he thundered, *I say you will lance this infection on my theatre before it grows another hour. Do not flatter yourself that I will allow your stupidity, your repugnant, filthy vice to bring down all that I have created. You shall do as I say, or I swear, it will be war between our houses. And when I am concluded, anyone associated with the name of Stoker shall count themselves fortunate if they can find employment kneel-scrubbing the wards in a debtors' prison. Do we have an understanding.*

Irving spun in his chair, showing Bram his back.

Love, he scoffed, almost spitting his disgust. *I believe you have an appointment in Spitalfields.*

Chapter 19

1.

His right hand is in front of him, pushing aside a curtain. He senses he has passed through this curtain before, perhaps more than once. It has a sticky feel. Inside is the fortune teller's tent.

The close air is full of drying herbs, hung all about in odorous bunches. Odd, Bram thinks—he so rarely smells, or tastes, anything in dreams. But the lucid moment fades again, and the tent is simply what is happening.

With mounting anxiety Bram looks around this unspoken place. Milky sea light comes from nowhere. Underneath the herbs is another smell, both disquieting and somehow familiar. He has come here to have his future divined.

The Seer sits in the dirt before him, hunched over on herself, muttering and shaking. Her entire person is concealed beneath a rotten cloak. The low, raspy voice has been whispering and chuckling under there for a long time, but he cannot discern what it says.

When she opens the cloak, Bram sees that she is two: two children, in fact.

Now the children stand before him, looking at him with curious youthful expectant eyes. They are sexless, hairless, their naked skins glossy. Their faces, bodies, even their expressions are identical, as if he were seeing some kind of mirror. They are holding hands—no, that is wrong; they are bound, bound tightly at one wrist.

Sweet, one whispers.

Sorrow, grins the other.

Bram understands that he must *part* these children, that this is his awful responsibility. He must part them both, and also *part with* one. But the words are confusing, like the ivory children themselves. It bothers him that they are tied together; it bothers him that he must bear the weight of decision, but cannot know which one to choose. He begins to search inside their mouths with his finger; this will allow him to determine which one. He feels the little child-teeth against his knuckle. But he cannot tell, he cannot tell.

Wordlessly, Bram attempts to explain his situation. Parting sweet from sorrow is difficult, even impossible to do. He has been given a terrible, an unworkable decision. How can he leave either? They must not both look at him with such need, such expectation. Surely they understand.

But instead the twins have begun a little nursery chant, writhing their fused bodies as they rise into what has become a vague and uncertain sky. Father Abraham had many sons, they sing, many sons had Father Abraham. I am one of them. And so are you.

2.

BRAM WOKE WITH A CHOKING SNORT. IT WAS MID-AFTERNOON; HE HAD fallen completely asleep during his lunch hour, sitting at a bench in a cake-and-coffee on Lossiter Courts. Last night he had not closed his eyes at all, circling only the little spare bedroom in his Chelsea home, seeking to avoid the coming day and its decision. Could he truly go through with Irving's plan? Could he *not*? The rubicund man pressed in next to him, a boiled egg raised to his beard, turned and frowned.

Forgive me, Bram tried awkwardly. *... forgive me.*

The automatic words had carried more weight than intended. He stood, blinking rapidly, and excused himself from the establishment.

Ah, Lujzi, he breathed out sorrowfully, supporting himself on a lamp post. The appointment with the mysterious Dr. Seward was in six hours.

A trailing wisp of the dream floated through his mind and he recognized the offensive odor, the one that was underneath the herbs. In the dream it had been coming from his own fingers. The smell of blood.

Chapter 20 (blood-red room)

1.

How had Irving made contact with the sweatshop on Goulston Street, how made his intention known with such rapidity? There was word recently of an 'acoustical telegraph' that might carry a man's voice across parishes in an instant, but Bram would just as well have believed the actor practiced black magic. That was the time in which they lived: steam wheels and type-writers and pipes crammed full of copper wire, machines merging with wizardry. Bram's arrival at the sweatshop door, as the dusk laid its vapors around London, felt horribly like courtship, as if he had returned to request from this young lady's mentor the pleasure of her company. Seeing him, Aiolfi enjoyed a moment of superiority, then disappeared into the building.

Miss Lujzi knew already as well, as she emerged silently and stood before him. Somehow the plan had been communicated: perhaps Aiolfi, more likely Bacco, had elaborated exactly what she must do if she would entertain any wish of retaining a roof from the rain. Bram flinched at the faint blue cloud he discerned on one of Miss Lujzi's cheekbones. In the desolation of his soul, where sand-filled winds moaned, he pictured with cruel precision the back of Mister Bacco's indifferent hand. Likely it had been swung without even malice, merely as routine, a way of underscoring instructions.

She stood a few feet away, refusing eye contact. Her expression, so animated when they first met, was empty as the dressmaker's dummy. Again there was the terrible resemblance to a swain taking his shy miss for an unchaperoned evening on the town. It struck Bram that to lean over now and peck gently Miss Lujzi's cheek would be, perhaps, the most purely Satanic act a man could undertake.

He wanted to say to her that he had no choice, that he had struggled mightily with this decision, that it had torn him as well... but he was under orders; they must proceed. As with the bulk of his life, everything was on a timetable.

Silently they moved through the immigrant-crowded street. He checked a public clock, plotting out their actions. The years of responsibility as a Dublin clerk had cruelly trained him in managing a schedule. Florence expected him back in Chelsea before supper; he had told her a lie about remaining for a Beefsteak function. This other business would need to be concluded expeditiously... but no, he could not take Lujzi, on the instant, to Dr. Seward's operating room. It would have been heartless, too efficient. Once out of sight of the sweatshop he stopped, the sunset bleeding west, and sat frozen on a stone bench outside a small Lutheran parsonage. The windows had been smashed in, their copper bracings looted; beside the weedy bench a cherub held up a dry fountain pipe. Miss Lujzi lowered herself obediently to the seat next to his. She was like a candle whose wick had been crushed down by a bailiff's indifferent thumb. He could lead her all the way to the rancid mudflats, Bram thought miserably, and instruct her to lie down with the water lapping over her nostrils, and she would do so, with neither comment nor complaint.

This parsonage was abandoned but the cherub still gleeful, its grinning cheeks spotted with moss. Bram stared at it, amazed that such an expression of joy had been carved by the hands of men. On what possible earth had the artisan lived? He turned toward Miss Lujzi. Around the greater city the first gasless lamps were being installed this season, and a public contest would be hosted next month—he had seen the placards—between traditional lighting and "electrical fluid mechanisms" for illumination of the embankment. In Whitechapel, though, even gas lamps were few, and as the clouds lost their luster overhead she waited among congressing shadows.

In Szentgyörgy I used to walk by myself, for hours; I had no real fear of the woods. To me, the forest was a room of a thousand voices. I think that was how I was able to go unafraid through this place after dark. I used to follow you in secret, Abraham, those nights you looked so sad. You never saw me there. But when I went to find you in your new home, for the first time, even walking in moonlight gave me fright. England is so different from what I have known, so much more wild. I asked one of the sisters in the costume shop to discover your address; all I knew was that I needed then to find you. It is a beautiful house, where you live. When your face appeared in the window, it was as if you had heard me outside, calling.

I was afraid you were not going to speak, Miss Lujzi.

I loved you, Abraham, when you were showing me English poetry, telling me about English plays. Sometimes I only pretended to understand the words you were pointing to. Other times I pretended not to understand, so that you would talk to me a little longer. Betl was also an artist; he liked to paint pictures, but more frequently he would dance. He adored dancing, more than any man I have ever known. It was childishness in him, but also a joy he could not be rid of. Whenever the harvesters built a fire in their stone ring, whenever there was music or singing in the fields, my Betl had to dance. He said it was his prayer. It was with his spirit that I danced, that day at the cemetery.

I wish I could understand your language, Miss Lujzi, Bram sighed, heavily. He rested his face entirely in his palms, massaging the fatigued skin. I wish that I could. It sounds like a lovely language.

Betl and I had a child, Abraham. No one knows this, and I will never tell anyone, not even you. Even if our lives cross again, after tonight, how could I bear to tell you? We had a child, Abraham, a beautiful daughter. We called her Kende, after my mother. She was so good, with little laughing eyes, as if she had opened them once to the world and what she saw there struck her as foolish. I had known her for only a month before she began to cough.

Please, Miss Lujzi. Please speak English.

I do not really want to be dead. Now I understand. I only want to be free. And I will be free. I still believe you will choose what is right. I believe you are a good man. But even if you make me do this terrible thing—even if I am forced—tomorrow, or next year, or the following year, I will find a way to escape this cursed island. And if you do force me to do this tonight, then may the Holy One, the Lord of the Sky and Sea, destroy you, Abraham, for taking out the life that is in me.

Miss Lujzi—

I am sorry, she said, in English once more.

I am sorry as well, Bram answered eventually, placing his numb fingers across her own. *For all that has happened.*

2.

When he could not delay any longer Bram walked her to the address in Spitalfields. It was a slum section in this world of slums, wretched to nose and eye. Black garrets crowded on top of one another like refuse bones heaped in a pile; indigents lounged under archways; on the street side, starving things pressed themselves against hot potato stands and whelk counters, begging scraps. With Miss Lujzi under his arm he passed a red brick alley where a soldier was driving a whore into the wall, bare buttocks clenching with something like hate. There was immigration in the flesh, Bram thought nauseatedly; within those abused loins swam the mixed seeds of the city entire, white, whiptail dragons thrashing each other in darkness.

He hurried Miss Lujzi past the vision, horror congesting around his lungs. A coffee seller, two negroes in sleeveless shirts, a small cadre of Chinamen stepping distastefully around a rummy so far gone he was hollering at the air. Among these expendables, too, were crowds of filthy Irish: coal heavers, carvers and carriers, persons his same age but doomed by a Catholic birth, unskilled and wholly replaceable. Was it possible this was the same London as the gentlemen's clubs with their twelve-course dinners served on warmed, gleaming plates, the opera goers in monocles and half-capes of offwhite silk, the department stores and luxury goods and specialty shops trading imports from around the globe? Here was a temporary shelter for paupers, jammed in like packed meat. Spotting him, a human stream emerged and grabbed at Bram's coat, trying to reach into his pockets. So rotten was both clothing and skin he could not determine their ages; they smelled like death. *Get away, get away. Leave us.* Four or five Orthodox Jews hurried past, long black coats, black hats, the dangling side-locks, all of their faces closed prayerfully in, trying to stay pure in a venomous world. Around the crowd, the heaps of windowless dwellings slumped defeatedly toward the water.

O Abraham, Miss Lujzi said in English. *I am afraid.*

They have gone their way. He was referring to two roughnecks in billycock hats who had taunted them, sizing up Bram's ability to defend himself with the cane. He held tightly to her with one arm, head hunched, as if they were weathering a storm.

Not of the men. Of...

She did not want to say the word.
Of the doctor? There is no need.
Will it be clean?
Very clean.

Bram felt her there under his arm, fragile paper. He tried to picture the illegal operating room toward which they were headed, but had nothing on which to draw. Only once had he seen an actual surgical theatre, when his brother Richard was studying medicine in Wales: walls of painted brick, a circular space, at its center a high table on which the sweating patient had been held down by volunteers. The surgeon, in his stained apron, sawed through the leg while ignoring the screams. The whole horrible production had been surrounded by ringed tiers of watchers, several of whom applauded at the end. It had all felt like a theatre of blood.

But none of that applied to an abortionist. Would it be merely a sitting room, a coal fire behind the screen, a shaded lamp—perhaps a wooden bucket to catch the business that must, in some fashion, slip free of her loins? Or would the expunging be forced on with chemicals? He had read something once in the *Dial and Examiner* about a pharmacist arrested for dispensing a drink that could empty the "overfull womb." And then, there had always been those oddly phrased newspaper adverts—powders for "undoing menstrual blockage" and "sweet relieving pills"—he did not know, he could not say! He had never had occasion to consider, in the remotest way, how any such nightmarish actions were performed, actions which, common as the nightside might make them, were too ghastly properly to envisage.

Yet was it unquestionably an evil in which he was engaged? The cessation of one life, to rescue another—the loss of a person not yet fully formed, an almost-person, with no future at all—was it killing, or sparing? Did Miss Lujzi's future prospects count for so little in the balance? Did his own? And what of his obligation (shall he confess the thought?) to his *actual* child—his lawful offspring—the son he hoped for, fervently, joyfully, from his union with Florence? Should all that person's tomorrows be rendered grime, should that child be consigned to a fatherless house, a family name blighted by ignominy, in order to spare this one?

Many were the infants who expired in their cribs. Many, most. Robust health could never be assured, a fact to which his own miserable youth gave evidence. Yet, should Miss Lujzi's offspring be born (*his* offspring, just as much! his own, his other child!), its life would, without question, comprise execration and brevity both. If it lived it might simply fall prey, as did many, to "baby farmers," those shadowy figures who took off unwanted children for a fee. The fortunate bastard was sold as a ready-made slave to one master or another, the unfortunate carried to the mudflats in a bag. Was *this* supposed to be Christian mercy, to deliver one's seed to anguish?

Bram's hot brain remembered, all unexpectedly, debate night at Trinity—the night when he strove to articulate the ethical value of *Frankenstein*. He had been struck by the passage where the young anatomist, having dared to "sport with life," determined to tear apart the female he had almost brought into being. Afterward, concealing the gory pieces, he must question whether his was an act of kindness or of mayhem; and if either, then to whom?

I am cold, Abraham.

Hold me closer. It will all be quick, and then the difficulty is done. Think only of that.

His own assurances sounded distant in his ear, and his fraught mind threatened to pass into numbness. The foul street's congestion was thinning out, the lighted building fronts giving way to long rows of unbroken tenements. Any moment could still bring the cutthroat's blade, but all he felt was the fragility of her small body beneath his arm. He was a child again in Clontarf, during the long period of his disability, waking one morning to find a crisp, single leaf resting perfectly on his window ledge. Extraordinarily colored, every copper twist in it a miracle; he had climbed onto the ledge with his arms just to witness the tiny wonder. *It is perfectly clean and safe,* he heard himself explaining. *Dr. Seward is an acquaintance of Mister Irving's, and a well-respected physician... a surgeon certified, I am quite sure, by the Royal College. He knows well how to undo such things, and tomorrow it will be as if they never were. There will be some small discomfort, I expect. But afterward, you will be just the same.*

Does he use a knife?

No, no. It will not hurt. It was not the question she asked. Bram had recoiled from that question, unwilling to come close enough to consider it.

The narrowing alley took a turn. A wagon trundled past, driven by brutish men. In the glow of a street lamp, an unexpected bobby was standing.

Bram hid his face. Under his boots, purple and sapphire stars winked off broken glass.

Will you be with me?

I am taking you directly to the door, Miss Lujzi. Afterward, when it is finished, I shall return you safely home.

You will not be with me?

I must—there was no time for concealment, for pretty evasions. Their footsteps echoed sharply on the closing walls. *I must not be seen by these men. By the surgeon, or his assistant, if there is one. Nor may I see his face. What we are doing, Miss Lujzi… the penalty in England for such actions is severe. No one is allowed to see faces, not even you. The room may be dark.*

I still believe you will save her.

The pain, billowing around his heart. She had spoken the last sentence in her foreign tongue, sparing him the necessity of understanding.

3.

A NOISY CROWD WAS COMING TOWARD THEM, ALL IN A MASS. NO, IT WAS not rowdies, but some anarchist agitation, so that they were constrained to take a circuitous route around some greasy pens. What had been a twilight fog was mounting to solidity now, foul smelling, polluting both his clothing and skin. Why did he circle once more, why delay so long in this dreadful arena? Here they were, at the appointed hour, arrived at the address on the card. Somewhere a church bell rang. The day I arrive in hell, Bram thought, the devil shall tell me I am punctual.

It was a tall, stained, faceless building, just one of a series, away from the main street with curtain-blocked windows. Dim markings above the doorway revealed the outline of a faded Eastern figure, peering over a crystal decanter. Another winter and the words underneath would be illegible: *Madam S—s, Phreno-Mesmerist! Egyptological Secondsight*. This has been, at one point, a table-tipping room. Now it was nothing.

In there, I am told, is where you shall find Dr. Seward. I shall return in one hour.

In there?

Do not be troubled by appearance. It will all be over quickly.

It was horrible, horrible: a mouth of hell. The brickwork was pitted and wet, the windows of the building like blacked-out eyes. By the weedy steps, in a bit of indentation, the remains of a small animal lay. And above it all, that faded image, like the eyes of some deity in ruins. Lujzi stopped.

I do not go in there.

We must. He meant: you must.

Turning to him she began to speak quickly again from her strange, foreign syllabary, so that Bram only sighed and shook his head helplessly. She had taken him by his fingers, her other hand clutching him partway up the arm. She looked directly into his face, as if straining to climb toward him, toward him through the miles that divided her life from his own; as if disregarding, like the telegraph cable, the too-limited world of space and making to leap all at once past his defenses.

Please, Miss Lujzi. For pity's sake, English.

Abraham… think now. Do not say me to do this.

I do not wish it, Miss Lujzi. Bram trembled in his core. *God in heaven knows I do not wish it. But we have no more choices. Neither of us.*

You have choice, yes, you have choice.

I have none! I will not see you ruined, Lujzi, and, Miss Lujzi, I cannot lose all that I have. My wife needs a husband—my own child needs a father!

She grabbed his fingers and pressed them on her stomach. Horrified, Bram tried to rip his hand away, but her desperate clutch held him fast.

In here is our daughter, Abraham. I know it is girl. I know, a mother knows. Believe her, Abraham, believe her, and believe me. I come here, this far, only because I know you do not want, you will not do this. I know you are good.

Stop, Miss Lujzi, stop. You destroy me!

He twisted free his hand. Still she was not satisfied, searching him almost frantically for more. *The mirror crack'd from side to side,* Bram chanted internally, fighting to keep himself from looking in her eyes. *The curse is come upon me, cried!* The hour was now, the street perilous. Mister Irving had ordered him, his wife expected him. They must not linger.

Go, Miss Lujzi, go inside. Let this moment be over, do not force us both to endure it. It is not a happy decision, for either of us. But tomorrow you may return to your former life, as if you had never met me.

Is it you, Abraham, who want this? Is it you?

Mister Irving—

Mister Irving is not God. He is not God!

Bram thrust her off. Passing figures noticed them, but did not react. The streets were filled with tragedy; theirs was of no moment. Bram turned his back but she embraced him from behind.

Believe her, Abraham, she whispered madly, close against his ear. He felt the sharp points of her clipped hair, that beautiful auburn that had been destroyed by his touch. *Almost alive. Almost alive. Save her now. Save her.*

The door to the surgeon's room opened a crack, revealing a candle. Turning to look, Miss Lujzi released him. When she saw what was beyond that door, she drew her shawl tightly about herself, as if in a chilling wind.

Bram took a leaden step, forcing himself not to turn. No one must discern, neither the surgeon, nor he himself; he must neither see, nor be seen. All was in darkness. And abruptly he remembered the Irish Traveler's warning, there, in a tent in the West Country: *I see a man with no face.*

The abhorrent truth of it came to him. Was he not, himself, in this moment, the terrible faceless man...?

Spinning around he grabbed Miss Lujzi, pulled her fiercely to himself. Damnation, hell and damnation! His heart was leaping, not with the low thud of exhaustion but a fierce, unrelenting hammer. Damn Henry Irving, damn the imbecile mob! Here was the answer he had been seeking all along, the solution to the vexation of life. *She* was the source of a bright, exuberant future; not Florence; not the Lyceum; joyous life with *her*, not a living grave among the respectable. She, she, a stranger without name or connection, wholly unworthy, she alone had filled his hollowness with vitality. On his soul, he would keep this, the one jewel of the world.

Abraham.

Lujzi. Lujzi!

What shall he do, then, how achieve his right ending? He will throw it all over—Irving, London, all—he will have *this* child instead, sweet instead of sorrow—*their* child, the child of his actual passion. Such relations between different classes and traditions would not always be forbidden. They must not! The century was shaking off its chains. He would take her away from England, tonight, this very hour. The British Isles were a scrap, a single jot on the broadly unraveling scroll of earth. Somewhere, anywhere! He would do this, he would forge for them both a fresh existence, the only two innocents in a lifetime that was still theirs for the living—

With a cry Bram collapsed to the wet cobblestones. The salty pain ran freely to his lips.

I cannot, my love, he wept. *Oh, forgive me, forgive me. I cannot.*

The surgeon, having seen them, had opened the door of her shop. *Her* shop, Bram realized: "Jack Seward" was a woman, doing, quietly, women's business. Doing the deeds that were needed, but not sanctioned, erasing all the loves that must never become known.

Lujzi. We will still be dear to each other. We can continue our conversations, as before... talking about art, and beauty, and about many things. I will find you a place, near me, not far. I will save enough to afford you a room. This child... this child we must give away tonight, we must. But that is not an end. The changes the doctor will make are in no way permanent. Your body will heal, it will forgive us. When you are ready, you may have another, with a better man.

The expressionless woman, "Dr. Seward," was waiting by the opened door, standing just past the point at which her features might be recorded. Miss Lujzi looked down at Bram for a time, her white face without expression as she examined him, as if at a mystery that had been disappointingly solved. The tassels on her shawl swayed lightly in a breeze. Then she took her hands away from his shoulders. Without turning, without language, she walked into the building.

Bram struggled up, stumbling and then walking and then running back into the night, running from the place. Lighted windows sailed past, blurred shapes of men. He ran, he raced; he was a sportsman, a hero; he could run without tiring, forever. The bleak, foggy air was changing around him, becoming flake-tossed. There was a sharpness to it that portended ill—strange, uncanny weather. He ran, street after street, boots pounding brick, the icy breaths whooping like knife blows into and out of his lungs.

My good lad.

Bram turned, gasping for air. A figure was there, pulled up on top of a coach. The old man was wrapped in a heavy cloak, densely bearded, his black pupils glittering from the roof.

Come in for the ride. This is no place for a sensitive nature.

Mister Whitman?

After our letters you call me mister.

Bram entered the carriage and the poet, alighting in a flash, cast a great cape around his shoulders like an enclosing wing.

There is drink under the seat if you want it. Some Ruskie thing.

The old man leapt to the driver's seat again and they rode. Shadow and form played across the cab's interior, revealing crimson wall panels richly embroidered with lace. Bram leaned out the window where the lights of passing lamps illuminated the poet's sculpted features from below. With each lamp he could see variant dimensions, as complex with grandeur as Longfellow's.

I am Mr. Henry Irving's manager, Bram tried to call up. *I—*

I know who you are, my boy.

It had begun to snow more heavily. Whitman cracked the horsewhip and the carriage rumbled on, winding now through a forest of lighted steeples.

Listen to them, Whitman said, his deep sonorous voice somehow present inside the cab. Bram closed his eyes. *The dock workers, the coopers, the lumberjacks and lumber haulers, the makers of oilcloth and whole cloth, the carriage makers and drivers, the wool mills' tireless worker, growing stronger with each day's labor, each day more filled up with vim and with fibre. That is the power that lies in this country... can you feel it?... the life, by God, the life of America.*

America? Bram whispered. *Sir, this is Spitalfields.*

Camden, by God!

Bram felt his hurt mind drifting, his heartbeat slowing, as the fast carriage rumbled over thickening newfall.

My lodgings.

The coach had come to a frame house with horizontal slats. The heaviest flakes had stopped; stepping down, Bram smelled clean waterfront, with no poison of industry.

Welcome to my house, Whitman laughed, swinging the knob widely. It was a fantastic gesture of greeting. Bram entered and the poet crashed shut the door behind him.

Eat, Whitman says. *You look bear-hungry.*

Bram sat at the small oaken table, on which his host had already laid round after round of steaming victuals. He felt strangely at home in this mysterious lodging, with the whale oil lamp and the river frost melting on the windows.

You must already have dined... Bram began. But the old man was attacking his meal with vigor.

The hell I have. I dine, I sup, and I snack! As it please me!

Whitman kicked back loudly after his meal, tossing the slop out the kitchen door and returning to lounge by the mantle.

Tell me about England.

Sir... you are the poet of America.

America I know. I want to know England the way an Englishman knows it. Correct me if I say the damnedest thing that's not Oxbridge.

Well... Bram was tempted to snicker.

Right there?

No Englishman would say damnedest.

The poet belly laughed. Then he tipped a purple glass to his eye, peering through its depths.

Drink, he said. *A fellow named Eakins gave it to me. What the Devil do I know about wines? It looks old.*

Gratefully Bram swallowed, the liquid burn falling inside him. It was the wine of forgetfulness, and he pictured the blue flame traveling his throat, dropping through his esophagus to his gut. In the flickering light, the corners of the room started to dance. They were stuffed with books, an impromptu collection: war correspondences, congressional reports, a well-used dictionary of plants. *Sonnets from the Portuguese. Franklin Evans, or, the Inebriate. Antigone. Representative Men.* Large stacks of raw paper were included between the piles, tied with string and bundled aside for future use.

Do you know I used to address him as Master? By the gods, I did! Emerson, I mean. Master I called him, like a groveling Tory.

... every man... has his master...

Praised him, I did, like a fool! Now Lincoln, there was one who might have been hailed as great, without lessening the self.

Bram eased back in his seat to listen; the old poet began pacing, rolling his glass in one fist. *Why a congress of politicians and not of poets? Why shan't the poet serve as representative of the nation? Hades, man! Let us send poets to France, poets to the Kaiser!* He talked of everything. Bram had no clear sense of the connection between ideas, but his mind was overawed at their glistening web. The woman issue—was it even a discussion? They stood in the American labor force, but only foreign-borns, and blacks, not in the professions. One heard bellowed down every civic meeting house that marriage been instituted by God to be that union on whose back society rests. But was it so?

Marriage, Bram sighed faintly.

Marriage! Whitman brayed back, his broad, well-set teeth enjoying themselves. *I have had three wives; never married in the law, but wives, by God! Fathered a slew inside em—no one knows how many. Even I don't know.* With every interchange he grew looser limbed, as if moving backward in time. Bram's head was fulsome with dancing light, the hours sidling past and the lamp wick twisting low in its socket. For how long had the man held forth on politics, the new Black Tide, on how the writer's calling eclipsed that of the priest? *Damned cornswaddlers! Drive a Catholic cur back to Rome with a mighty howl! Shall I serve two masters now?* Hour after hour, and while the poet grew stronger, Bram himself tired, faded, sinking now into a settee, his cheek by a pillow. Finally it was over. Bram lay his head heavily against the worn quilting. A slow heat came over his brain; he entered a somnambulatory state. Whitman was silent, well sated. Bram could not see him but could feel his seated presence by the fire, his breathing low, rhythmic. Time drifted and eddied, like the snow.

Walter, Bram whispered. *Will I ever see her again.*

The poet, who had been facing away, turned, and Bram saw his father's face.

Always, my dear boy. You will never stop seeing her.

The figure loomed over him; Bram felt two dry hands embracing his head, pulling him close in affection.

Is it over, Papa? Bram asked faintly, his cheek pressed against someone's sorrowful ribs. *I must return now, to take her home. She will be very tired.*

Dear boy, there is no hurry. The scalpel has done its work. The blood has sung its song. Your beloved is already cold where she lies.

The hands disappeared; the figure to whom they belonged was now standing by the window, arms spread wide, hailing the reddening dawn. Bram's face opened in a silent howl. Softly, in a sympathetic voice, the ancient poet sang to the sun.

TRICKLE, drops! my blue veins leaving!
O drops of me! trickle, slow drops,
Candid, from me falling—
drip, bleeding drops,
From wounds made to free you
whence you were prison'd...

From my breast—from within
where I was conceal'd—press forth,
red drops—confession drops;
Stain every page—stain every song I
sing, every word I say, bloody drops;

Glow upon all I have written...

Conclusion

The Beautiful Uncut Hair of Graves

> And at the closing of the day
> She loosed the chain, and down she lay;
> The broad stream bore her far away...
>   Alfred, Lord Tennyson

> This was my Message from the Dead.
>   Bram Stoker, *Personal Reminiscences of Henry Irving*, 1906

Chapter 21 (who haunts the haunters: London, 1897)

1.

SOME STORIES ARE QUICKLY FORGOTTEN. OTHERS HAVE THE ABILITY TO continue on almost indefinitely, maintaining their existence by virtue of what they withhold as much as what they reveal. Irish writer James Joyce once quipped of his own work that filling it with puzzles was the best way to reach immortality.

Actual lives, by contrast, have absolute conclusions. Death, knowing no sequel, places its definitive period after each, and the breathing, human person behind all biography must retreat into silence. The memorable artists have each strutted and fretted their individual hour upon the stage, at last to be heard from—as Bard, and bird, agree—nevermore.

Real life, in other words, has a final chapter. This is the final chapter in Bram Stoker's life.

After it comes only celebrity, and the beginning of that false afterworld known as *biographical criticism*. After it come only fans, both high and low; the fusty speculation of scholars; and the deeply felt gratitude of generations.

Which is to say, the grave.

2.

Bram walks the blustery streets, fending off with his umbrella point scraps of newsprint that cling to his pant cuffs like hectoring spirits. The newspaper at century's end is weak stuff, steam-heated *papier mache* that withers and crumbles in the wind. Always these days the capital is marked by floating bits of text, loose words, whispering about the cobble like voices.

Almost two decades have passed, two decades of the achievement of his dream. Acting Manager to the elderly Henry Irving and Ellen Terry, those unrivaled toasts of all Britain. Organizing hand behind the great Lyceum Theatre. Financial success, solvent enough now to wear Mother of Pearl cuffs, a cream-colored dress shirt with gathered sleeves. The half-breed Irishness of his origins is all but elided; seeing him, one salutes a well-heeled member of Empire. Who was it that told him, once (amusing recollection), that anyone can have readers, but true artists have victims?

It is 1897, sharp edge of the century.

#

Of coincidental interest:

1845-52: The Great Famine in Ireland. Survivors emigrate to East London.

1880: Agricultural failures in England. Travelers, "Gypsies," squatters crowd into urban areas.

1881: Assassination of Tsar Alexander III. Pogrom waves crisscross the Russian Empire, like echoes of a macabre song Christianity is doomed to sing.

1883: Marx dies. Mussolini born.

1884: The fountain pen.

1885: The machine gun.

1885: King Leopold II of Belgium declares Congo Free State his own.

1886: Post-Impressionism.

1887: Arthur Conan Doyle publishes *A Study in Scarlet*.

1887: Barbed wire.

1888: Around the gutters of England's greatest city, two novelties make their appearance. One is the cheaply printed word; a slew of half-penny newspapers is currently being produced for a mass British audience, flashing such come-hither titles as *Shocking!* and *Illustrated Arrests*.

The other is blood. Recent weeks have seen the first repeat murderer—only much later will the term "serial killer" be coined—emerge from the smoky retreats of Whitechapel. He is a figure whose imprint on history will be as much a phenomenon of a rapidly spreading literacy as the other rapidly spreading pools he leaves behind.

The predator works his strange craft after dusk with a surgeon's skill, removing organs from prostitutes' bodies and performing other deeds "whose intimate nature precludes their mention in this paper," as the dailies titillatingly have it. The penny pages dub him *The Ripper*, after a letter he himself sends the Central News Agency, outlining his crimes. This letter begins a series of increasingly graphic correspondences (including one wrapped around a partially consumed human liver) that become instant media successes. The decades will debate his identity—surgeon, Freemason, agent of the Crown—but in a segment of the popular mind, "Red Jack" comes to stand for the brutal conditions of the East End itself. The Ripper is workhouse, bawdy house, sweatshop; he is the war on immigrants, seasonal workers, the poor; he is the murderous contempt for all that is Other, given physical form and quite physical knife.

Next, rumors spread that the stolen female organs of increase (for the papers soon overcome their squeamishness) that are being discovered on doorsteps have been soaked in wine, leading some to suspect a Catholic connection. Men whose religion bids them ritualistically drink blood and eat flesh now suspect the killer may be merely the wrong *kind* of Christian. Perhaps "our Jack," as the *Telegraph Crier* rakishly has him, is a Popish literalist, taking transubstantiation into his own capable hands. Suspicion falls quietly on the Irish.

The Ripper falls on the Irish as well. The most horrifically rendered of his victims—she will be found with her spleen nestled in one armpit and her liver between her feet—is Mary Kelly, born in County Limerick, Munster, and transported to London in the service of prostitution. In a work of sociological fiction she would no doubt stand for the way in which her culture is being utilized as an import resource. Unaware of such ironies, however, on Friday, November 9, Mary enters an unoccupied chapel, confessing her week's load of the necessary sin of concupiscence to a statue of her namesake. Afterward she dozes lightly in her pew, thinking for no sensible reason at all of a childhood sweetheart named *Chawlie* who used to push her in the public swing, so high he pushed her! Fly, Mary, fly! he'd shout, and little thing, she flew, flew high as Mount Corran, high as the clouds. Smiling at the reminiscence she rises from her bench, kisses the foot of the Virgin under which a marble snake lies coiled and grinning, and walks calmly into the fog.

1889: The tabulating machine.

1894: The gramophone.

1895: Oscar Wilde is convicted of moral outrage. Said the presiding judge, "It is the worst case I have ever tried."

3.

IT IS 1897. ABRAHAM STOKER, KNOWN AS "BRAM" BY HIS FRIENDS, of whom there are few, has dedicated his entire career, indeed his entire life, to the promotion of another man. He has avoided the various diseases that plague the age—the hurrying black carriage has yet to find him—but from the general appointment with mortality there is no exemption.

His literary ambitions have amounted to nothing, the dream of finding "his book" a fantasy. None of his novels has made more than a passing impression: *The Snake's Pass, the Water's Mou', The Shoulder of Shasta*. None of his stories holds particular merit: "The Crystal Cup, " "The Red Stockade," "Death Doom of the Double Born." His best-selling work, by an absurd reach, is the unreadable *Duties of Clerks of Petty Sessions in Ireland*. He cannot even bring himself to lift its cover.

Excellent, Henry Irving muses, on the day he is informed of plans to have himself knighted by the Crown. His name will be written in the marble of Westminster Abbey, beside Milton, Chaucer, Shakespeare. *Thus I join the immortals.*

Bram is not yet at the cool edge of confinement, he reminds himself often. There will be more life to come, perhaps even a decade. But his best years are not merely past the prow, but foundering in the wake. In reaching out for that fresh, new existence he envisioned as a young man, he has been forced to accept certain decisions, to make certain choices that cannot be reversed. Unlike the magical Count, he has no power to wind back the clock's slicing hand.

And so he sits—a serving-man in a library carrel, alone, as is now his confirmed habit—sits, a merely adequate pen—sits, and begins the final chapter of this, what will prove to be, by far, his most interesting novel. And here the critic, winding back the hand of time indeed, notices something odd. All of Bram Stoker's other attempts he hurries out in a mere span of months, while to this book, alone, he dedicates seven entire years.

Why?

It is a version of the larger question, having to do with successful art: Why did one story live, when all the others died?

Bram dips the ink and settles his thought. The hero is closing in, with his kukri knife in hand; the wicked Count is now the hunted, and vengeance rideth fast. His heart begins to beat. Following Whitman's advice, he has written "the song of himself"—but hidden, a secret memoir wrapped inside a thriller, one where reminiscence and fantasy, dream and waking, coexist. Of his wife Florence's whereabouts, Bram has no notion. It strikes him that he cannot even say when he stopped caring. At some point, a child came into their lives: one upon whom Bram doted excessively, as if covering up for feelings of uncertainty. A healthy boy it turned out to be, the son for whom he had longed—; and who, as he has grown, has shown a particular stoop of the spine, and a tendency to limp when he walks.

It is a small deficiency. Only a father's eye would notice.

This child he unexpectedly names "Irving Stoker," a combination name for a combination offspring, as if paternity were a matter of degree. One of the most striking elements in the concluding chapter of *Dracula* is the announcement, in the final pages, that Mina Harker is going to have a baby, but that the child's name will be a kind of code. The Harker boy will include, in his long designation, the birth names of all those men whose blood went into his mother, with the notable exception of one—that dark prince whose bloodline she is carrying, and whose secret insertion into the Harker family tree is the book's subtle, and chilling, *dénouement*.

Many years later, as an adult, "Irving Stoker" will go by his middle name, Noel, denying this second family inheritance completely. When he dies, it is as

Noel Stoker that his ashes will be mixed, in Golders Green Crematorium, in the urn with Bram's own. Florence's ashes will be scattered.

Noel Stoker, for his part, will explain to the curious throughout life that he refused the name "Irving" in order to redress some imbalance that he felt had occurred in the family before his birth; that he came to believe the famous stage actor had overwhelmed his father in some way, stealing away something fundamental to his life.

4.

WHAT IS THE NOVEL *DRACULA?*

Originally conceived of as a drama in which the English actor Henry Irving was to play the villain's role, it may be Bram Stoker's revenge—a cleverly concealed portrait of a monster who walked the streets of London. Dangerously close to autobiography, and yet not, the book tells of a naïve clerk who becomes victimized by an older man with a wild, hypnotic power. Clear references to Shakespeare are throughout: *Macbeth, Othello, Hamlet,* even *Merchant.* There is a method to Renfield's madness; Dracula's brides are called *weird sisters;* "I sympathize with poor Desdemona," Lucy writes in her journal; "Quick, my tablets," Jonathan misquotes in his. The actress Ellen Terry is mentioned by name.

The bulk of the novel was executed in Whitby, a lonely fishing village far north of London on the Yorkshire coast. Stoker took himself, his wife, and their son Irving there in the 1890's for a rare vacation, away from the duties of theatrical life. Whitby forms the dramatic backdrop for much of the action, for which it appears made to order. The roofless walls of a medieval Abbey loom over a seaside cliff, at the base of which beetling waves blow in at all hours. Rainswept, fog-haunted, the moody town provided the perfect gothic setting for this strangely intimate tale of a bloodsucking aristocrat who menaces two women, seeking to perpetuate his own, unholy life, forever.

At the surface level, the dramatic precursors are easy to spot: Mary Shelley, Wilkie Collins, Sheridan Le Fanu. There is anxiety over the late Victorian era's spike in prostitution and the syphilis that raged at its heel, the omnivorous pan-sexualities of Byron, Whitman, Wilde, the scary gender politics of the New Woman. No doubt Stoker's own childhood during the waning years of Ireland's Great Hunger played a role as well. And a protracted childhood illness—common to gothic writers from Coleridge to Hawthorne to Stephen King—may have formed the first impressions in his mind, blending the nuances of both yearning for, and fearing, the all-powerful father. According to his three-volume *Personal Reminiscences of Henry Irving*, written after the actor was gone, Bram Stoker (he changed his name from Abraham the year his father died, as if to signal a profound change) began life as a cripple. About this time he says little, noting only that *In my babyhood I used, I understand, to be often on the point of death. Certainly till I was about seven years old I never knew what it was to stand upright. I was naturally thoughtful and the long illness gave opportunity for many thoughts which were fruitful according to their kind in later years.*

At some point, however, something more fundamental than any of this seems to have entered Bram Stoker's mind. Unlike his other potboilers, something invested this story with *life*, that inexplicable spark that may leap, on occasion, between the conducting electrodes of brain and heart. In a stroke was born the most famous villain in gothic literature, more recognizable than Ahab: *Drakul*, the Dragon.

The tension between the clerk and the vampire, their evil cat-and-mouse play, is palpable on the page. Fluid metaphors of sexuality, of a tortured *ménage a trois*, bleeding sadomasochism, of dominance and submission, wander its halls in gauzy attire. Grave cerement and wedding gown fuse; men love the dead, and the dead respond. If *Frankenstein* is about motherhood and its terrors, *Dracula* is just about sex—all the ways in which true wife and husband may conceal bedroom monsters. It is a surprisingly subversive take on what is now called "Victorian Morality," depicting *fin de siècle* London as a city with a Dark Half, where grinning lusts shuffle the streets.

In one paralyzing scene, Count Dracula will be discovered shirtless in bed with Mina Harker while her husband sleeps beside them. This demonic threesome (she is engaged in swallowing fluids directly from his body, as he has been indulging in hers) is an image of many things. Conspicuous among them, however, is the hero's obliviousness to, if not complicity in, his own wife's infidelity.

Critics have sought to interpret Count Dracula in numerous ways. He is an English landlord, bleeding the Irish of life; he is an immigrant, heralding an invasion of the same; he is the Freudian Id, violent, rapacious dream-life of a century. Biographical criticism, in its heyday, will see pieces of Dracula in Tennyson, in Whitman, in Jack the Ripper. That "Harker" is "Stoker" seems obvious, at least as much so as that K is Kafka and Pym is Poe. The noble foreigner "Abraham Van English" (as "Helsing" might anagrammatically be called; the book exhibits a surprising affinity for wordplay) likely derives from the elder Abraham Stoker, Irishman but loyal servant of the Crown. Mina Harker, the solicitor's infiltrated spouse who expresses weird sympathy for the villain and secretly carries his blood, will be found in Florence Balcombe, to whom Bram Stoker remained married all his years, but with whom he shared no personal life following the birth of their only son.

No one will search for that other female presence, the one who so drives the narrative that readers have found her far more interesting than the actual heroine: that curiously unexplained *second* damsel in distress, whose ruin, at the vampire's hand, forms the novel's most riveting section; the character whose very superficiality—beautiful flirt, dream lover, ghost—has served to curtail any speculation about her possible reality. The one with whom all the heroes, and perhaps even the author himself, fall in love; whom everyone fails to save; and whose terrible death scene, half marriage bed, half murder, forms the book's actual high point. Who was behind Miss Lucy Westenra?

Probably no such original existed. The critic must leave room for mere invention.

If such a person were to be posited, however—unheard, without status, erased from all history—the surprisingly layered novel *Dracula* would be something else again. Between its lines, Bram Stoker's true love would lie interred, the nameless woman through whom he was finally able to produce his one, enduring tale. From this strange book of mirrors would emerge, then, the most gothic family secret of all: for this inspiring person would be mother to Stoker's text; the book itself would be *their* baby; and that baby would go on to achieve a worldwide fame—millions of copies sold, hundreds of stage and film adaptations, an entire subculture that is growing to this day—in comparison to which the achievements of the now largely forgotten "Sir Henry Irving, Actor" would seem like the most transient flicker in time.

Herein lies the irony of the vampire's bite. One cannot take blood without sharing blood. Victim and perpetrator merge; all borderlines exist only inasmuch as they are crossed. It is indeed through a vampire coming into his life that Bram Stoker is destroyed, along with all that he had loved. And yet he dies only to waken again in a new shape, in a new world; only to unfold, by starlight, the tenebrous wings of his own immortality.

Epilogue

Early in the Twentieth Century

1.

It is just twilight, the rawness gilded by the reflection of sunset on the newly painted fences at Highgate Cemetery. The air is chill, whispering the change in seasons. Along the tombstone-covered hills, already, trees are made golden by angular light.

As this is supper time, the man—elderly, by the standards of his generation—has the expansive cemetery to himself. He is a frequent visitor at this quiet hour, walking its dim avenues, lost in meditation. Sometimes he goes directly to his chosen spot, as if for an appointment, and waits there, his attitude projecting eagerness—never finding, apparently, what he seeks. Other times he wanders, seemingly without direction, for much of the evening. Always, though, his final destination is the same: a particular leafy hill, with, at the top of it, a sad angel carved in white.

Tonight is no different than any other. See him now, head inclined, his once-red beard threaded over with gray. See him as he makes his way through the Egyptian Avenue, past the Cedars of Lebanon, approaching the usual location. See his large hands seeking to steady his weight on his umbrella handle. He has spent an hour, already, in meandering contemplation. But as he reaches his final objective, tonight, he stops.

Someone is up there. A second figure is standing next to the angel, half-hidden behind its drooping wing. The man starts; his tired eyes look again;

he begins to run, losing his umbrella as he stumbles off the path and up the leaf-scattered embankment.

But when he reaches the top, he is alone once more. The sad angel can tell him nothing. The man teeters, looking wildly about.

Lujzi! he cries, a peculiar, foreign-sounding word you do not understand. *Lujzi!*

Like a lost soul, he staggers through the empty graves, long after dark. Shadow and light dance away, fading; who can say if anything had ever really been there at all.

About the author

William Orem's first collection of stories, *Zombi, You My Love*, won the GLCA New Writers Award, formerly given to Louise Erdrich, Sherman Alexie, Richard Ford and Alice Munro. His second collection, *Across the River*, won the Texas Review Novella Prize. His first novel, *Killer of Crying Deer*, won the Eric Hoffer Award, and has been optioned for film. His second novel, *Miss Lucy*, won the Gival Press Novel Award. His first collection of poems, *Our Purpose in Speaking*, won the Wheelbarrow Books Poetry Prize and was published by MSU Press, and he has been nominated for the Pushcart Prize in poetry, fiction and creative nonfiction.

Meanwhile, his short plays have been performed around the country, winning both the Critics' Prize and Audience Favorite Award at Durango Theatre Fest, and thrice being nominated for the prestigious Heideman Award at Actors Theatre of Louisville.

Currently he is a Senior Writer-in-Residence at Emerson College. Details at *williamorem.com*.

More from Gival Press

Barrow's Point by Robert Schirmer
The Best of Gival Press Short Stories edited by Robert L. Giron
Boys, Lost & Found by Charles Casillo
The Cannibal of Guadalajara by David Winner
A Change of Heart by David Garrett Izzo
The Day Rider and Other Stories by J. E. Robinson
Dead Time / Tiempo muerto by Carlos Rubio
Dream of Another America by Tyler McMahon
Dreams and Other Ailments / Sueños y otros achaques by Teresa Bevin
The Gay Herman Melville Reader edited by Ken Schellenberg
Guess and Check by Thaddeus Rutkowski
Ghost Horse by Thomas H. McNeely
Gone by Sundown by Peter Leach
An Interdisciplinary Introduction to Women's Studies edited by Brianne Friel and Robert L. Giron
Julia & Rodrigo by Mark Brazaitis
The Last Day of Paradise by Kiki Denis
Literatures of the African Diaspora by Yemi D. Ogunyemi
Lockjaw: Collected Appalachian Stories by Holly Farris
Mayhem: Three Lives of a Woman by Elizabeth Harris
Maximus in Catland by David Garrett Izzo
Middlebrow Annoyances: American Drama in the 21st Century by Myles Weber
The Pleasuring of Men by Clifford H. Browder
Riverton Noir by Perry Glasser
Second Acts by Tim W. Brown
Secret Memories / Recuerdos secretos by Carlos Rubio
Sexy Liberal! Of Me I Sing by Stephanie Miller
Show Up, Look Good by Mark Wisniewski
The Smoke Week: Sept. 11-21. 2001 by Ellis Avery
That Demon Life by Lowell Mick White

Theory and Praxis: Women's and Gender Studies at Community Colleges edited by Genevieve Carminati and Heather Rellihan
Tina Springs into Summer / Tina se lanza al verano by Teresa Bevin
The Tomb on the Periphery by John Domini
Twelve Rivers of the Body by Elizabeth Oness

For a complete list of Gival Press titles, visit: *www.givalpress.com*.

Books are available from Ingram, Follett, Brodart,
your favorite bookstore, the Internet, or from Gival Press.

Gival Press, LLC
PO Box 3812
Arlington, VA 22203
givalpress@yahoo.com
703.351.0079

CPSIA information can be obtained
at www.ICGtesting.com
Printed in the USA
LVHW030327090121
675854LV00003B/82